BURIED
with HONOR

BURIED
with HONOR

GARY J. CROSS

CO-AUTHOR
MATTHEW T. CROSS

TATE PUBLISHING & *Enterprises*

Published by Tate Publishing & Enterprises, LLC
127 E. Trade Center Terrace | Mustang, Oklahoma 73064 USA
1.888.361.9473 | www.tatepublishing.com

Tate Publishing is committed to excellence in the publishing industry. The company reflects the philosophy established by the founders, based on Psalm 68:11,
"The Lord gave the word and great was the company of those who published it."

Published in the United States of America

ISBN: 978-1-61739-069-2
1. Fiction, War & Military
2. Fiction, General
10.10.08

ACKNOWLEDGMENTS

I would like to acknowledge co-author Matthew T Cross for his candid opinion on plot analysis and character development of Garrison and Williams. I would like to thank my loving wife, Barbara, for her review of final edit. I would like to thank my son Wyatt for his candid opinion on the story line. I would like to acknowledge the staff at Tate Publishing, in particular, Melissa Huffer and Rachel Sweeden for showing a new author the ropes and adding clarity where needed; the conceptual editor and copy editors; cover designer, Lauran Levey; and the marketing rep.

PROLOGUE

"Can ya trust him?" asks Smith.

LaDeau's piercing eyes takes on a more sinister glare, and the tension creeps in as if the temperature dropped like a cold wave from a passing thunderstorm on a hot, humid summer day and with a tension so thick you can cut it with a knife. The eyes give away the intent, taking on a glare that is ever so threatening and menacing that it makes Smith feel like he is the target. The glare... the glare sends the message by signaling the fight or flight mechanism you feel in the back of your neck when you know your life is in danger and you need to leave the area immediately. The glare... the glare that gives one the impression that if LaDeau had a pet dog he would probably would have slaughtered it right there on the spot and eaten it in front of you.

"He knows better to open his mouth. And when this job is over, he won't be around to count his money," responds LaDeau; and from that response, Smith knows what is in store for Manning.

"Now we are talking about murder," Smith responds, in a weak voice that sounded like it had not quite reached puberty.

"Yeah. We are talking about murder, and we are talking about murder in a third-world country that's at war where murders occur all the time," LaDeau responds with an air of confidence.

"Even if someone finds his body, they'll think it's one of de local Iraqis killing another American. Don't worry, Bubba. There's no FBI over here. No one will suspect us." And again, the look of confidence has not changed.

"You forget I'm Manning's first-line supervisor, and I are the one that reports his attendance at work, so it will be me that will report to BCKR. I'll report that Manning constantly complained about being homesick and finally came to me and said that he was leaving. I'll report that I cut his last check and that was de last I saw of him," he said in a confident Louisiana drawl.

The look of confidence reflected in LaDeau's face has now appeared in Smiths as if moonlight had reflected across two adjacent pools of water. Yes, the sinister duo knows they have all the angles covered and now it's time to move on to the next subject at hand.

MID-WINTER IN IRAQ

The year is 2003. It's winter in Iraq, and the temperature is sixty degrees Fahrenheit, which is cold by Iraq standards. Violence is the norm, as US soldiers maneuver the country, hunting for Saddam Hussein and his henchmen. US soldiers must take care when maneuvering the main supply routes, for the weapon of choice among insurgents and Al-Qaeda is the IED or improvised explosive device. US soldiers are keenly aware of this danger and rehearse battle drills for IED's and anything else that might come their way. Baghdad is sixty-five miles away, and in the small desert towns along the southern major highway the drab sandstone color of their buildings mirrors the color of the terrain. The only sense of color comes from the graffiti that occasionally shows up on the sides of buildings or the multi-colored minaret tops of the towers that mark the temple for the Muslim call to prayer. Along the major highway south of Baghdad, the date palm trees and grass almost give the soldiers from the states of Florida or California, where palms flourish, a false connection to their home. But that connection is broken when you come across a burnt-out car on the highway or the bullet holes in some of the sandstone buildings. The light shade of beige seen almost in every town seems as if it has risen out of the ground with a life of its own, devouring whatever color the buildings had, and replacing it with the color of the desert.

Traveling farther, an occasional cellular tower pops up, its shadow reflected across a plowed field where farmers attempt to grow crops as close to the Tigris River as possible. It is the nearest source of water for the starved crops. Farther south, the trees disappear, and the desert starts to crawl in with its long fields of sand between fields of date palms and grass. It is a landscape that might make a perfect training ground for the military force now at Camp Trigger, a base south of Baghdad in the Babil province. Like most American bases, it is heavily fortified and fenced with a military barbed wire called concertina wire. The wire coils along the ground in a slinky toy fashion with each coil sporting sharp, double-barbed razors along the arc of the coil as if it was a snake with a body armor of thorns saying, "Watch it. I will bite." Entering Camp Trigger, one finds trailer-like buildings called cormacs that are similar to the trailers you would find on the back of a semi trailer truck. These buildings are sometimes used to house the soldiers, and the ones that are not so lucky are housed in tents. The cormacs all reside on one side of the street with the tents on the opposite side, side by side, as if they were soldiers standing in formation who are about to be addressed by a commanding general.

Nestled in between the cormacs and tents are occasional configurations of cormacs that are labeled with enlarged signs found outside of the restrooms identifying male and female cleaning facilities. A common complaint among soldiers is the odors that emanate from these buildings, especially after the noon meal, when some soldier has visited to relieve himself. Space is at a premium, and what genius would have thought of building the restroom facilities into the same area that soldiers would have to shower? BCKR does not care, for it is the American contracting corporation that performs all the mundane, day-to-day tasks of cleaning these facilities and constructing them as well. BCKR is truly an army in itself with its ranks not being soldiers but the local nationals, Shiite in this case, who live in the small town just outside of the base. With the economy being well below the norm of any standard, these jobs are a prize to be had by most of the Shiite locals. BCKR is truly a friend to the locals and to the US soldier as well, for gone are the days where the soldiers living on these base camps would have to perform all the mundane labor tasks such as cleaning restrooms or washing dishes. This is a great help to the soldiers, for as they travel outside the base camps on combat missions they are not tired from the day-to-day tasks of maintaining the camps, and therefore they are sharper and more alert to the combat task at hand.

Outside of one of these cleaning facilities, two US army soldiers are in conversation. One of the soldiers is sporting chevrons that identify him as a sergeant first class in rank, comparable to the gunnery sergeant in the US Marine Corps. Along with the chevron, there are patches on both shoulders of the sergeant that are the hundred and first airborne patches, an elite US Army airborne unit. On the left shoulder and above the patch are two other patches in banner form with the top banner spelling out "Airborne" and the second banner below it "Ranger," indicating that this non-commissioned officer has had elite training. This sergeant wears a vest of body armor with the sergeant first class chevron patch dead center over the heart area. Attached to the body armor are two Velcro tags. The one on his left spells out "US ARMY" and the one on the right spells out his last name, "HAZARD." Across from Sergeant First Class Hazard, stands Sergeant Purdue, who is sporting the same 101st airborne patches on both shoulders but without the elite training ranger patch that

Sergeant Hazard wears. This is Sergeant Purdue, as his name tag states; and this is not his first rodeo in Iraq. In fact, this is his second tour and Sergeant Hazard's third tour. Both sergeants are carrying holsters on their legs that contain the nine-millimeter pistol; and each is carrying the M4 rifle, which is one of the army's favorite assault weapon. With each tour comes a wealth of experience that is combined with expert training that makes them a force to be reckoned with. Sergeant Hazard is giving Sergeant Purdue the briefing on the next mission coming up.

"The mission starts at o' dark thirty," instructs Sergeant Hazard in military jargon for bright and early in the a.m.

"I want you to get your squad up and run them through the battle drill for the day."

"Start the prep training off as usual with having them function check their weapons and then run them through drills."

"I have already given the other three squad leaders the same brief, and I will brief the entire platoon with the op order when we get ready to move out."

The skilled non-commissioned officer runs down the exercises he expects each squad leader to exercise during battle drill, and we leave these soldiers to visit what appears to be a civilian who is standing opposite the soldiers across a small dirt road.

Bowe LaDeau is an American employee of BCKR. He sports a trucker's cap with a picture of a deer and the words "John Deere" right above it. Bowe is wearing a bulletproof vest that most American contractors wear in this environment. The vest is sloppily worn with the front open, offering no coverage at all, for Bowe figures he is at an American base camp and he should be safe. If Bowe had to button the vest, it would be quite difficult to fit over the pot belly, if it could fit at all. When the shooting starts, he will close the vest if need be. Being a civilian, he does not march to the same standard that American soldiers march to.

Bowe is about six feet two inches and weighs about 230 pounds. He is wearing blue jeans and Reebok track shoes. Beneath the John Deere cap is a mid-thirties, balding head with gray on the sides, which is the only place where hair will grow. He has not shaved in two days. He has hair growing out of his nose that needs constant trimming and a bushy mustache that hides the unlit end of the cigarette hanging from his mouth. One noticeable feature on Bowe is his eyes, which are light blue and piercing while retaining a rat-like appearance. Yes, Bowe can be a rat and a vicious one.

Bowe is originally from a small, rural town outside of Alexandria, Louisiana and was first employed by BCKR back during the war in Bosnia, where he has worked his way up to BCKR supervisor, a position where he is currently in charge of local national Iraqis who are employed on the base. BCKR employs a large number of technicians and craftsmen who handle most of the logistics on the bases. This contracting agency employs Americans who are willing to take a risk working in a combat zone and are paid top dollar for working there, not to mention the tax break since seventy percent of all monies earned there are not taxed. The big bucks are appealing to most Americans and, for some, the job is a way of providing a service for their country—some of whom probably never joined the military for some reason or another but are patriotic as well. However, LaDeau is clearly the exception to the rule; he is a criminal who is there to make as much money as possible illegally. Patriotism does not factor in.

Bowe's tours in the Balkans and Afghanistan have led to many criminal endeavors that were small-time scams. But Bowe, a lowlife opportunist, is always looking for the big one. Some of Bowe's criminal activities include overcharging the US government and pocketing the cash, a criminal activity that his brother in-law, Duke, and Bowe conspired in. There is the prostitution ring out of Bosnia that Bowe had set up with a Bosnian madam with whom he was having an affair. They both made a tidy profit; and when his tour was over, they both shut the ring down by turning the Bosnians who worked for them over to the United Nations police force operating in that region. The Bosnian prostitutes feared the madam, who would have her cousins take their lives in a heartbeat if they gave the madam up. There is no honor among criminals. Then there were the diamonds that were stolen from the diamond mines in Africa and smuggled through Sudan, across Iraq, into Pakistan and Afghanistan. Bowe managed to smuggle these back to the US, where he had his sidekick brother-in-law, Duke, fence them for a tidy profit.

Bowe is very greedy; and most of this greed probably spawns from his childhood days growing up in rural Louisiana. A sibling in a family of seven and the oldest son, Bowe's days were filled with going without and family violence. Bowe's father was in and out of jail mainly for driving while intoxicated; bar-room fights; and driving unregistered, uninspected vehicles. His father worked as a common laborer, which involved back-breaking jobs in some of the large cities like Alexandria or Baton Rouge. He drank most of his salary; whatever was left over, the family would get for food. His mother took jobs as a waitress in restaurants and secondary jobs cleaning people's homes. They were able to obtain some sort of state subsistence in the form of food stamps, which Bowe hated. He often saw other people stare at his mother and him when they were in the store purchasing food, and he hated to see the food stamps come out. You could see the disgust on people's faces; and although Bowe was twelve, he could hear the term "white trash" muttered from some idiot standing in line. If Bowe ever had the chance, he was going to get out of Louisiana; they could all kiss off.

On occasions when his father would come home drunk, there was a severe beating. There was one beating in particular where he had just returned from a baseball game with the local neighborhood kids. He went to the kitchen to make a sandwich out of peanut butter, unaware that his father had just tiled the kitchen counter area where Bowe was spreading the peanut butter on his sandwich. Just then, his father walked in, and he caught Bowe buttering his sandwich on the new countertop that he had just installed. Pissed off at the world and worried about where his next nickel would be coming from, he spun Bowe around and punched him in his eye. Bowe, who was twelve years old, immediately saw stars flash before his vision and went straight to the floor. The power from the blow had a loud ringing affect in Bowe's ears and was complemented by very pronounced throbbing on the side of the face where Bowe was struck, as if the throbbing was beating to a drum beat all of its own.

This did not stop his father, who jumped on top of Bowe and was raising his hand for yet another blow when he stopped to say, "Ya rotten little rug rat! I just got done tiling that countertop there and you are not going to screw it up," with eyes that were glaring and glazed over from sheer hate. He was about to swing again when—.

"Bowe senior! Ya'll get off that kid right now," screamed Bowe's mother in her Louisiana drawl. "What in hell duh ya think you are doing?"

His father glanced up at his mother, and at that moment the glazed-over look was replaced with a look of fear—yes, the fear you would probably have seen in a juvenile who just got caught doing something illegal. Meanwhile, Bowe was crying and holding onto his left eye, which now clearly swollen and immediately turning blue, and his mother did not stop.

"Do ya want to lose your kids? If de neighbor calls de cops, that is exactly what is going ta happen."

His father got off the top of Bowe and was arguing with Bowe's mother, who immediately scooped up Bowe and took him to his room.

Bowe's siblings, cowering before their father, followed their mother into Bowe's room.

"Look at his eye," his sister, Mary Sue, said, half in fear and half in childlike wonderment.

Bowe had finished crying and was busy whimpering from the event, his body shaking as if he was in below-zero weather without the proper clothing. The shock from the blow had produced the feeling of an approaching illness that was almost feverish had overcome him. The happy little twelve-year-old that was hungry and only wanted something to eat was totally confused from the beating.

He sobbed as his mother tried to comfort him. "What... what... what did I do wrong?"

"You did nothing wrong, Bowe... It's just your dad... its de way he is... He's just mean, Bowe... Shh... Don't cry now... Everything is all right... Don't cry," said his mother as she tried to comfort her son.

The shock and the effect from the beating had left Bowe with the feeling that his entire psyche had fallen into a deep hole, a deep hole that would always leave scars across his entire life. His mother would always pull him out of this hole; after a few days, Bowe would look back and learn from the event. For Bowe, this would make him the better man. His mother would always break in, pushing her husband away and standing in between both of them. This particular event would require that Bowe junior stay in the house for a week until the swelling in his eye went down.

Bowe's mother attempts to hold what family they had together by making up lies. "If someone asks, just say that you got hit in the eye with a ball. Don't tell um your father did this."

But it was the constant of going without and the sneers from people in the grocery stores whenever his mother broke out the food stamps that funneled Bowe's hate and greed. It was these events that were the underpinning of Bowe's drive to obtain as much as possible in his miserable life, even if it was obtained illegally. His mother had died five years later, and not before his father had drove his car into a tree in another drunken stupor and was killed.

As LaDeau eyes Sergeant Hazard and Sergeant Purdue from the opposite side of the road, up walks another BCKR employee, Joe Manning. Manning grew up in Boston and attended an electronics school when he graduated from high school. Manning barely made it out of the electronics training but obtained a transcript that enabled him to get a job as a BCKR employee. Unlike LaDeau, he was more of a technician that would repair some of the HQ office equipment and some military electronic equipment as well. Joe had a high school personality that was immature and was always looking for other's admiration.

Unlike LaDeau, Manning was involved with minor, juvenile, criminal activities along the order of stealing fruit from the outdoor vendors that might inhabit the Boston inner-city area. Manning likes to play these criminal activities up and would make others believe they held up the fruit stand just to add the drama to a non-dramatic event. LaDeau spotted Manning for exactly what he was, a "wannabe criminal." Another thing that LaDeau did not like about Manning was that Manning had few siblings and his parents paid for his education beyond high school. It was an indicator of upper class to LaDeau. Manning did not belong to the same lower class cut that LaDeau was made of. Manning was not much to the appearance, five feet four inches and weighed about 120 pounds—possibly another reason why he was always looking for attention and the reason he played up his criminal endeavors to make him look larger than his physical appearance.

Manning has a cockney Boston accent hiding most, if any, proper English. "Aye, sucker, What are ya up ta?"

"Not much, Yank," answers LaDeau.

Manning did not mind being called Yank and was pretty proud of it, although he never called LaDeau Reb, which was probably due to fear of, and not respect for, LaDeau. LaDeau sensed this and kept this nickel in his pocket in case he would have to spend it at a later time.

Both Manning and LaDeau like to one-upmanship spar as they exchange the local shop talk going on at Camp Trigger. Manning immediately strikes up a conversation. "Did ya hear about what the troops found in the semi truck that they confiscated from the insurgents?"

"Yeah, and BCKR bought it from de US Army," says LaDeau. He immediately deflates Manning's achievement at knowing what was going on in the fight against insurgents.

"Did ya hear about the secret room in the back of the semi? They say it was loaded with explosives and that it was about to detonate somewhere in Baghdad," asks Manning. Manning tries to trump LaDeau's knowledge; and here is where LaDeau recognizes that Manning likes to enhance the base rumors from what they really are.

"Nah. Ain't no explosives. They're smuggling in silk linen stolen from Iran," says LaDeau. Again, another trump card as LaDeau eyes Manning with a glint of satisfaction.

"They was going to sell it to de local vendors in Baghdad," answers LaDeau in another blow to Manning's credible rumor.

LaDeau educates Manning on BCKR business. "I plan on keeping the semi for our future supply loads."

This sparring on local news continues, and we leave LaDeau and Manning to their conversation and drift back to Sergeant Hazard and Sergeant Purdue.

Sergeant Hazard wraps up the instructions to Sergeant Purdue. "And that's about it."

"Okay, Sergeant Hazard. I'm on it."

"Hey, it's about chow time, ain't it?" asks Sergeant Hazard.

"Hell yeah. My stomach has been growling for the past hour." Both Sergeants head for the dining facility.

On their way, Sergeant Purdue breaks off from Sergeant Hazard's direction and heads over to one of the tents to pick up his squad for chow. After all, that is the army way—"Take care of your people"—and Sergeant Purdue follows the army way quite well.

Sergeant Purdue enters the tent and yells, "Chow time! Okay. First squad head over to the mess hall!"

Five soldiers playing video games wrap up their game quite quickly and grab their weapons. Almost like a cheer from a football stadium, there is a loud, "Hooah!" The band of soldiers begin to head outside the tent. As they fall into a single line formation facing Sergeant Purdue, they come to a position of attention with their feet together but their weapon always in the ready position, a position that points the weapon to the ground but with both hands on it, ready to fire if necessary. They await Sergeant Purdue's order, which then comes.

"Attention! Right face!" barks Sergeant Purdue. Together, they face to the right, giving the appearance of a single-file line of people.

"Route step. March!" They begin to walk toward the dining facility at a comfortable pace and not in cadence.

THE MISSION

Outside the dining facility, the soldiers arrive and stand in a line that extends outside the facility to double doors that mark the entrance. It is one minute to chow time, and a local national unlocks the doors to allow the soldiers in for the evening meal. The solider at the front of the line walks up to a red barrel that is filled with sand and is tilted forward, supported by sandbags to ensure its posture. The soldier rifles through the steps to check and clear his weapon before entering the dining facility, a procedure to ensure that a round is not in the breech when entering the facility and lower the risk of an accidental shooting, should a weapon be dropped. The last step in the process is the soldier pointing his weapon at the barrel and pulling the trigger. With no sound of a discharge comes the assurance the weapon is not loaded, and the soldier puts his weapon on safe and enters the building.

The next soldier in line steps up to the barrel and repeats the process. As the soldiers enter the building, they are greeted with a number of wash basins. When you are operating in a country where disease is prevalent, it is common practice to wash your hands before eating. This is a common US army practice with signs above the basins reminding soldiers of the practice. Each soldier washes his hands and enters a door to the dining facility, where he is greeted by a local national sitting behind a desk that has a large number of clipboards. The soldier signs in and then proceeds to the cafeteria line to obtain his meal. The local national eyes each signature, ensuring that no spaces are skipped and providing an empty sheet whenever the roster sheet has filled. Inside the dining facility are cafeteria-style, glassed counters with a large number of different main-course meals such as spaghetti, chicken steaks, salmon steaks, liver and onions, and small beef steaks to choose from.

Dishes augmented with a number of different side dishes and complete counters filled with deserts of all sorts are aligned side by side. Individual slices of blueberry pie covered with a vanilla icing, mixed fruit bowls with whipped cream topping, slices of both chocolate and white cake, puddings of all sorts covered with whipped cream and a cherry on top. A counter is devoted to salads of all sorts with the many salad dressings peaking out of the stainless steel serving decanters each with its own ladle. Plenty of drinks are found in both glassed-in refrigerators and on separate countertops: juices, teas of many sorts, and always coffee. The display is truly a king's banquet by solider standards. BCKR has the contract for providing the dining facility, and it is first-class, with very few, if any, complaints on the food from any of the soldiers.

Sergeant Purdue and first squad sign in and make their way through the many different counters of food; as each first-squad soldier fills his cafeteria-style tray, he stops and waits on his fellow first-squad soldiers to obtain their meal. Sergeant Purdue is the last first-squad soldier to fill his tray. He links up with his squad, and they choose a table to sit down to together. Sergeant Purdue, always the leader, takes care of his troops and ensures that first squad is served first before he himself is served, the army way. Usually, there are a lot of compliments on the many different dishes from the first-squad soldiers as they butter their breads and stir their drinks.

Always upbeat on the day and very hungry, they chow down. It's not long before small talk on the combat mission ahead and some shop talk on their assault weapons ensues. These are infantry soldiers who are experts with their weapons. If one soldier is having problems with a maneuver tactic or weapon malfunction, they come together and analyze the problem and always come up with a solution. These soldiers are Cracker Jack. If their squad leader is taken out during a combat mission, any one of the other soldiers can jump in and take his place. They are all well-versed on tactics, which make them a deadly force in combat. They chow down, and after the meal is complete, Sergeant Purdue announces to his squad that he needs to attend a non-commissioned officer meeting being hosted by Sergeant Hazard and then departs first squad. He searches the dining facility, locates Lieutenant Armstrong, and joins him. "Sergeant Purdue, first squad standing tall and ready to roll," responds the sergeant as he sits down to the table with Lieutenant Armstrong, a West Point graduate.

"How's it going, Sergeant Purdue?" asks Lieutenant Armstrong.

Sergeant Purdue enjoys these meals with Lieutenant Armstrong, whom he has a great deal of respect for. "Hooah, sir,"

They make small talk on the football games that are going on back in the US, and each gives his expert opinion on what should have happened on the games that they were able to see or read about during their hectic day.

Lieutenant Armstrong sports the same combat patches that both his sergeants wear and has the same elite Ranger training to boot. It is not long before the squad leader sergeants from the remaining three squads arrive and take a seat. There is the same warm greeting extended to them by Lieutenant Armstrong and returned in favor by the sergeants. Small talk again breaks out. As always, it's about the football games and current events that they might have read on some news article. It's not long before Lieutenant Armstrong breaks in with a brief overview of tomorrow's mission.

"Troops, we are heading back to a troubled area where there has been some small fighting in the past, but nothing like what we have experienced on other combat missions," Armstrong explains.

"This is pretty much routine. But we need to be aware of highly valued targets like maybe Saddam or one of his cronies.

"With that said, I will turn it over to Sergeant Hazard, who will give us instructions on where he wants to conduct his brief." Armstrong glances toward Sergeant Hazard, who had been cradling his coffee between his hands. Sergeant Hazard places his coffee cup down and takes control.

"Let's finish our drinks, and we can meet over at the ops area, and I will brief you from there."

The sergeant squad leaders immediately rise from the table, grabbing their food trays to dispense of them in one of the tray racks. A number of local nationals are talking in their mother tongue, dressed in the familiar white work uniform that all kitchen help wears. They grab the tray racks, which are on small wheels, and roll the racks through double, swinging doors to the kitchen area behind the same counter where the food was served. There are a lot of guttural sounds that emanate from the Shiite dialect that almost seem alien to the English speakers. As the sergeants place their food trays into the tray racks, they pass the local nationals; and the body odor is quite pronounced. It emanates from the local nationals, who do not have running water at their homes. Because of this lack of resource, water is at a premium and is used sparingly. There are plans to develop the local wells in the small town that the locals come from. However, those plans have not come to fruition, and so they make do with what they have.

The sergeants are used to the odor and pay it no mind. They drop their food trays off and head for the exit, following Sergeant Hazard and Lieutenant Armstrong. Sergeant Hazard waits outside the dining facility on the remaining sergeants and takes a head count.

"Okay. Let's move out to the ops," barks Sergeant Hazard. They start down a small dirt road to the ops area just outside the motor pool.

The ops area is nothing more than an open area roughly a hundred yards from the motor pool, not a formal briefing area with chairs and tables but an open field of rocks and dirt that is sparsely patched with grass. This is the briefing area that most US Army sergeants prefer to conduct their briefs, for the army sergeant is an outdoor, muddy boots sort of person. He is a Johnny Appleseed character , but instead of planting apple trees, he plants ideas on leadership and training.

"Take a knee," barks Hazard as they arrive at the field. The troops form a semicircle around Sergeant Hazard. The sergeants pull out their small, green notepads and prepare to take notes.

While Sergeant Hazard is conducting his brief, Sergeant Purdue's first squad has arrived at their tent to continue the video game and card game they left. They all gather around a foot locker, a rectangular, wooden box used to store their personnel belongings. They pull out the small chairs and take a seat, using the foot locker as a table with a small-screen TV on top. Private Billings is working the hand control, as is Private Bixby, and small talk ensues.

"Can you believe that shot Sergeant Hazard made?" announces Billings.

Billings respects Sergeant Hazard partly due to his elite airborne ranger training and the thought that he is always looking after his troops.

"No joke," another soldier chimes in.

"He wasted two insurgents at an easy four hundred and fifty meters," Billings continues.

"Did you see how quick that happened? I bet he aimed, pulled the trigger, and aimed again all within two seconds easy."

"Man, how I wish I was that kind of shot," another soldier pipes in.

"Yeah. That Sergeant Hazard is something else. I sure am glad he is on my side," says Billings.

They all nod their heads in agreement.

"Sergeant Hazard is pretty good to us," Billings continues.

The soldiers at the card table yell "Hooah," in agreement.

"I mean, he is hard on us when it comes to training, but he is always looking out for us. Remember that time we were just setting up forward operating position in area two thirty-nine and we did not even have anyplace to take a shower and nothing to eat but MRE's. It did not take Sergeant Hazard more than six hours to get a portable shower tent set up and to have food airlifted to us," Billings recalls.

"Yeah," replies Private Bixby. "We thought we were going to eat MRE's for a month."

"Not to mention being able to take a shower for a month," Bixby continues.

"Sergeant Hazard and Sergeant Purdue both know how to take care of their troops."

And another, "Hooah," is shouted out as the soldiers continue their card game.

It is not long before Sergeant Purdue enters the tent and takes a seat at the makeshift table.

"Deal me in on the next round," Purdue shouts. "Looks like we are headed back to the little town Al Hila," Purdue explains as he gathers his dealt hand from the card table.

"Another search-for-Al-Qaeda exercise?" asks one soldier as he reviews the cards he was dealt.

"No. It's a search for Saddam, but we always have to be on our toes like it is Al Qaeda we are after," explains Sergeant Purdue. "And, team, when we are through with this hand, we need to get cleaned up and get some sleep because when it is o' dark thirty hours and, well, you know the drill," announces Purdue. "Is everybody tracking?"

The card table and video game table erupt with a, "Hooah!" from all the soldiers.

As the video and card games continue, let's leave our band of brothers to their favorite pastime, for outside the tent night has fallen rapidly. The wind has picked up slightly, and the sky is full of stars. An occasional breeze whips up the dust from the dirt roads that navigate the base and cause an occasional tent to billow against the breeze. It won't be long before another day breaks the horizon.

It's o' dark thirty, or early in the a.m., and the soldiers are starting to stir from their tents. Although it is dark outside, they manage to stand at attention with their weapons at the ready and pointed toward the ground. There are four ranks of soldiers facing in the same direction with about seven soldiers to a rank. SFC Hazard is taking roll call, and he calls out each soldier by their last name, to which they respond, "Here, Sergeant." SFC Hazard goes down his list, checking off each name. When everyone is accounted for, he announces the op order for the day.

"Today, first platoon will battle drill in preparation for reconnoiter of the little town of Al Hila just outside the oil refinery about thirty clicks from our location. Now, we know the town has been pretty peaceful and we have not had too much trouble, but first platoon is always ready for trouble. Hooah."

All the soldiers standing in rank respond. "Hooah."

Sergeant Hazard continues with the operation order, "We will be a passive reconnoiter, where we will be knocking on doors and asking the locals if they have seen anything out of the ordinary. Now, I am thinking since it is a small town that everybody knows everybody else's business and if something is strange, it will be exposed by the locals. We have been good to the locals, and they have helped us in the past, and we do not want to ruin that trust.

"We will battle drill, get some downtime for personal hygiene, grab some grub at the dining facility, and then report to the motor pool, where we will mount up no later than zero six hundred hours. Now we have to move out quickly because I want us to be at the town when the sun is barely rising. Hooah!"

The platoon responds, "Hooah!"

Sergeant Hazard pauses and then commands, "First platoon, attention."

The platoon snaps to the attention.

A pause. "Right face," yells Hazard; and the platoon performs the movement.

"File from the right column right," commands the next movement; and three of the squad leaders at the front of the four formation lines yell, "Stand fast."

The fourth squad leader yells, "Forward."

Sergeant Hazard breaks in with, "March," and the soldiers peel off in single file to the battle drill area.

With battle drill over and first platoon completing personal hygiene followed by dining at the dining facility, all soldiers report to the motor pool as instructed.

The vehicles are in their standard combat formation, with engines running in preparation for leaving the base. It's a serious business for the air guards who are soldiers that stand through a circular hole known as the ring mount in the Humvee roof directly behind the fifty-caliber machine guns mounted on top of the roof are prepared for battle. The lead vehicle in the convoy begins to move out and in single file. The other vehicles follow as they drive toward the exit for Camp Trigger. Upon immediately exiting Camp Trigger, the lead vehicle makes a left and heads down an adjacent road to the main highway. It's a dirt road about a quarter mile from the main highway providing the sand that is billowing in a dust cloud behind each vehicle. Gradually, the dust cloud drifts away from the road as it is coaxed by a morning breeze, clearing the driver's view from the vehicle following.

The lead vehicle enters the main highway and heads toward the right, toward Al Hila. The sun has not quite risen, but the twilight offers enough light for the drivers to see down the distant highway. It is about forty minutes into the drive when the sleepy little town of Al Hila is seen from the distance; and as predicted by Sergeant Hazard, the sun is just rising. Not far from the town, a few of the lead vehicles break off and head toward a small hill that provides an overwatch area for the squad that will pull security. They quickly move into their combat positions that provide them the advantage point for viewing all that can be seen. A few more vehicles peel off and head toward a main street of the town while another set of vehicles heads toward the back side of the town.

They all stop before starting their patrol, as soldiers hop out of the Humvees, and quickly move to a presence patrol position for a foot march into the town. The soldiers line up on both sides of the road, and the vehicles follow not too far behind. The air guards' fingers are on the triggers of their fifty-caliber weapons, each pointing in the opposite direction of the other, providing the cover needed should an ambush pop up. The sleepy little town is barely waking up. As some of the locals open their doors to step outside, they are greeted by the interpreters and the squad leader of each foot patrol. The greetings are always friendly, and the interpreters communicate the request to search the home. The greetings are always accepted as the soldiers enter the residence, weapons at the ready, in team formations, searching each room as they go. This process repeats itself on the opposite side of the street, where third squad is searching the Shiite homes.

First squad is in the lead, and they are the squad that reaches the end of the small town that is bordered by a series of warehouses used to contain oil refinery machinery. As they complete searching one of the homes, it is Private Bixby who runs into the little girl who is playing outside her home. Private Bixby has been schooled to treat the kids with respect and offer them candy whenever possible. The little girl is about eight years old with very dark eyes and a very friendly smile. She grabs the stick of gum and unravels the wrapper. Her eyes getting larger at every corner the wrapper reveals. She finally reaches the gum and, with a very large smile, sticks it in her mouth, smiling all the way.

"Saddam," responds the little Iraqi girl between a couple of chews as she points to the warehouse.

Private Bixby is as surprised with the response as the girl was when she was unwrapping the gum.

"Sergeant Purdue!" yells Bixby; and Sergeant Purdue, standing close by, glances in his direction, ever alert.

"Over here, Sergeant Purdue."

And Sergeant Purdue immediately heads in Bixby's direction. "What's up, Private Bixby?" asks Sergeant Purdue.

"The kid pointed to the warehouse and said, 'Saddam,' Sarge." Private Bixby pulls his M4 assault weapon closer as if it were a child he was comforting, readying him for the next expected explosive moment. As he stares off toward the warehouse with eyes wide-open, one can see that his pupils are quite enlarged as if to let in more light in a darkened room. This is the adrenalin that has kicked in, and the fear has already set in.

"It's not time to get scared yet, Bixby. Save it for when we breach the building, and don't worry. Everything is going to be okay," said Sergeant Purdue as he comforts the soldier.

"Just remember your training and everything will be okay. Hooah." Sergeant Purdue pats on Private Bixby on the shoulder while Bixby responds in like.

"Hooah, Sarge."

Sergeant Purdue nods in approval.

"Wait here, and we will consolidate first squad before we search the warehouse," barks Sergeant Purdue.

Sergeant Purdue is well-skilled in advancing toward a building that has yet to be searched, and so he consolidates his squad giving commands on the approach.

"This is too big of a building for a single squad to search, and I will need to give Sergeant Hazard a call for further guidance. First squad, take up a security position," barks Sergeant Purdue as first squad immediately moves into position, some of them kneeling while others peer behind the corners of buildings along the street.

Sergeant Purdue grabs the radio microphone in his hand and speaks. "Big Red One." The radio cackles and the Sergeant continues with the call. "Big Red One, we are north of the warehouse and got a tip from one of the local kids that Saddam is housed in the building."

"It's too big for one squad to cover. What are your directions? Over."

There is a pause and then, "This is Big Red One. Stand fast, and I will bring the remaining squads with me. Big Red One out." And the radio goes dead.

Sergeant Purdue motions to his people to stand fast as he waits in position for Sergeant Hazard to show up. Not long after, a number of Humvees turn the corner of the street; and the remaining three squads take up a security position.

"Take up a security position along both sides of the warehouse, and you air guards stay sharp," barks Sergeant Hazard.

The air guards are standing through a ring mount circular door in the roof of the Humvee with one air guard standing behind the M2, a fifty-caliber machine gun, and the other air guard shouldering the M248B machine gun. From the intense look in their faces and the firmly yet skillfully positioned weapons it is clear that these soldiers are ready for a gunfight. The Humvees drive off in a plume of fumes and dust, each taking up a position along the sides of the warehouse. Sergeant Hazard motions to the squad leaders of the soldiers positioned along the sides of the streets, and they run across the street in Sergeant Hazard's direction. They link up with Sergeant Hazard, who immediately takes charge. The instructions come quick as the tension builds for what will come next.

"Second squad and third squad, you will enter the east and west corners of the building, breaching the windows for access," barks Hazard. "First squad will enter the center door first, followed by second squad through the east window and third squad by the west window. Fourth squad will pull security outside the warehouse both east and west along its longest sides."

The squad leaders are listening intently. The smell of sweat and gun oil from the previous maintenance inspection of their weapons that day fills the air around the huddle.

"First squad, toss a flash bang before entering and take up a concealed position once inside. If you take on fire, provide cover for second squad as it breaches the east window."

"Second squad, once inside, you will provide cover along with first squad while third squad breaches the west window."

We can see that the look among the squad leaders is becoming more intense.

"If we do not take on fire, I want all squads to begin clearing the building. Okay. You know the drill. Is everyone ready?" asks Hazard as the squad leaders respond with, "Hooah."

The squad leaders break contact with Sergeant Hazard and beat feet across the street to their respective squads. A motion from Sergeant Hazard, and the squads begin to move out in tandem toward the warehouse. First squad approaches the center of the building, just right of the door, with their shoulders against the building. Private Denton is the first to take up position next to the door, with Private Bixby behind him and Sergeant Purdue following in the rear. First squad has their weapons in the ready position, pointing forward. Sergeant Purdue gives the order to Private Denton.

"Flash bang."

On cue, Private Denton opens the door and pops in grenade simulator.

Moments later, *Bang!* The echo is heard outside the building, rolling across the ground.

Without a moment's notice, Private Denton rushes through the door and takes up position behind a supporting column, followed by Private Bixby, who travels right to another supporting column. Sergeant Purdue enters the door and dives behind an old Arab supply truck with his weapon pointing toward the driver window, which appears to be empty. Without hesitation, second squad kicks in the east window, jumps through the window, and takes up a concealed position behind another supply truck, followed by third squad breaching the west window.

With all squads in place, the squad leaders order their troops to search the floor of the warehouse. The warehouse contains a number of old Soviet supply trucks possibly brought in from Afghanistan during the war between Iraq and Iran. The soldiers cover each other meticulously as they search both the driver and passenger sides and work their way to the back of the truck. Some of the trucks have a canvas tarp covering the back, and these are the most dangerous since a combatant could be hiding behind the canvas. The squads make their way along the warehouse floor only to find the trucks empty. Meanwhile, Sergeant Purdue and first squad spot a stairwell going down beneath the floor of the warehouse. Sergeant Purdue signals the other squad leaders, indicating that his squad will search that area.

The light from inside the building shines down the stairwell enough so that soldiers can see the bottom of the stairwell. Sergeant Purdue lines his men up to descend the stairwell, and they slowly begin their descent. This is a tense moment that is almost like diving into a frozen lake during the wintertime with nothing on but a bathing suit. The affect is the same in that it nearly takes ones breath away and the cold, numbing feeling of the ice water is replaced with the cold, numbing feeling of fear. The order of descent is Private Bixby, Private Denton, and Sergeant Purdue. Private Bixby descends to the bottom. The bottom of the stairwell is dark , and it is clear they will need light in order to search.

"Sarge, it's pitch black down here. I can't see a thing."

Before he finishes the sentence, Sergeant Purdue has already popped a chem light and tossed it into the darkness. The soft, green light slowly fills the room; and dark objects toward the walls of the room begin to take shape as if rising out of the water of blackness. Sergeant Purdue pops a few more chem lights and tosses them about the floor of the basement. The center of the basement is barren except for the chem lights that are rolling across the floor. With the added chem lights, the basement becomes well-lit. It is clear to see that objects that had risen from the blackness earlier are nothing more than office file cabinets.

WE STRUCK GOLD

"Okay, men. Let's search the file cabinets, and be careful. They might be booby trapped," instructs Sergeant Purdue as the soldiers begin to search all sides of the file cabinets, looking for anything that might look like a trip wire. With nothing found, Sergeant Purdue orders his troops back away from the file cabinets.

"Private Bixby, I want you to slowly open the top drawer of the file cabinet while ducking down below the door," barks Sergeant Purdue. "Before you do that, I need you to remove your body armor and hold it front of you so that you are standing behind both of the armor plates," cautions Sergeant Purdue. "That will give you added protection in case there is a detonation."

Private Bixby executes Sergeant Purdue's command, removing his body armor, which is snapped shut by Velcro. As Private Bixby peels away the Velcro, the sound fills the room as the Velcro releases its glue-like hold. The body armor contains two armor plates, one in the front and one in the back to protect the soldier from bullets or shrapnel.

Standing behind the two plates gives Bixby double protection in the case of a booby trap going off. Bixby positions the plates between his torso and the file cabinet while reaching around in front of the plates and slowly begins depressing the slide on the file cabinet. This is a long moment for Bixby and his compatriots as they wait intensely for what the next moment might reveal.

The clear, crisp, and distinct sound of a metal latch releasing its grip on the file cabinet drawer can be heard. Bixby begins to slowly pull the file cabinet drawer open. The wheels of the file cabinet drawer ride across the attached rail like a trolley car pulling up and parking in one of the Boston underground subways. The wheels reach the end of the rail and are greeted with metal on metal sound as if two trolley cars had collided while breaking for a stop, indicating the file cabinet drawer has reached the end of its journey.

There is a moment of silence. "Clear," barks Sergeant Purdue.

"Okay Bixby, check it out," comes the next command. Private Bixby rises up to peer inside of the drawer.

The basement had the odor of most basements, that of musk and dirt, but when the file cabinet drawer was stretched open, the odor of old paper begins to enter the room—yes, old paper that has the distinct odor of money.

"Sarge, it's full of money!" yells Bixby.

Sergeant Purdue and Private Denton had taken cover behind their body armor in the same fashion as Private Bixby, and Sergeant Purdue's head pops up behind the body armor.

"Money? Are you sure, Bixby?" asks Sergeant Purdue in a bewildered response.

"Yes Sarge! It sure is full of money," responds Private Bixby.

Sergeant Purdue and Private Denton rise up and approach Private Bixby. By now, the smell of money has spread throughout the basement; and Sergeant Purdue and Denton peer over the top of the file cabinet drawer. All three have a childlike look of wonder and amazement. There, in one of the most puzzling places to store money in the world, are what appear to be one-hundred-dollar bills, stacked one on top of the other. Stacks, that rise up from the bottom of the twelve-inch-deep file cabinet and fill its full three-foot length.

"Whew! There must be a million dollars right here," announces Sergeant Purdue as he looks across the basement to five-foot cabinets all of the same size lined up as if in military formation. There are twelve cabinets across each side of the basement wall, with the back wall holding about eight cabinets. The eerie glow of the green florescent light emanates from the chem lights across the basement, and the smell of money is almost intoxicating.

"We must be close to Saddam," remarks Sergeant Purdue.

"This must be some of his blood money that he milked from the poor Iraqis."

"Okay. I need to radio this into Sergeant Hazard pronto. I need both of you to repeat the exercise that we just did for each file cabinet door that you open. Do not get lazy and just grab a file cabinet door and open it. You know the procedure. Follow through," barks Sergeant Purdue as he begins to ascend the basement steps.

"Hooah," yell the troops he left behind. He reaches the top of the stairs, and yells to the squad leaders who were congregating around the far end of the warehouse.

They all walk over to Sergeant Purdue's location.

Sergeant Purdue begins to fill them in on the discovery. "You aren't going to believe what we just found!"

"I have to check this out myself," responds the sergeant of second squad.

"Me too," says the third squad leader; and they begin to descend the basement stairwell with Sergeant Purdue right behind them.

The squad leaders descend the basement steps. By now, Private Bixby and Private Denton have opened only one file cabinet and have many more to go.

"Sarge, we finished clearing the first cabinet," responds Private Bixby; and they begin starting on the second using the same methodical approach.

"Hold up! We need to check this cabinet out," commands Sergeant Purdue as he opens the top drawer and the remaining squad leaders peer in.

The battle-hardened faces began to soften, and their faces begin to light up as if in awe of a sunset just appearing over a hill on a crisp, clear, cloudless day in the Rockies of Colorado. Their jaws drops open.

"Wow! Man! There must be a million dollars here!"

They begin to open the remaining drawers of the file cabinet, and they all reveal the same content. Benjamin Franklin, in his light, striped, collared coat with a neckcloth, the smirk, all stacked on top of each other, one on top of the other. When the last file cabinet drawer is opened, another choir of Franklins appears.

"Bingo! We must have four million dollars here!"

The squad leaders slowly peer around the room, looking at all the file cabinets that line the walls.

The third squad leader speaks up. "It is clear we need to follow protocol with the opening of the file cabinets, and it looks like first squad will need the help from our squad and second squad as well."

The other squad leaders nod in agreement.

"This is probably blood money," remarks the second squad leader. Again, they all nod in agreement.

The third squad leader speaks up. "I'll get the other soldiers down here to help out." The squad leaders head for the stairwell and begin to ascend the stairs.

Sergeant Purdue stays behind and assists Private Bixby and Private Denton with the opening of the second file cabinet using the same precautionary steps while opening the file cabinet drawers. As they open each drawer, the same content appears with Benjamin Franklin and his smirk peering out of the file drawers. By now, the smell of money has filled the basement and continues to get stronger. Meanwhile, on the floor above, the squad leaders have rounded up their soldiers and created a semicircle huddle around the second and third squad leaders.

"Take a knee," commands the second squad leader; and all the soldiers lower to the floor. "Here's the situation," barks the second squad leader. "We have about thirty file cabinets in the basement below, and we need to open each file cabinet and examine its contents. Now, we know we are just not going to walk up and open the drawer without using some precautionary steps. You all have been trained in how to conduct the search. Right now, we are going to take you downstairs and have you open each of the drawers for our inspection. Once you have the door open, we want you to call your squad leader over to the drawer so that we can verify the contents of the drawer. Any questions?" asks the second squad leader. After a moment of silence he says, "Okay, move out."

The troops respond, "Hooah."

The soldiers head down the stairwell and join first squad in clearing procedures to ensure that the file cabinets are inspected thoroughly before attempting to open the drawers. With each squad lined up against a wall of cabinets, the inspection starts to pick up speed. When the soldiers ensure that the file cabinet drawer can be opened, they call over their squad leader to investigate the contents. Each squad leader takes inventory and annotates the contents in their pocket notebooks, a standard non-commissioned officer tool used to take notes in their day-to-day work.

During the inspection, the squad leader reports loud enough so that the other squad leaders can hear, "We struck gold." They continue on with their inspection of the drawers. Not all the drawers contained money, as the soldiers discovered during the inspection. Of the thirty file cabinets, only twenty-two cabinets contained money, with the remainder of the file cabinets either being empty or containing documents photos of Iraqi personnel. When first discovered, Sergeant Purdue thought this might have belonged to a watch list that Saddam's henchmen were using to monitor suspected dissidents.

Purdue reviews the different photos. "Probably some sort of file on people whom Saddam wanted to do in or people whom he might have killed."

"She's a knockout." The second squad leader remarks as he and Sergeant Purdue review the photos of an Iraqi female close to their age.

"Something for the intel folks," remarks the third squad leader. All the squad leaders nod in approval.

The inspection proceeds forward with all the thirty file cabinets inspected. Almost thirty minutes later, and all of the file cabinets have been inventoried. The squad leaders get together for a huddle and to compare notes.

"I had nine cabinets filled with money and two cabinets filled with photos," reports the first squad leader to Sergeant Purdue.

"I have six cabinets of money, one cabinet that is empty and two filled with photos," reports the second squad leader.

"I have seven cabinets of money, one cabinet that is empty, and two cabinets with photos," reports the third squad leader.

"Okay. I will go upstairs and report to Sergeant Hazard what we found," announces Sergeant Purdue.

"Sergeant Pulley and I will stay here and keep track of the inventory and prepare to move the file cabinet drawers to the top floor," reports Sergeant Beaman, the third squad leader.

Sergeant Purdue heads up the stairwell to the top floor and makes a call over his radio to Sergeant Hazard.

"Big Red One, this is Little Bullet. Over."

Not long after, the radio squawks. "This is Big Red One," answers Sergeant Hazard as his voice blares out of the speaker.

"Big Red One, we have secured the warehouse and, in the process, found a basement filled with file cabinets and discovered a large amount of money. We need your assistance for guidance on how to handle this. Over."

There is a pause

"This is Big Red One. I will be there in five mics. Out," and the radio call concludes.

HAZARD IS
INFORMED

Five minutes later, and Sergeant Hazard appears through the door with his driver; and they both walk across the warehouse floor.

In a few strides, he clears the warehouse floor and reaches Sergeant Purdue. "Sergeant Purdue, what do we have?" asks Hazard.

Sergeant Purdue responds. "Follow me, Sergeant."

With that, they both head down the stairwell to the basement. At the bottom of the basement, Sergeant Hazard is greeted by the remaining squad leaders, Sergeant Pulley and Sergeant Beaman.

"We struck gold, Sergeant Hazard!" yells Sergeant Pulley.

"A whole lot of gold," said Sergeant Beaman.

"We found about twenty-two cabinets with the drawers filled with hundred-dollar bills, and about six cabinets filled with what looks like some sort of personnel file on Iraqis. Not sure what that is about, but it could be one of Saddam's hit lists. And the remaining file cabinets are empty," Sergeant Purdue explains.

"Well, let's see what you have," commands Sergeant Hazard. The squad leaders escort Hazard over to the file cabinet where they first found the money.

As they open the drawer, the same magical smirk appears on Benjamin Franklin's face.

"Whoa!" responds Sergeant Hazard.

"You weren't kidding. There must be a ten million dollars in this drawer alone! Well, we are going to need a supply truck to move the contents," instructs Sergeant Hazard. "We might as well leave all the money and the records in the file cabinets. We will get one of the five-ton trucks and load the file cabinets onto the truck. We will need to secure each of the drawers so they do not fly open while in transport back to base camp. Sergeant Purdue, get on the horn and radio to base camp requesting a five-ton. Ask the drivers to bring with them a number of rolls of duck tape so we can secure the cabinets during transport. When you are done making that call, make another call to Lieutenant Armstrong and tell him we need him here."

"Hooah!" yells Sergeant Purdue. Purdue heads up the stairwell to make the radio call.

"Okay. Let's inventory what we have," commands Sergeant Hazard. "Now, I know we are not going to count each and every hundred-dollar bill, but we need to count the stacks of hundred-dollar bills that we have in a drawer. We also need to take a best guess at the number of Iraqi records that we have in the drawers and keep track of that count. If you squad leaders can get with your personnel and take that inventory and report back to me that would be great."

The squad leaders take their positions among their squads, opening each file cabinet drawer, noting what each drawer contains within their notebook. The squad leaders and their troops maneuver among the file cabinets, taking meticulous counts and recording the contents. It is not long before all the file cabinets have been inventoried and the counts tallied. The squad leaders compare notes and then walk over to Sergeant Hazard, who has been monitoring the inspection.

"Here is what we have, Sergeant," responds Sergeant Pulley. "For the drawers that contain the money, we have thirty-two stacks of hundred-dollar bills, with each stack filled to the top of the drawer There are five drawers to a file cabinet, and we have eight file cabinets filled with money, so that's forty drawers with each drawer containing thirty-two stacks of hundred-dollar bills."

Sergeant Beaman interrupts. "We have what appear to be three hundred folders each containing an Iraqi personnel record, and we have six file cabinets with five drawers each. That gives us a total of thirty drawers with roughly about eighteen thousand Iraqi personnel records. The remaining file cabinets are empty."

As Sergeant Hazard and his squad leaders are theorizing why both the money and Iraqi records were found together, they hear footsteps walking across the warehouse floor.

"That must be the lieutenant," reports Sergeant Hazard. It is not long before Lieutenant Armstrong and Sergeant Purdue descend the stairwell and head over to Sergeant Hazard and the squad leader's huddle.

"How is it going, Lieutenant?" asks Sergeant Hazard.

"Okay, Sergeant. What do you have?"

Sergeant Hazard runs down what his squad leaders have found.

The chem lights continue to glow the eerie, fluorescent green; and as the light reflects off the huddle with Sergeant Hazard, the squad leaders, and Lieutenant Armstrong, it casts an eerie shadow across the basement wall. The fluorescent green light is reminiscent of what one would see as one peers through night-vision goggles. The hand gestures from Lieutenant Armstrong and Sergeant Hazard add to the eerie phenomena, along with the strong scent of money emanating throughout the basement. The soldiers in the huddle have their weapons shouldered so that the assault weapon is resting over their shoulder with their arm through the rifle sling. Each soldier has an M9 pistol attached to his leg, and the shadows projected against the basement walls are somewhat reminiscent of a bunch of cowboys huddling around a campfire out on some range in the far West, with each cowboy carrying the tools they need to ward off varmints or cattle rustlers. After a number of hand gestures, Sergeant Hazard walks Lieutenant Armstrong through each of the contents of the file cabinets, comparing the notes of what they have and validating the counts. It takes some ten minutes to validate the count.

"Looks like we have inventoried as best as we can," remarks Lieutenant Armstrong. "And now we need to call up to higher headquarters on what was found. When the five-ton gets here, let's go ahead and secure the file cabinet drawers and label each file cabinet such that we can tell which file cabinet has the money and which has the records. We could use something like two small strips of duct tape for the file cabinets with money and one small strip for the file cabinets with Iraqi personnel records. Getting a file cabinet full of money up these steps is going to be a challenge and perhaps we should remove the drawers and have the soldiers carry the drawers up the stairwell and then assemble the drawers within the file cabinets once we have the file cabinets upstairs."

As Lieutenant Armstrong and Sergeant Hazard work out the details, one leaves the warehouse to see the five-ton truck finally showing up at the entrance of the sleepy little town of Al Hila. The five-ton truck is being heavily escorted with Bradley escort vehicles, an indicator to anyone thinking of picking a fight that there might be some risk. The five-ton truck weaves through the small streets and down to the warehouse. It is fourth squad that is pulling security motions to the five-ton truck and gets it in place to be loaded. The fourth squad leader gets on the horn and radios to Lieutenant Armstrong that the five-ton truck is in place.

By now, the file cabinets have been carried up to the top floor of the warehouse and the only remaining task is to button down the file cabinet drawers with duct tape so the drawers are secured during transport. The soldiers have positioned the file cabinets close to the exit doors and begin to hoist the file cabinets through the doors and up and onto the back of the five-ton truck. The five-ton truck is a behemoth of a truck and is made for rough terrain. It resembles the huge dump trucks that are used in road construction, with the exception being that the frame is made of steel. The wheels are all-terrain wheels, and the truck runs on diesel fuel. As the five-ton behemoth is backed up, the strong scent of diesel fuel fills the air. It overrides the stench of the small town that has the odor of human feces that permeates the streets of the small town and is probably due to the human waste not being properly disposed of.

With the five-ton in place, the soldiers obtain the duct tape from the driver and begin to button up the drawers of the file cabinet by circling the file cabinet with the duct tape, securing the drawer in place. They label the file cabinets appropriately and begin the tough task of transporting the file cabinets through the doors of the warehouse and hoisting them up onto the bed of the five-ton truck, a job only built for soldiers; and by design, the soldiers can handle the job. There are some grunts and groans and shouted warnings to each other as to where they are stepping. When it comes time to hoist the file cabinet, there is a, "And on three. One, two, three, and lift. "Each file cabinet is hoisted onto the bed of the truck and moved to the back, where it is lined up one next to the other. Meanwhile, fourth squad is pulling security and monitoring the perimeter of the warehouse and any area that might appear as an avenue of attack. Similar to African army ants, fourth squad represents the soldiers that will go on the attack if any of the workers that are loading the five-ton truck are attacked. It is not long before the truck is loaded and the file cabinets are secured.

Sergeant Hazard does not waste time and orders his soldiers back into the warehouse for a quick safety brief. He runs down the typical procedures of what his drivers should be doing and what the air guards should be watching for the trip.

The briefing is quick and ends with, "Are there any questions? If not, hooah."

The soldiers respond with "Hooah," and they break from the meeting and head toward their vehicles. It's not long before the vehicles are running and the smell of diesel and gasoline fumes fills the air.

BACK TO BASE

The convoy has grown larger with the addition of the five-ton supply truck and the Bradley escort vehicles. Sergeant First Class Hazard is the convoy commander, and he gives the Bradley vehicle drivers and the five-ton supply truck driver instructions on the position they will take during the convoy back to base camp. It is not long before the convoy leaves the sleepy little town of Al Hila as they snake their way through the small town streets, kicking up dust as they go. Between the smell of diesel fuel, the dust in the air, and the odor of a septic tank backing up, the odors are almost unbearable as the convoy traverses the streets. The Shiites who dominate the town are up and out of their homes, watching the convoy as it leaves the town. The small children run along some of the vehicles. Some throw rocks in front of the vehicles in a childish attempt, thinking they can flatten the tires when the vehicle runs over it. It is not long before the convoy has cleared the town and they are on the major highway, heading back to base camp.

Private Denton is one of the drivers of the Humvee trucks, and riding shotgun is Private Bixby. Private Bixby grew up in Lansing, Michigan. He graduated from high school at seventeen and was the youngest of three siblings. His mom worked in a restaurant while his dad worked as an auto mechanic. They were working-class people. They lived in a mobile home that, although was small, was home for their small family. His parents did the Cub Scout thing and saw him through Boy Scouts, attending most of the scout meetings as best as they could. They attended a Methodist church and attended PTA meetings when they could spare the time. Although he graduated from high school at an early age, Private Bixby was an average student. His parents made enough money to get by. With all the bills coming in, they lived week-to-week on paychecks that came in, saving money when they could. Private Bixby was enthused with the characters that stood for what was good and the right thing to do; he always cheered for the good guy or hero while watching television shows or movies. It was that connection with the characters that Bixby identified with. It was because of this connection that Bixby thought the US Army was a home for him, full of people he could identify with.

"Wow, man. Did you see the cash in those drawers?" asks Denton as he drives down the highway.

"Hell yeah. I bet there must be ten million dollars," answers Bixby.

"Nah. There has to be a heck of a lot more, fifty million at least. I wonder what they are going to do with the money?" asks Denton.

"My guess is they will store it at base camp until they can figure out where it came from. It is probably money that Saddam ripped off from his people," answers Bixby.

"That would be my guess, and I think Sergeant Hazard had it right that its blood money."

"Yeah. Blood money," says Denton.

" It's blood money. But it makes you wonder why all that money and those personnel records of Iraqis were stored with the money? I wonder what was going on there," asks Bixby.

"It's probably a hit list of people Saddam killed," answers Denton. "My guess is that when they try to find all of those people, they won't turn up."

"Yeah. They have been snuffed more than likely," remarks Bixby.

"But, wow, that money. Boy, when I opened that drawer and saw that money and the smell... wow. It almost took my breath away," says Denton.

"Yeah. Sweet," remarks Bixby. They both clench their fists and knock knuckles as their Hummer makes it way down the highway.

In another convoy vehicle, Sergeant Hazard puts his paperwork down for a moment and watches the highway for the next unexpected event that might occur. Directly behind Hazard is the air guard with half of his body peering through the circular hole in the roof with his finger on the trigger of his M248B machine gun. With his desert goggles on, he is scanning the highway, looking for the next possible location of an IED or a possible ambush from an insurgent. The desert palms drift by with small fields of crops of beans and tomatoes.

In the same vehicle, Lieutenant Armstrong looks at his watch and realizes that he needs to make the call back to base. He picks up the hand microphone and presses the key. "Big Sky, this is Red Leader. Over."

There is a pause in communications, and the speaker begins to squeal.

"Red Leader, this is Big Sky," echoes the voice from the other end.

"Big Sky, we have found a cache at objective one that appears to be a large amount of personnel records and a very large amount of money. Over," explains Armstrong. "The money appears to be in the millions of dollars, and we are not a sure exactly how large. Over."

And then conversation continues.

Meanwhile, back at the base camp, LaDeau is standing next to a convoy that is about to depart the base. LaDeau is reviewing some construction work that his hired local nationals had performed when he overhears the radio message that just came over the radio of a Humvee that was sitting in a convoy formation getting ready to leave the base. He recognizes the person calling as Lieutenant Armstrong and has overhead that a cache of dollars, possibly in the millions, was found. LaDeau's piercing eyes begin to widen and change to something like a child in awe of their first sight of a butterfly that might have landed on their hand. With eyebrows raised somewhat and his mouth half-opened, it is clear to see that LaDeau had made a most amazing discovery.

Millions of dollars? he thinks to himself. The wheels of greed begin to turn in LaDeau's squirrel cage brain. It's an almost animal instinct that has risen up, looking for its next meal. *Hmm. That money will be back at base quite soon, and the army will want to secure it.* He ponders the situation. *I need some of that money, but not all of it. No sah. Taking all of de money will draw attention. But if they are missing a few hundred thousand, who's to know? How am I going to do that?* LaDeau's sinister mind continues turning. *I need a plan.*

Back at the convoy, Lieutenant Armstrong has closed out his call and has made his first SP, or scheduled point. When all of a sudden, *Kabang!* A loud, deafening sound fills the air, and for an instant it is all that can be heard. As the sound dies out, Lieutenant Armstrong recognizes that one of the Bradleys was hit with an improvised explosive device, or IED, and it's blocking the road. As the deafening sound rolls across the ground and begins to die out, there is a the sound of automatic gunfire coming from a clump of palm trees in the distance on the right side of the road and is followed by another report of automatic gunfire from the left side of the road. They are caught in crossfire, and this is not a good place to be. The Bradley is totally destroyed, with all of its occupants killed. The air guards spring into action and answer the call by sending down range a hail of gunfire from the fifty-calibers and M248B machine guns. The traffic has come to a standstill, and action must be taken to clear the road. Immediately, the driver of a Humvee that was following the Bradley attempts to drive around the Bradley. *Whoosh!* A rocket-propelled grenade just missed the Humvee passengers and hits the front of the engine. *Kabang!* Another deafening explosion. Lieutenant Armstrong immediately assesses the situation and knows that he needs his convoy to clear the roadblock and he needs to answer with overpowering firepower. There are two Bradleys; and he knows that the other Bradley is heading down the highway, not knowing what has happened to its counterpart. He immediately gets on the horn.

"Big Lightning Two, this is Red Leader. Over."

Almost immediately, the speaker crackles.

"Red Leader, this is Big Lighting Two. Over," echoes the voice of the Bradley.

"Big Lightning Two, Big Lightning One has been hit with an IED. We need your fire power now. Turn around now!" Lieutenant Armstrong responds frantically.

The Bradley slows to a halt as the driver whips the Bradley about and begins to head in the opposite direction. The tank commander who is sitting on top of the Bradley motions to the five-ton driver to stay in its position, and the Bradley heads back down the highway to come to the aide of its soldiers.

The Humvee that was hit has some injured soldiers, and Private Denton and Private Bixby are right behind them.

"Sarge, what are we going to do?" asks Denton. But before Denton can finish the sentence Sergeant Purdue cuts him off.

"We are going to get them out of that Hummer and into ours," commands Sergeant Purdue, who was sitting directly behind Private Bixby. Private Denton takes control of the situation.

"But we are supposed to punch through. We can't stop and pick them up," cries Denton frantically.

"We are not leaving them, Denton. Now pull up to the back of the vehicle and stop. I will get them out."

Denton begins to follow Sergeant Purdue's order. "Sarge, are you sure?"

"Denton, we need to stop and pick them up."

Sergeant Purdue opens the door as the Humvee is approaching the disabled Humvee; and while the Humvee is moving, Sergeant Purdue jumps out of the Humvee and runs over to the disabled Humvee. By now, the gunfire is intense and the dirt is kicking up around both of the Humvees. Private Denton jumps out of the driver side and begins to return fire with his M4 assault rifle. Private Bixby jumps out and on top of the disabled Humvee and attempts to remove the air guard who is sticking out of the top of the roof and is clearly bloodied and disabled. Private Bixby unstraps the air guard and begins to lower him down into the Hummer, into Sergeant Purdue's arms.

It is an Audie Murphy moment, and the disabled Humvee engine compartment is on fire. As Sergeant Purdue is pulling the wounded soldier out of the Hummer, Private Bixby jumps into the hole that the air guard had taken up and twists around into the direction of fire. He immediately returns fire with a fifty-caliber weapon in the direction from where it is coming from. *Plink! Plink! Plink!* Enemy fire begins to ricochet off the disabled Hummer. Sergeant Purdue has the wounded soldier out of the Humvee, throws him over his shoulder, and runs over to the Hummer that Private Denton is hiding behind. He immediately throws the wounded soldier into the available compartment and runs back to retrieve the driver and assistant driver in the disabled Hummer. Meanwhile, Private Bixby is cranking the M2, a fifty-caliber machine gun, and is tearing up the palm trees in the direction where the fire is coming from. The other vehicles in the convoy begin to drive around the disabled Hummer and, once they are on the other side, begin taking fire from the left side of the road. The soldiers respond in like, with weapons hanging out of the windows. Sergeant Purdue stops one of the vehicles and places the wounded driver into the Hummer and motions the driver to clear the disabled Hummer and then returns to pull the assistant driver out. Meanwhile, the fire is getting more intense; and Private Bixby and Private Denton are responding with gunfire in the direction from where enemy activity is occurring. Sergeant Purdue removes the assistant driver from the front passenger side of the vehicle and runs over to the next vehicle in the convoy and tosses the wounded soldier inside.

Private Bixby stops for quick reload on the fifty-caliber and cranks it up again. The fire is beginning to enter the compartment of the disabled Hummer, but that does not slow Bixby down. The enemy insurgents make another futile attempt with an RPG round; and this time, it hits home. The disabled Humvee is hit, and Private Bixby is immediately killed. The shock of the direct hit and the proximity from where Private Denton and Sergeant Purdue were standing throws them to the ground. They recover and, looking up, they can see Private Bixby slumped over the fifty-caliber machine gun. All of a sudden, there is a repeat from a twenty five-millimeter cannon that is lighting up the direction from where the RPG round originated from; and the shooters are immediately killed. The Bradley has arrived on the scene and, unfortunately, just a little too late for Private Bixby. The Bradley immediately springs into action and heads off the road into the direction of the palm trees, where the fire had originated from, all the time firing the twenty five-millimeter cannon. The insurgents on the right side of the highway are getting their butts kicked and losing their lives in the process.

Sergeant Purdue runs to Private Bixby's side and pulls him out of the top of the disabled Humvee. From the waist down, Bixby has lost both legs and has excessive trauma to his lower abdomen.

"It's going to be okay, Bixby!" shouts Sergeant Purdue as he pulls him out; he knows he is lying to himself, and he can see that Private Bixby is dead.

This is a crushing moment for both Sergeant Purdue and Private Denton, and they do not have the time to reflect other than clearing their Hummer from the area. Sergeant Purdue places Private Bixby in the backseat of the Hummer and takes the shotgun position of the Hummer just to the right of Private Denton, who immediately pulls around the disabled Hummer. Meanwhile, in front of them, the Bradley that had just put down the gunfire on the right side of the highway has turned its attention to the left side of the highway and is screaming toward the position where automatic gunfire is being reported. It the same case, the twenty five-millimeter cannon is barking while the Bradley is on the move. The Bradley rushes across the highway and toward the direction of fire, and Denton stops his vehicle so that the Bradley can clear the highway and then punches it. Humvees are not fast, but it eventually picks up speed and catches up to the remainder of the convoy that has cleared the attack area. It is clear that the Bradley has overpowered the insurgent activity and is now in control of the situation. Lieutenant Armstrong has caught up with the convoy and has ordered it to stop until the remainder of the vehicles has joined. It is not long before Sergeant Hazard has joined the convoy in his Humvee and both Lieutenant Armstrong and Sergeant Hazard take roll call by going from vehicle to vehicle to see who is hurt and whether they need medical attention.

They arrive at Sergeant Purdue's vehicle. "Private Bixby is dead sir," announces Sergeant Purdue before they can ask a question.

LADEAU NEEDS A PLAN

LaDeau's mind is churning over the last radio message that he overheard while instructing local nationals who were working on a landscape project next to the motor pool. His proximity to the convoy that was about to depart had been within hearing distance of the last radio message that appeared over the radio. The radio squelch is again broken.

"Big Lightning, this is Red Leader, over."

After a pause, the transmission continues. "We have been hit with an IED, and have lost one Bradley and one Humvee. All the soldiers in the Bradley were KIA, and first platoon lost one of its own."

The radio crackles with a few more instructions. By now, LaDeau is oblivious to the ongoing conversation. One of the local nationals conducting the work that LaDeau has assigned him walks up to LaDeau with a question, to which LaDeau is quick to respond with, "No. Not now," and LaDeau walks away, thinking to himself. *A plan… I need a plan. He rubs* his chin, which is stubby from the days without a shave. *The Army will come to BCKR to assist with the movement of that cash, and they will probably come to me for de vehicle transport since I am the lead supervisor for BCKR.* LaDeau's plan slowly begins to take shape. *Hmm.... they probably did not count de money... that would have taken too long.*

LaDeau happens to spot Joe Manning walking his direction about a hundred feet away.

Hmm.... they will probably come to us for de electronic money counters that we loan out to the army finance team. Like the cogs of a Rolex watch, the plan continues to turn in LaDeau's brain. Some distance away, Manning spots LaDeau and yells out, "Hey, Country boy!" LaDeau ignores him, knowing he will probably come in his direction uninvited and open up with some stupid conversation. As LaDeau ponders to himself, it's a eureka moment for LaDeau. It's as if he walked into a brick wall that halted his forward movement. His eyebrows suddenly rise up, and he stops suddenly.

That's it! That little turkey has electronic skills... I bet he could change de electronic money counter to count every other bill! LaDeau's piercing eyes begin to widen ever so slightly. A grin begins to form below his mustache, causing it to change from its drooped position to almost as if it was a curtain at a Broadway musical that opened to show the next scene. *But can I count on that little twit to keep his mouth shut?*

Manning is slowly closing the distance, where LaDeau had stopped in his tracks moments earlier.

I have to trust to him... crap... but that does not mean I have to split de take. The same animal response that kept hunter gathers alive over the hundreds of thousands of years almost kicks in, for LaDeau knows what he has to do with Manning's body once the job is complete. But for now, he has to trust him.

LaDeau presents his best brotherly warm greeting. "Hey, Yank. Stop and listen ta some of my bullshit," announces LaDeau in a

Southern, warm tone of voice. A tone that mesmerizes Manning and LaDeau knows he has that power over that little creep.

Manning makes it over to LaDeau's location and stops to chat.

"Have I got a deal for you." LaDeau looks around through his piercing blue eyes, scanning the horizon like a predator hawk, scanning close and afar for anyone who might listen in on this very private conversation. LaDeau then turns to Manning and has done something Manning did not quite expect and places his arm over Manning's shoulder as if he just greeted a long-lost relative. "Step over here, bro, and listen ta my proposition."

And six-foot-two-inch LaDeau spins Manning around and, with one arm around his shoulder, begins walking Manning to a remote section of the base where he feels that no others can hear the conversation, all the while talking as he is walking along.

"Bro, de army has just ran into a cache of money, and it sounds like it might be in the millions."

Manning's eyes widen as in the excitement of a little kid who just peeked into one of his Christmas presents that his parents had hidden from him.

"How many millions?" Manning asks.

"That I am not sure of at de moment, but I do know it is worth millions," responds LaDeau. "Now, we don't have much time here. De army will come to us for our electronic money counters, you know, the money counters we loaned de Army's finance team every month so that they can count their money."

With that, Manning nods and LaDeau continues on.

"We are going ta loan them de money counters as usual, but I need for you ta change the electronics so that the counter display—. You know de digital electronic window that tells you how much money has been counted."

"You mean the LED display," Manning breaks in with a response that Manning knows confuses LaDeau; and at the same time, he makes himself look like an expert in front of LaDeau, whom he respects.

"Yeah, that LED thing you said. Change that thing to say… count every other bill… ?" asks LaDeau in a raspy voice that beckons like the biblical snake in the Garden of Eden.

Then Manning comes to a complete halt that stops LaDeau as well.

This abrupt stop almost has lost LaDeau's confidence, and he thinks to himself, *Can I trust this little twit? If this little twit squeals on me, I will kill him before the week is over.*

And as Manning looks up at LaDeau, LaDeau eyes begin to shrink away as a child would who is about to receive physical punishment for not paying attention; and his head rises just a little, like a male leopard searching the horizon for the next kill.

"Well, hell yeah, Reb!" remarks Manning. He has never called LaDeau a rebel in the past, but he has lost all fear of LaDeau now that he knows he has LaDeau over a barrel.

For a brief moment, LaDeau almost wants to hug that skinny little five-foot-four-inch creep.

"Can ya?" asks the biblical snake with its hypnotic stare that absolutely mesmerizes Manning. Again, LaDeau needs reassurance that he can trust Manning.

"Like I said, Reb, hell yeah! For half of the cut that is."

And for a brief moment, they toss the percentage cut back and forth between them, with LaDeau asking why Manning should get a 50-percent cut when it was his discovery in the first place. The debating and arguing goes on for ten to fifteen minutes, with LaDeau finally conceding to Manning.

"Okay, Yank. Ya got me. Ya win."

And with that, LaDeau extends his hand in a gentleman's handshake. Manning takes hold, and when he does, LaDeau pulls him close and gets right in his face.

"Now, Yank, I can trust ya, can't I, Yank?" asks the biblical snake in its most mesmerizing enticing voice as its coils of deceit tighten its grip around Manning.

The question, although inquisitive, is also threatening; and at this close of a range to LaDeau's face, Manning realizes that this is not the small little thefts that he had conducted in the past and that although he worked with LaDeau, he really did not know LaDeau.

"Don't worry, Reb. I will make us both rich."

And with that, LaDeau loosens his grip and retracts his distance. "Great. I knew I could count on ya. The South and the North, what a team, huh, Yank? Nobody can beat us."

And they both begin to grin and chuckle as if they were two middle-schoolers skipping school. The chuckling goes on for about five minutes; and finally, LaDeau breaks in and, in a chuckling sort of way, says "Hehe. Now, Yank, the army will probably come ta us for transporting the money, and I've got just de semi truck they can use."

As Manning finally composes himself, he asks, "What's that?"

"We've got that semi with de false room in the rear of the trailer. You remember, the one the army captured from de insurgents that were smuggling silk to the Baghdad vendors," he says as he begins to spin out his perfect plan.

"Oh yeah. Did you guys tear out that concealed room?" asks Manning.

"Heck no," answers LaDeau.

"It's still concealed in de back of the semi trailer, and we can access it from underneath the trailer. It has a trap door," reveals LaDeau.

Manning breaks in with, "But how is this going to play out?" in a confused but inquisitive sort of way.

"Well, we need ta transfer the money from de file cabinets to a much larger container. That way if they ever catch on that de money was missing they will have a hard time ta track where in the process it failed. That will buy us time," answers LaDeau as he begins to spin his web.

"Over in our BCKR supply warehouse, we have all de ingredients we need. We need ta store some equipment in the concealed room, and you and I need ta hide in the concealed room while the count is being worked out among the soldiers."

LaDeau stops to light up a cigarette, reaching into his pocket to grab the wooden match stick; holding it between his thick, hairy fingers as if an anaconda had captured a prey it was about to crush, he snaps it with the tip of thumbnail. The head of the match explodes into a ball of flame as LaDeau guides it to the cigarette and takes a puff long enough just to light it and then exhales a plume of blue smoke.

"And then, I figure once de trailer is locked up tight, the army is going to want to transport it immediately ta Kuwait."

He stops to take a long drag on his cigarette, the embers growing ever red and the sound of him sucking on the filter like it was a fountain drink purchased from a drive-up gas station.

"During that trip, you and I will collapse the wall from the other side of de concealed room."

During his conversation, smoke is being exhaled in blue plumes that spiral out between the concealed lips of the mustache as if it was exhaust from a car that burned way too much oil.

"I have already checked out de concealed room, and I know that it is possible to collapse it from the hidden side."

He exhales the remaining smoke.

"Once we collapse it, we need to remove half de money from the containers. I will load up duffle bags in de concealed room, along with some wire banding material that will be used to restrain the money containers to the wooden pallets during de transport."

Manning is listening ever so quietly, taking in as much detail as LaDeau will allow.

"Can we take one of de money counters with us, and will it work on batteries?" asks LaDeau as he throws Manning a bone.

"Yeah. I am almost sure we can operate the money counters off from some D-cell batteries. But why recount?" asks Manning.

LaDeau grins at Manning's lack of scheming skills. "Because we want the count to be as close as the count that the soldiers will be counting," answers LaDeau. "However, our counter will be conducting a normal count. We will count all the money first, and then we will count half of that money and package it away in the duffle bags."

LaDeau stops for another long drag on his cigarette, the embers ever glowing bright red. Again, the sound of sucking sounds filling the air.

"Once we have removed half the money, we will recount again just to make sure we have taken half of de money. When that is done, we will build a false bottom and place it in de bottom of the container that will appear to raise the bottom of the container up by a couple of feet." explains LaDeau.

"Well, won't the soldiers notice that?" asks Manning.

"Probably so, but you know soldiers. They will only focus on de task at hand and will not give it a second thought." LaDeau is half blowing out smoke during the response. "We then return the other half of the money to de container with the new false bottom and move on to de next container."

Manning's eyes widen. "Next container?"

LaDeau gives that evil grin of his. "That's right, Yank, de next container."

They begin to cackle like a bunch of jackals that have found a new dead carcass.

"But what happens once we get to Kuwait?" asks Manning in the middle-school voice that LaDeau has come to love.

Huh. Some criminal, LaDeau thinks to himself; and once again, he begins to grin and goes on to explain.

"Once in Kuwait, we will drop out of de trap door and go over to the motor pool at the Kuwait base camp and retrieve a BCKR vehicle. We will then go back to de motor pool and unload the semi trailer after the soldiers have removed de containers."

LaDeau takes another drag of his cigarette, which, by now, is burning right into the filter, just the way LaDeau likes to smoke them.

"The soldiers will park de semi trailer in the motor pool, and we will return to get de cash."

LaDeau flips the cigarette off onto the dust of the dirt road.

"I have a buddy in Kuwait who will then transport de money back to the States, where we will pick it up."

This brings an almost immediate response from Manning.

"What you mean you have another bud? Won't that screw up the split? Won't your bud want a cut?"

For once, Manning is asking the tough questions that LaDeau was prepared for.

"Look, de only way we can get the money is to get it back to the States. Once we get it back to de States, we can have my brother-in-law pick it up and hide it for us."

And again, Manning interrupts. "Your brother-in-law? Now we have a four-way cut. What to hell is that going to leave us?" asks Manning. LaDeau was prepared for that as well.

"Remember I said it was in the millions?" LaDeau waits for Manning to respond.

"Yeah. I remember."

LaDeau begins to grin again, that long, slow grin. "I would say it is about six hundred and fifty million dollars, and our take of that will be three hundred and twenty-five million, split four ways... well, you do de math."

Manning's eyes begin to widen as the displaced smirk begins to fade away into the once-again grin that was there not moments ago. "Three hundred and twenty-five million?" asks Manning.

"I figure about eight duffle bags full," responds LaDeau.

Slowly, Manning begins to chuckle in that middle-school-kid, high-pitched chuckle and is joined by LaDeau in his low, monotone voice. The chuckling becomes louder as the look of surprise covers both of their faces. Their hands are slapping their thighs as they continue their long bout of laughter.

The laughter continues moments afterward, until Manning interrupts. "But how do we get it back?"

HOW DO WE
GET IT BACK?

"You just can ship it back in plain sight." Manning begins to kick into whinny mode. "If it gets traced back to us, we're screwed." Manning's paranoia gets the better of him. "I tell ya, LaDeau. I am not going in on it unless I know it can't get traced back to us." Manning deals a threat to LaDeau.

LaDeau raises his hand to stop the whining in its tracks and to ease Manning's paranoia. LaDeau did not want to convey all the facts of the shipment, for his experience taught him that the more you know, the more of a chance you can compromise the job if you are caught. Against his better judgment and knowing that he needs Manning's assistance, he gives in.

"Yank, we won't ship it back in plain sight." LaDeau's eyes again show a look of confidence in knowing that once Manning does his job, he would get rid of the loud-mouth Yankee.

"I have an old partner that I used to run with back in my younger days." LaDeau pauses. "You know, back in de burglary and auto theft days," remarks LaDeau knowing that Manning had no idea of what he was talking about as Manning is nodding his head.

"Yeah. Sure, Bowe, I know what you are talking about. I did a few of those," answers Manning, all the while lying through his teeth as he attempts to gain acceptance from a person he looks up to.

"My partner runs de mortuary out of Kuwait. BCKR has the contract for processing dead soldiers' bodies as they leave Iraq and are shipped back to de States."

Manning is now hanging onto every word coming out of LaDeau's mouth.

"We are going to line the coffins with de stolen cash." LaDeau raises one of his eyebrows, making him look even cleverer, and waits for Manning's response.

"Wow. Man, is that good," Manning applauds LaDeau's wit in a middle-school sort of way. "Who would have thought of that? Only you, Bowe." And the boyish grin widens on Manning's face. "We're rich, Bowe. So, who's your bud?" asks Manning in the Boston cockney accent.

LaDeau raises his hand again and, after a pause, says, "Don't worry about de bud. That's for me to know," in a pleasant tone of voice, not wanting to anger Manning at this point. "You just focus on changing de electronic counters. Run over to our BCKR warehouse and check them out and start working on them." LaDeau pours out the instructions. "And if that nosey twit of a supply clerk asks what de mission is for, just tell him its routine maintenance and if he needs more of an explanation, he can call me." LaDeau's expression changes too as his eyes widen just a little and reveal a sparkle that could be taken as threatening glare.

LaDeau hated the supply clerk that worked the BCKR warehouse. He was always correcting him on his English whenever he wrote out the supply checkout slip.

"What does *ain't* mean?" asked the supply clerk in one of his most snotty responses. "Where did you go to school anyway? Did they ever teach you how to spell?"

The supply clerk was an opinionated turd as far as LaDeau was concerned, but not worth killing.

"I hate the smart aleck myself. He's always asking me where I learned to speak proper English," Manning remarks sarcastically. Manning applauds LaDeau's response to the nosey supply clerk.

"Okay, Joe. You gotta get moving on de job at hand." LaDeau takes control of the task at hand.

"I'm on it." Manning heads off toward the supply warehouse.

"Keep a zipped lip," LaDeau shouts after him. Manning raises his hand in a receptive wave. *I really do not trust that little twit,* LaDeau thinks to himself. *He likes to brag, and bragging will getcha caught every time.* LaDeau eyes Manning, who has now distanced himself from LaDeau and is closing distance between the BCKR warehouse and himself. *Oh well. Yank will not be around long. I will be sure to take care of that.*

LaDeau turns and heads off toward his office on the other side of Camp Trigger. LaDeau's pace is lumbering slow, and he whips out his cell phone to make a call. Cell phone communications are available at Camp Trigger, for the setup and maintenance work on all the cell towers was brokered through a contract that BCKR had made with an Arabian company that provides cell phone service in Iraq and throughout the Middle East.

LaDeau speed dials his partner, Bill Smith. Smith and LaDeau grew up in rural Louisiana, and Smith's background is pretty much the same as LaDeau's. Both have a criminal history that entailed burglaries and car thefts from some of the larger-neighboring towns. Neither owned a car so they would ride their bicycles into town cruising the streets, all the while casing the place they were going to rob. They would then head home. When LaDeau's father would pass out from being drunk at home, LaDeau would sneak out his window and run over to Smith's house, where Smith had been waiting. Tossing a small stone at the window would get Smith's attention, and Smith would crawl out his window. The duo would head over to a neighbor's house who they knew was almost deaf. How that neighbor ever obtained a driver's license was beyond them, but they would sneak into the deaf neighbor's yard and break into the car. After a quick hotwire, they would slowly back the car out of the driveway and head toward town, where they would commit their crime. They both paid attention to detail during their burglaries and were never caught or suspected of stealing their deaf neighbor's car. The next day, they would get a bus ticket into Alexandria and take their booty with them to pawn at the Alexandria pawn shop. Neither had a driver's license, and so the stolen goods that they pilfered were always small enough so that they could carry them on the bus. The bus ticket to Alexandria and back was a few bucks, and their stolen goods returned enough profit to pay for the bus trip and then some. They continued down this path and never got caught. Surprisingly, they graduated from high school. It was that year when they decided to both to become correctional officers at the Angola state prison. They attended the six-week training program, and both had started working at Angola. It is here where they had listened and overheard many of the prisoners tell their tales of the schemes that had gone wrong. As correctional officers, they sat in on many parole board hearings and listened as the criminals would spill their guts on the crime they had committed and how they got caught. They would meet after work and, over a six-pack of beer would talk bull about the convicts at the parole board.

"Yeah, and this idiot actually thought he could get away with it. He should have known better."

LaDeau would chime in much like a member of Baptist choir, "Where he made his mistake was letting too many people in on his caper." From there on, it was normal during their conversations about convict capers to discuss what the convict should have done in order to get away with the crime.

BCKR had a branch office out of Houston, and when they got word that BCKR was hiring it did not take them long to fill out the job application. Through conversations with other former BCKR employees that they knew, they were schooled into what not to put down for job experience and what to put down. So they both lied on their application forms, stating that they held logistic positions at the Louisiana state prison, Angola. This was enough to get them in; and from there, they both branched off in separate directions. With the war in Kosovo, Smith had tapped into the local nationals, Albanians, who were involved in the white slave trade, and made some money on the side by hiring the local Albanian girls and prostituting them outside the local NATO bases. Smith could tell from the start in his short conversations with the criminals he did business with whether or not they would get caught. After all, both LaDeau and he had worked around all the criminals that got caught. It was a matter of reviewing what their criminal counterparts had set up for a base of their crime and how well they conducted it. LaDeau had dealings with the white slave trade himself when he was working in Bosnia. He knew enough to hire a madam who would strike fear into the hearts of the Bosnia women who were being prostituted. They knew well enough to keep their mouths shut. Otherwise, the madam would not waste any time in beating them down or having their family members tortured and killed. LaDeau and Smith both headed for Afghanistan, where they were quick to pick up on a diamond smuggling trade. While in the Balkans, they got a tip from a crooked United Nations security officer that a diamond smuggling route existed that stretched from Africa through the Middle East and through Afghanistan. It was easy for Smith and LaDeau to figure out the port of entry for the stolen diamonds, and they both ran a little caper themselves. After a year in Afghanistan, they put in and took a job in Iraq, where they are both now employed.

LaDeau's cell phone continues to ring. Smith answers on the other end. "Hello," he said in his best Southern drawl.

"Bubba, how ya doing, brother?" asks LaDeau, a truly warm greeting from an old-town buddy.

"Hey, Bowe. Whatcha know?"

Both were glad to hear from an old friend.

"Are you in a place where nobody can listen in?"

With that question, Smith knew what was going to come next. "Give me a minute." Smith, who was working in the mortuary in Kuwait, stepped outside on a loading dock, distancing himself from the employees he worked with. "What's up, Bowe?" asks Smith.

"We hit the mother load, brother," rejoices LaDeau.

"Give me a second. I need a cigarette." LaDeau reaches into his pocket for a smoke and pops it into his lips, which are hidden behind the thick mustache that he sports. He strikes his match that he retrieves from his pocket and takes a long drag that causes the embers to glow and burn through almost one quarter of the cigarette. Without exhaling, he begins. "I need you to catch this next helo ride to Camp Trigger."

"Look me up, son, when you get to Camp Trigger, and I'll give you the rundown," LaDeau goes on. "Hop a flight tomorrow, and we can yak at each other when ya get here." With that, LaDeau hangs up.

On the other end, Smith closes his cell phone and pauses as he looks at it. *What in the hell did Bowe run into?* Smith thinks to himself. *Mother load, huh? I hope it's better than de diamond caper.* Smith slowly walks back into the mortuary.

The cell phone call with LaDeau constantly nagged at Smith throughout the day. *Mother load, huh? Come to think about it, I never heard him so happy,* Smith thinks to himself. The constant nagging thoughts and the replay of LaDeau's conversation only make the day drag on. When it comes time to break for supper, Smith drops by the flight pad and puts his name on the next day's manifest for Camp Trigger. The flight pad is run by the US military. Before you book your flight, you have to show up in advance to ensure your name is manifested. The flight out will be on Chinook, a US Army troop helicopter. After booking the flight, LaDeau heads over to the dining facility on the Kuwait base. The dining facility is where all US military and US contractors have their daily meals; and it mirrors the same facility at Camp Trigger, both of which are run by BCKR, who has the contract for the US military. Smith drops into the dining facility, signs in on the roster, and pays for his meal. Once again, nothing but the best for BCKR has a really good spread when it comes to presentation. Several main-course dishes are available and augmented with many side orders of your choosing. There are salad bars that can compete with the best American eateries. Awesome desserts are presented to the dining guests. Although it is cafeteria-style, the food is great. Smith gets in line and walks his tray down the main course bar, placing his order to the local national that serves the dish. Smith works his way down the many different self-serving bars and, when he goes to sit down, picks a small table where seated are a number of US soldiers who have completed their meal and are getting ready to leave.

"Mind if I have seat?" asks Smith.

"Not at all, sir. Have a seat, and take a load of your feet," said the soldier in a warm welcome that most US soldiers give to American contractors.

It is the bonding that goes on between Americans in general, and it is always good to meet another American when you are deployed in a foreign country. Smith has a seat, and they make small talk about Camp Kuwait. The great thing about being an American contractor on a US base outside the combat zone is it's always good to rap with the US soldiers. Smith cherishes these moments, even if he is a criminal. In Smith's mind, he is doing a service to his country by helping US soldiers. Smith is getting rich at the same time, even if it is through illegal methods. It is a twisted sort of logic, but it works for Smith. After supper, he heads back to his cormac, the housing units found at Camp Trigger and the same housing units used by US contractors in Kuwait. Once he opens the door to his cormac, one sees he has all of the amenities of home. Instead of having one cormac like most US soldiers would have, Smith has swindled a deal where he has configured two of them side by side, giving him twice the living space—"Working de system." It is a phrase Smith is well-known for. The double-sized living quarters has all the amenities of home: a wide-screen TV, a bar, a contemporary sound system, and a queen-sized bed. Smith steps into his personal shower and performs his personal hygiene for the day and, when complete, returns to his small dining table in the corner of his cormac. "Hmm. I wonder what de mother load is," Smith mumbles to himself. "Oh well. Guess I'll have to wait until tomorrow."

COLD FEET

Wop! Wop! Wop! The helicopter blades could be heard in the distance. *Wop! Wop! Wop!* The drum beat from the rotors grew louder, announcing the new arrivals. *Wop! Wop! Wop!* What appeared to be a small flock of birds grew and grew until they took on the image of helicopters.

"I hope he came alone," LaDeau mutters to himself.

LaDeau has been up since six o'clock in the morning and has had breakfast and stopped by to brief the local nationals from the neighboring town on their tasks for the day. After the brief, LaDeau beats feet over to the helo pad to wait on Smith's arrival. The helo pad is small but will allow for a number of the larger transport helicopters like the Chinook, a cargo and troop transport. This helicopter is large enough to carry up to thirty-two soldiers and has two main helo blades on both ends of the aircraft. There is no waiting room here. Most of the cargo is positioned behind a two-story tower as well as the troops or BCKR personnel who have to catch a hop. To LaDeau's right is a casket, Sergeant Hazard, Lieutenant Armstrong, all of first platoon, and most of the soldiers on the base who could make it and who were not out on mission. Higher headquarters has showed up for this is an event where all of the soldiers say good-bye to one of their own, Private Bixby.

Wop! Wop! Wop! The Chinook has gotten quite louder, as its image grows larger. It's about three hundred meters away, and the sound is becoming quite deafening. *Wop! Wop! Wop! Wop!* Now the sound is like thunder as it approaches its landing zone just about seventy-five feet from the ground. The whooping sound has been replaced with what sounds like a large herd of horses riding in front of the observer, and it is as if one can almost feel their hoof beats rumbling across the ground. The heavy hoofs hammering the ground are augmented by the deep, loud, low rumbling sound as if a violent storm is approaching. The smell of jet fuel fills the air; and the breeze from the rotor blades is quite strong as it lowers its frame to the ground, kicking up sand and dirt as it attempts to land. On touchdown, hearing and speech is severely inhibited as the sound of the blades and the engine is the only sound that can be heard. Yes, the herd of horses is truly in front of the observer now as they rumble past in a full gallop. This continues for what is about one minute, and the sound has notably descended an octave or two and thirty seconds later, a few more octaves. The herd of horses has disappeared along with the rumbling of thunder it brought with it. The thundering sound of the engine has declined to the point where a high-pitched whine of the sound of the twin jet engines that power the blades is now heard. The high-pitched whine can be heard for about thirty seconds and begins to descend the ladder of octaves as the engine winds down. Finally, it's only a fraction of the noise of what it used to be as the twin rotor blades have slowed to a crawl and have come to a complete stop. The engine is quiet now, and the airmen working the small flight line run around the Chinook, checking its tires and starting the refueling process. At the opposite end of the helicopter from where the pilots are seated, the back gate begins its slow crawl downward. The back gate is used as a ramp for boarding soldiers and loading and unloading cargo. The back gate of the helicopter drops to the ground and provides a ramp for the soldiers and some US civilian contractors who are exiting the helicopter.

The helicopter is about seventy yards from the tower, LaDeau, and the soldiers of first platoon. LaDeau recognizes Smith right away, who is about six feet tall with a somewhat stocky build but no pot belly like LaDeau sports. Smith has dark hair and eyes, belonging to his Louisiana Cajun heritage, and a beard sporting a two-day growth. The eyes... the eyes are somewhat trustworthy, not like LaDeau's. Perhaps this is a signature of stealth for a person who people trust to prepare a soldier for his last journey home, for Smith works in the mortuary in Kuwait and on a US base known as Camp Kuwait. It is not long before Smith closes the distance between him and LaDeau.

"Howdy, Bubba. How's it going, brother?" asks LaDeau with a warm welcome.

"Not bad, Bowe," Smith responds. After a handshake and a slap on the shoulder from LaDeau, they start making small talk. Meanwhile, the casket with the body of Private Bixby is being wheeled onto the Chinook along with the other cargo. The casket is modest and is more of an aluminum cargo container than a casket—humble entombments for a soldier, for soldiers do not ask for much. The colonel in charge of Camp Trigger issues a command as the casket is wheeled up the ramp of the Chinook.

"Camp Trigger, attention," comes the loud, booming command. The soldiers respond by snapping to attention, hands down by their sides, and a loud thud echoes like two large blocks of wood were suddenly struck together as the heels of their boots slap together.

Sergeant Purdue is present at the ceremony, and his mind drifts off. The day before, the formal ceremony for their departing comrade had taken place with the Brigade Chaplin and Private Bixby's boots, M4 rifle with bayonet affixed and stuck in the ground, and goggles wrapped around the helmet that rested upon the butt of the rifle.

"For although I travel into the valley of death... I will fear no evil," chants the chaplain as he goes onto to read from his small military Bible. Upon completion of his readings, the chaplain signals for each soldier to come up to pay his final respects. This is a difficult moment for Sergeant Purdue, for he never lost a man in his squad. His thoughts race through the history of first meeting Private Bixby and up to just talking to him days before. There is a feeling of loss accompanied with the guilt that Private Bixby jumped into action to defend Sergeant Purdue and the soldiers in that disabled Hummer. Guilt is always the byproduct when one of your soldiers in your squad is killed.

I should have stopped him from mounting that M2 on top of the Hummer. It's my fault. Why couldn't I have mounted the M2 myself? Why Private Bixby? Why not me?

Yes, guilt is tough to shake for it will haunt Sergeant Purdue for some time to come. These feelings of loss run deep, and it's only the many training sessions from his military leaders and comrades in arms that give him the tools to handle this day. Sergeant Purdue and every soldier attending the ceremony walk up in line one at a time and kneel on one knee and say a small prayer.

The sound of the command, "Present arms," comes from the colonel that commands the military unit; and all the soldiers who are at attention snap a sharp salute. This command brings Sergeant

Purdue back to reality, and he watches as Private Bixby's casket is loaded into the back of the Chinook. A few other soldiers accompany the casket, and the Chinook is ready for its return flight. When the casket is out of sight, the colonel barks the last command, "Order arms," and the soldiers snap their right arms down to their sides. "At ease." The soldiers stand with feet spread apart and hands behind their backs in a relaxed position. There are minor whispers, and they are waiting for the Chinook to start up again and take off. It is protocol to salute the helicopter as it leaves the base, giving the final salute to their fallen comrade.

Meanwhile, leaving the soldiers to their duty and drifting across the base to LaDeau and Smith, who had walked away during this ceremony, a disrespectful move that goes unnoticed.

"Okay. How much money are we talking about?" Smith asks and is quick to get to the topic that brought him here.

"I'm guessing we will get three hundred and twenty-five million."

Smith stops walking and looks at LaDeau straight in the face. The trusting look has now taken on one of disgust, as if a bad joke had been cracked.

Before he can get another word out, Smith interrupts. "Look. I did not fly all the way from Kuwait to hear a joke."

"Three hundred and twenty-five million is what I figured, but you tell me, how many stacks of hundred-dollar bills can fit in a standard five-drawer filing cabinet? And we have twenty-two cabinets filled with hundred-dollar bills, and we are going ta steal half of it."

A more a serious tone in LaDeau's voice signals to Smith that this is for real. The trustworthy look has now taken a more serious appearance. The dark, Cajun eyes have now become somewhat sinister. Yes, Smith has come to read LaDeau's tonal signals that his voice projects. This is for real.

"Well, how in hell are we going to lift three hundred and twenty-five million dollars?" asks Smith. LaDeau begins to fill him in on the scam.

LaDeau goes over the details on how Manning and he will doctor the electronic money counters to count every other bill.

"Can ya trust him?" asks Smith.

LaDeau's piercing eyes takes on a more sinister glare, and the tension creeps in as if the temperature dropped like a cold wave from a passing thunderstorm on a hot, humid summer day, a tension so thick you can cut it with a knife. His eyes give away the intent, taking on a glare that is ever so threatening and menacing that it makes Smith feel like he is the target. The glare... the glare sends the message by signaling the fight or flight mechanism you feel in the back of your neck when you know your life is in danger and that you need to leave the area immediately. The glare... the glare gives one the impression that if LaDeau had a pet dog, he would probably would have slaughtered it right there on the spot and eaten it in front of you.

"He knows better than to open his mouth. And when this job is over, he won't be around to count his money," responds LaDeau; and from that response, Smith knows what is in store for Manning.

"Now we are talking about murder," Smith responds in a weak voice that sounded like it had not quite reached puberty.

"Yeah. We are talking about murder, and we are talking about murder in a third-world country that's at war where murders occur all de time," LaDeau responds with an air of confidence. "Even if someone finds his body, they'll think it's one of de local Iraqis killing another American. Don't worry, Bubba. There's no FBI over here. No one will suspect us." Again, the look of confidence has not changed. "You forget... I'm Manning's first-line supervisor, and I are the one that reports his attendance at work, so it will be me that will report to BCKR." LaDeau continues to weave his web of deceit. "I'll report that Manning constantly complained about being homesick and finally came to me and said that he was leaving. I'll report that I cut his last check and that was de last I saw of him."

The look of confidence reflected in LaDeau's face has now appeared in Smith's, as if moonlight had reflected across two adjacent pools of water. Yes, the sinister duo knows they have all the angles covered. Now it's time to move on to the next subject at hand.

"How are going to get it off this base?" asks Smith.

LaDeau gives Smith the run-down onthe semi truck that BCKR had acquired from an illegal smuggling operation that US soldiers had uncovered. To be legal, the semi truck belonged to the government of Iraq, which was just being formed. BCKR had ponied up the cash for the semi truck, and the Iraqi treasury department agreed to sell it for a price that was almost one tenth its appraised value—pretty much a steal. It was LaDeau who had swindled that one. Yes, the combat zone has its benefits; and negotiating with a country that does not have money is quite easy and legal. LaDeau explains the false room that exists at the very back of the semi trailer, how it was constructed, and what illegal activity it was used for.

"I have crawled up inside de room. You can get in by opening a trap door just under the trailer. The US Army will want to transport de cash to Kuwait, and the way I figure it, they will come to us for the transportation. They will come to us for the electronic money counters and containers for shipping de cash." LaDeau's eyes begin to take on a glaze of confidence. "Manning and I will board de semi trailer and wait there until the money is loaded and the truck is in convoy and on de road. Once we get moving we can disassemble the concealed room from de concealed side. I have already checked it out, and it's held together with a bunch of mechanical latches." And the spider web continues to spin. "How are you going to know exactly how much money to steal?" Smith goes down a checklist of questions that he is now forming.

"Not a problem. I will have de Yank bring a battery-operated money counter with us. That way we can do a recount of each container with what it actually holds and half of what we will steal. Once we remove half of the money, we will insert a false bottom at the bottom of the container to raise it up from de inside."

"Won't they be able to figure that out and notice de false bottom?" asks Smith, who is worried.

"Relax, Bubba. We do this all the time when we ship common produce. It's common practice and is used to protect the produce from getting wet in case de container is set outside."

LaDeau tries to calm Smith's fears. "Heck. They are almost expecting a false bottom to show up in a shipping container."

The confident look again returns. Once again, the trusting eyes of Smith return.

"Well, I guess its money in de bank, Bowe."

And with that, both laugh. They make their way over to a small little Toyota and jump in. The Toyota is the BCKR vehicle of choice for shuttling BCKR employees around the base. With LaDeau at the wheel, they head toward a local hamburger shop on base, a soldier's favorite, where French fries, soft drinks, and hamburgers are the . Another BCKR contract, this small little fast food shop is a building designed out of cormacs. Once again, the BCKR general contractors make use of the cormacs that they snap together as if they were children's building blocks. BCKR attaches a walk-up, covered deck and throws a wooden roof over the top of the building; and its appearance is almost of an outdoor eatery one would find at home. LaDeau drives up to the building and parks in a designated parking area. They both exit the vehicle and walk up the steps to the double door as soldiers are exiting. As one enters the building, there are a number of tables and chairs with soldiers sitting down to their prize meal, body armor and weapons slung over their back, some wearing leg holsters with M9 pistols. There is a walk-up counter much like one would find at a McDonald's. The walk-up counter has registers with some of the local nationals working behind the counters, busily preparing the orders and packaging the food. LaDeau walks up to one of the counters, and Smith and he place their orders and pay for the meal. They receive the receipt with a number that is called when the meal is ready, and they both find an empty table and grab a seat. They make small talk, being careful not mention their scheme while they are out in public. It is not long before their number is called, and they walk up to the counter to claim their meal and return to their table. Not much talking takes place as they begin to chow down. The meal is gone in no time, and it's not long before the conversation drifts toward the next flight out. Smith will not be staying at the base and will be heading out in few hours. They finish their meal and exit the building and hop into the Toyota, and LaDeau backs the Toyota out as Smith strikes up the conversation.

"Yes, this is de mother load, Bubba, and we need to be careful on how we go about spending it."

"I hear that," responds LaDeau.

Smith rambles on. "I figure we could buy a nice pad over in Macedonia or maybe even Greece. The money won't be traced there, and they always is an influx of tourist both American and from all over de world."

"Yep. I'm for Greece. One hell of a nice place, and plus, we can live like kings," remarks LaDeau.

The Toyota lumbers along at the mandatory base speed of ten miles per hour. The sputtering engine almost gives one the impression that it will conk out at any time.

"Kings. Yeah. I like that." Smith turns on his Louisiana accent, grinning at the thought of the money.

"Yep. We will be the only bayou kings in Greece!"

And they both laugh.

"Bayou kings." LaDeau laughs. "That sho enough is us."

And they chuckle as the Toyota makes it back to the flight line for the next flight out. They finally arrive at the flight line, and LaDeau kills the engine and is about to unbuckle his seatbelt when Smith stops him.

"Bubba, are you sure you can get rid of Manning without getting caught? We go way back, and I really don't want you taking a risk that can put you away for life."

This catches LaDeau off guard for a moment, and he appears to be surprised.

"Don't worry. Like I said, this is a third-world country and people die here all de time. No one is going to miss this little twit."

With that statement, Smith raises his hand as if to wave. LaDeau grabs it as if they were to arm wrestle.

"We're rich!" says Smith. LaDeau responds in like, "Rich bayou kings!"

Smith exits the vehicle and heads for the flight tower to register on the manifest for the next flight out.

COUNTING THE MONEY

It's the following day. Sergeant First Class Hazard is several miles away, returning to base from a dismounted patrol mission. His platoon is tired, and the morale is low since they lost one of their own. This is a critical time for the platoon, and Sergeant Hazard had pulled his people together to restore their confidence in their training and their mission right after they had shipped Private Bixby's body out. As the convoy travels back to base camp, Sergeant Hazard's mind drifts off to yesterday's events.

Once the Chinook had cleared the pad, Sergeant Hazard gathered first platoon together and then marched them over to a field area not too far away from the motor pool but far enough to where they could not be disturbed. Once they arrived, Sergeant Hazard had them in a platoon formation and had them form a semicircle and have a seat on the ground. Standing before them, Sergeant Hazard spoke.

"I know how everyone is feeling, and I am feeling the pain too." As he speaks, he can tell that there is tension in the air thick enough so that you can cut it with a knife. He knows that the tension is from the loss of one of their own, and he continues.

"It seemed like yesterday when Private Bixby was standing before me and had completed all of his advanced individual training and we were his first assignment. Boy, he sure did look green and was anxious to prove himself. Did he not look green, Sergeant Purdue?"

"Yes, Sergeant. He sure did. In a way, he reminded me of myself when I had returned from training. I was new and wanted to earn all the badges and medals that come with combat," replies Sergeant Purdue.

"Yes, Sarge. He reminded me of myself as well, excited about the mission and wanting to prove myself," remarks Sergeant Hazard.

This breaks some of the tension as some of the other soldiers join in. "Yeah. That was me." Others say, "Me too." Almost choir like, a few others say, "I was that soldier." Sergeant Hazard continues to speak.

"Some of you reminded me of Private Bixby when you first arrived as well so, in a sense, Private Bixby has never really left us. He lives in us all in the army code, which is the way we live our lives."

After Sergeant Hazard speaks, one soldier speaks up. "He's not gone but up there in heaven, standing guard at the pearly gates."

And another soldier says, "Hoping that his relief can show up so he can get a shower and something to eat."

While another soldier speaks up, "I hope I'm not his relief... not yet."

And the platoon starts a mild chuckle. Sergeant Hazard knows that if he can get a small chuckle out of them that it is not the total cure but a temporary Band-Aid for the weeks to come.

Just then, the radio squelch barks, "Red Leader, this is Big Lightning. Over," and Sergeant Hazard's memory from yesterday is gone and he is back in the moment. Lieutenant Armstrong, who is riding with Sergeant Hazard, grabs the mike. "Big lightning, this is Red Leader. Over," he says and awaits further instructions.

The instructions from the radio come quick, and Sergeant Hazard and his patrol are to return to base and report to the warehouse where they had dropped off the money. The money had been under guard for a few days and was heavily guarded. The warehouse is actually a half-moon shelter that BCKR had been contracted to construct and contained some supplies and was used by the motor pool team to pull maintenance work on Bradleys and tanks since it was large enough to house them. As they approach the entrance of the base and are waved through by the guards, they decrease their speed and barely crawl through the small streets to the warehouse.

The warehouse is heavily guarded and has been that way for the past days, with guards all along its perimeter as if they were army ants guarding the queen. The doors to the entrance are guarded as well, and Sergeant Hazard dismounts from his lead Humvee and instructs his soldiers where they should park their vehicles. Sergeant Hazard, Lieutenant Armstrong, and Sergeant Purdue approach the entrance of the warehouse and enter. The warehouse floor is part concrete with the center portion at the entrance solid ground and used for parking the heavy, armored vehicles like tanks and Bradleys that require vehicle maintenance work. Today and the past few days since the money arrived, there are no vehicle maintenance activities going on in this building. There is fluorescent lighting suspended from the ceiling, and on the center of the concrete floor are two small tables with the money counters resting on them. The tables are placed side by side, and the opposite ends of both tables butted up against them are two long tables.

"Sergeant Hazard, glad that you could make it," booms the voice of the Lieutenant Colonel, who is the officer in charge. In a commanding voice, he says, "Over here, Sergeant Hazard."

And Sergeant Hazard, Lieutenant Armstrong, and Sergeant Purdue walk over to the Lieutenant Colonel who is standing by the money counters. The Lieutenant Colonel is standing in front of the money counter, and behind each money counter are LaDeau and Manning. LaDeau is standing with his hands resting outside of his front pants pockets with his thumbs hooked inside the pocket, holding them in place as if he is about begin the dance in the musical *Oklahoma*. He stands there, bowlegged with a glint in his eyes. Manning is wide-eyed and continues to look toward LaDeau with that elementary school kid look. "What's next?" However, LaDeau ignores him and continues staring at the Lieutenant Colonel. Off to the left of the long table where LaDeau is standing and in front of it, about ten feet away, are three large containers that are resting on wooden pallets, the containers that LaDeau had his local nationals placed earlier. Off to the right of Manning and at the end of the long table reside the twelve large file cabinets with an armed soldier standing in front of each file cabinet and an unarmed soldier standing adjacent as well. Standing behind LaDeau and Manning and about ten feet away are armed soldiers with their weapons at the ready who continue to glance around as if awaiting an attack. The sergeants approach the Lieutenant Colonel, stop about a few steps in front, and await their instructions.

"Okay, gentlemen." The Lieutenant Colonel takes control and, in a commanding voice, says, "Here is how it will play out. We have the money counters being operated by BCKR employees." He points to LaDeau and Manning. "We have the money in the file cabinets and an armed soldier each assigned to the file cabinet." He points in their general direction. "And we have the soldier who will carry the money from the file cabinet to the table to the right of the BCKR employee Mr. Manning."

As Manning hears his name, he waves his hand.

"This soldier is known as the loader." The Lieutenant Colonel points to one of the soldiers. "The loaders know who they are, and they will retrieve the money one stack of bills at a time and drop it off on the table and then return to their assigned file cabinet. Mr. Manning and BCKR employee Mr. LaDeau will retrieve the money and feed it into the money counters." The Lieutenant Colonel points to the electronic money counters. "Notice the money counters have a digital readout that is currently displaying zeros."

The money counters have nine illuminated red digits representing the number zero as if they were eyes on some sort of underwater fish yet known to be discovered.

"Now, I understand that these money counters are quite fast and so can count the money as fast as we insert it. Once the money has cleared the input tray, Sergeant Hazard and Sergeant Purdue will retrieve it and place it on the long output table at the end where Mr. LaDeau is standing."

Bowe reaches up and grabs the bill of his hat as would a cowboy who was greeting a young lady; and Bowe nods, returning his hand to rest near his pocket.

"When the output table becomes full, we will stop the counting and the loaders will walk over and take the money from the output table and begin to stack it in this first container closest to the long output table." The Lieutenant Colonel points to the motionless, large, plastic container that is used to ship supplies across Iraq by BCKR.

"Both Sergeant Hazard and Sergeant Purdue will be monitoring this process. Once the container becomes full, the loaders will place the lid on top of the container and wrap this half-inch wire banding material around the container and through the pallet so the container is affixed to the pallet and cannot rock back and forth during transit. Now, does everyone know their task?"

The Lieutenant Colonel looks around at all the soldiers, who nod as in agreement.

"Then are there any questions?" asks the Lieutenant Colonel. The soldiers look around at each other, shaking their heads as if to say no.

LaDeau raises his hand.

"Yes, Mr. LaDeau," responds the Lieutenant Colonel.

"Yes, sir. Jest so de soldiers know, we have included a false bottom at the bottom of each container. This is common practice when shipping supplies from one location to another," states LaDeau; and for a minute, he almost loses his breath when Sergeant Hazard walks over to inspect each container and then returns with a nod as if agreeing to Bowe's statement and signals the Lieutenant Colonel that they are good to go.

"As always, safety first. Be careful of the banding material that it does not snap when its being buckled since it could snap back and catch you in the face, perhaps tearing away some flesh or, heaven forbid, ripping out your eye. Oh, yes. Once all the money is placed in the containers, we will load it onto the semi trailer that BCKR will provide and then have another brief on the next mission. Okay, loaders. Take your positions by your assigned file cabinets and, Sergeant Hazard, you take charge from here."

"Yes, sir," replies Sergeant Hazard. "Is BCKR ready?" asks Sergeant Hazard.

Both LaDeau and Manning nod.

"Are the loaders ready?"

Together, as if at a football rally, they respond, "Hooah." The loaders' reply echoes the response across the warehouse.

"Okay, team. Let's load it up."

The process begins. The soldiers begin to open the file cabinet drawers and start to remove the money one stack of bills at a time, all while the armed soldiers are standing next to them, watching every move. When the soldier has the stack of bills removed and piled up in his arms, it is hand-carried to the table, where it is placed in a stack.

"Now let's not try to overdo it," announces Sergeant Hazard. "One stack at a time. We are not in the Olympics here." He manages the task of moving the money.

As soon as the first stack hits the table, Manning picks it up, places it in the feed tray of the electronic money counter, and hits the start button. As promised, the electronic money counter makes quick work of the feed tray, fanning the money as it counts. The red eyes of the money counter flicker as every other bill is counted, racking up the cash count. The aroma of money soon fills the area around the counters. Once the stack of money clears the feed tray, the stack of money is grabbed up by Sergeant Purdue and hand-carried over to the table adjacent to where LaDeau was standing.

LaDeau is not idle and has been watching the money being stacked onto the table. For once, the rat-like squint within his eyes has disappeared with eyes that almost appear to have widened as if he was watching the results of a Nevada gambling coin machine about to roll all sevens. As another stack of bills hits the table adjacent to Manning, LaDeau almost appears to have jumped up as if he was a gazelle attempting to flee an attack from a hungry lion and walked over to where the stack is, clearing the distance in less than 3 strides. Yes, LaDeau's greed has him motivated today; and this is the quickest this evil toad has ever moved.

LaDeau's normal movement is slow, almost sloth-like; but not today. Today, LaDeau's pace has quickened to the beat of millions of dollars coming his way.

Like a leopard that is ready to pounce, LaDeau grabs the money and returns to the money counter, closing the distance in two strides or less. Almost feverishly, he inserts the money into the counter and hits the start button. The aroma fills the tabled area of where the cash is being loaded, counted, and deposited to the output table. Yes, the aroma drifts through the warehouse as if it was a fresh pot of coffee being brewed on a cool fall morning and it drifts out of one's neighbor's opened window and into one's front yard. Yes, the aroma is that strong and grabs everyone's attention, quickly beckoning one for a cup of coffee. The soldiers pick up on it as well and begin to crack jokes.

"Wow. Can you smell that money?" one soldier speaks up. "Smells like the jolly green giant opened his wallet," he says. This obtains an immediate applause of laughter from all the soldiers.

"Okay. That was funny, but let's stay focused on the task at hand," responds Sergeant Hazard as the laughter dies out.

The counting stops after the first container is filled. Lieutenant Armstrong, who is carrying a clipboard, walks over to the container and peers over it. As two soldiers attempt to place the lid on top of the container, he motions them to halt.

"Wait a minute," announce Lieutenant Armstrong as he continues to peer over the money.

"What is it, Lieutenant Armstrong?" asks the Lieutenant Colonel.

"Sir, I was expecting a larger count than what I am seeing on the money counters."

Almost immediately, LaDeau speaks up. "We almost always overestimate de money we have, especially when it's on a scale like this."

But this does not deter Lieutenant Armstrong, who walks over to the money counters and the figures he has recorded on his clipboard and walks back over to the container. By now, Manning's eyes look like they are going to pop out of his head. He continues to glance up toward LaDeau.

"Sir, you still have a lot more money to count and a convoy to Kuwait in front of you," announces LaDeau, who is trying to draw attention away from the situation. All the while, LaDeau is thinking, *Stay cool. These are typical army officers questioning everything we do. Stay cool. He will move on, and we will be on the road before we know it.* LaDeau is correct.

Lieutenant Armstrong motions to the soldiers to continue with buttoning up the container. Manning almost looks like he is going to pass out, but he catches himself by holding onto the table. LaDeau glances over and nods to him as if to say, everything is okay.

THE SEMI
IS LOADED

Once the container is buttoned up, the counting continues. *Whir!* goes the money counter as the digital counters change rapidly as if the digital counters were eyes rolling back in the electronic money counter's head. The aroma of money fills the air as if one had walked through a garden of roses. LaDeau's face has a grin that is hidden through his five-day growth of beard. Yes, there is nothing like counting millions of dollars. It is not long before the loaders stop loading the second container and the counting stops. Once again, Lieutenant Armstrong eyeballs the container and the values reported by the money counters in their digital display and then records the data onto his clipboard and signals to the soldiers to button it up. They move onto the third container, and it is not long before the container is filled up.

At this point in the work effort, LaDeau speaks up.

"Lieutenant Armstrong, Mr. Manning and I have other tasks across de base that need attending to and we need to get de semi that will load these containers. Have you got all de information you need from these money counters?" LaDeau wants to press

Lieutenant Armstrong for the task at hand, and he needs the money counters.

Manning has been sweating all through this exercise, and it is clear that he is sweating now. Lieutenant Armstrong looks at his clipboard and records the last figures and nods to LaDeau.

"Okay. I'm through."

LaDeau asks, "How much do you have, Lieutenant?"

Lieutenant Armstrong reviews his numbers and double-checks with his calculator and responds, "Looks like three hundred and twenty-five million dollars, Mr. LaDeau."

LaDeau nods in approval and says, "Wow. That sure is a lot of money."

Manning chimes in with, "You can say that again."

Before he can get out another word, LaDeau intervenes. "Come on, Mr. Manning. We need to get going." They fetch the money counters and close the distance between the work area and doors to exit the building.

They both head over to the motor pool, which is out of sight of the warehouse. It's not long before the semi truck is in sight.

"Dere she be." LaDeau nods with his head in the general direction of the semi trailer as if he was a sailor aboard a clipper ship who just spotted a whale. LaDeau has this all planned out, and he knows the semi truck is out of view of the warehouse so they can't be seen. LaDeau and Manning crawl underneath the bed of the trailer, to the opposite end of the doors that are normally used to load the trailer. The trailer is not connected to the semi truck. Underneath, is a hidden door that LaDeau pushes open and then hoists himself into the darkness. With the trap door being small and LaDeau's pot belly being larger than the entrance, this is a birthing experience for the great whale of the semi trailer.

"Ugh. Crap. This is tight," complains LaDeau. "Dem insurgents' must have been your size, Joe. Ugh," grunts LaDeau.

"Come on and get your fat butt through there, Reb," Manning cheers LaDeau on in a Manning sort of cheer.

Finally, the big man hoists himself through the entrance.

"Pass me the counters," commands LaDeau. Manning passes the electronic money counters up to LaDeau and is followed by Manning, who makes quick work of squeezing his skinny body through the entrance. Although the room is concealed, the trailer has minor holes that were a patchwork from the outside to cover up bullet holes from previous missions. BCKR will run its equipment until the wheels fall off or the semi is blown up. It was from these previous missions and soldiers' chatter that LaDeau got wind of the concealed room in the back of the semi. As seen from the outside of the semi, the patchwork of square metal sheets barely riveted to the body of the trailer gives the appearance of a man's shaven face that was cut in many places and toilet tissue was used to stop the bleeding. On the inside of the trailer, this patchwork does not stop all the light from filtering in, and there is barely enough to see the images within the trailer. LaDeau closes the door into pitch dark blackness and turns the switch on a small camping lantern. Suddenly, there is light. The light casts a large shadow of LaDeau against the concealed room wall, covering the wall opposite of LaDeau, who is now sitting on the floor, while opposite him is Manning, who is standing.

"Have a seat, Yank."

Manning, who is looking around, squats to the floor and takes a seat. LaDeau's shoulders have about a three-foot clearance from the back of the semi trailer to the concealed wall, making movement limited. The wall is latched to the walls of the semi trailer that holds the concealed wall in place. A stack of twelve duffle bags are on the floor behind LaDeau. On top of the stack appears to be a stack of wire banding material and large wire banding metal clippers with two large, orange handles that appear as if they belonged to a long-legged clown you would see in a circus.

The large, crablike claws set on top of the long legs are closed, as if the crab was at rest. Directly behind Manning are three small pallets with three large, plastic, square covers leaning up against the wall that will represent the false floors once installed and about the same size in width and length and color as the containers that will contain the money. LaDeau catches Manning eyeing the containers. "This will raise the floor of de container to provide a false bottom," he announces, grinning like a shark that is about to have its long-awaited meal.

LaDeau pulls out his cell phone in his top shirt pocket and begins to type in the cell number for his Akhmed. The cell phone is quite small, and LaDeau's fingers are so large that they almost appear to cover the entire cell phone. After a brief moment of punching numbers, he raises the phone to his ear. On the other end of the call, on Trigger Base and in a BCKR office, the phone rings.

Akhmed picks up the phone. "Hello."

And before he can get a sound out, LaDeau says, "Get your butt over to de motor pool and pick up semi one fifty-five and drive it over to the warehouse!"

Akhmed already knows who is on the other end.

"De soldiers have a load of supplies that needs to be driven to Kuwait, and when you get there, you will spend the night and drive back the next day." LaDeau's commands come in quick succession.

Ahkmed replies in broken English, " Sir, my family are expecting me…"

And before he can continue, LaDeau says, "I don't care about your damn family. You get your butt over here'n drive that semi. Otherwise, quit." LaDeau ends the call.

Akhmed's face goes from shock to sadness almost immediately, for he knows that in Iraq, the only work available is work on the base. "That son of a donkey," mutters Akhmed . Akhmed stands there for a moment and then knows he has to rely on his friend to notify his family that LaDeau has sent him to Kuwait for another overnight mission. One of these days, he will have his revenge on this man, Allah willing. Akhmed walks off to find his friend and ask yet another favor.

In back of the semi trailer, LaDeau ends the call and places the cell phone back in his pocket.

"Lazy knuckle head," he mutters. "Okay. Let's review de plan, Yank."

And before LaDeau can get another word out, Manning intervenes.

"When will I get my cut?" asks Manning, to which LaDeau responds, "Look. We haven't even loaded de money. When it's loaded and dropped off in Kuwait, my bud will ship it ta the States, where it will arrive at my relative's funeral parlor—."

And before he can finish, the questions come in rapid succession.

"What relative? What funeral parlor? Look, LaDeau, if you are trying to stiff me—."

Before another question can be heard, LaDeau raises his hand, placing his stubby finger to his lips.

"Shh. Quiet," LaDeau whispers.

"Someone's coming. Must be Akhmed." LaDeau turns the lantern off.

The pitch blackness returns, and it's accompanied with the sound of approaching footsteps and a conversation in an Iraqi dialect. The footsteps come closer, and the conversation becomes louder. It's Akhmed, and he has brought another friend to assist with the hooking up the semi trailer to the truck. The conversation continues when one of the voices drifts off as if the person is walking away while the other voice stays constant in volume, indicating that the person is standing near the semi trailer and is not moving.

Off in the distance, the silence is broken as a long, low, monotonous growl from the engine is heard. The growl is broken as the engine turns over into the steady of a race horse that has completed a short gallop getting ready for its next race.

The sudden acrid smell of diesel appears as if a coal fired steam engine driven close by, and the odor can be detected even within the trailer and the concealed room. The race horse bolts, and the semi truck jumps forward and immediately goes into a quickened pace as Akhmed, the driver, gives it the gas in low gear. The pace is slow until Akhmed shifts into higher gear and the truck moves at a little faster pace. From inside the semi trailer and in the dark, LaDeau's mind is putting together the scenario that is taking place outside the trailer. He knows that Akhmed is approaching closer to the trailer and that he is in position to hook up the trailer. LaDeau braces himself, for the semi truck will get into position and then backup into the trailer, causing it to jump up enough so if one is not prepared it can startle one.

Should I warn that little twit? LaDeau questions himself. Hmm. *What if he gets rattled and hurts himself?* Again, LaDeau questions himself. *Why bother? I'm only going to kill 'em anyway.* He tries to reason the work effort of warning Manning to its outcome. *Hmm. What if he cries out? Then I would be in trouble.* LaDeau knows he has to warn Manning.

In the dark, some light filters through the semi trailer through cracks in the metal skin, enough light so that LaDeau can make out Manning's image. He reaches out to touch the outline of the image.

Manning responds in a loud whisper. "What?" asks Manning.

"Brace yourself, Yank. They are hooking up de trailer, and it will bolt on ya."

The soft whisper comes with the warning that Manning comes to respect coming from LaDeau, for Manning respects

LaDeau and truly looks up to him. Little does Manning realize that this will be last trip with LaDeau and the last trip on the planet. The racehorse has slowed its gallop as the semi truck slows to a stop. *Screech!* The sound of the air breaks signals the stop. Akhmed works the accelerator by depressing and then letting up and quickly accelerating again as he begins to back up the semi truck. The semi truck lurches backward and begins its slow crawl toward the back end of the semi trailer where Manning and LaDeau are housed in the concealed room. Akhmed's assistant is guiding him backward with hand signals; and when in position, the semi truck lurches backward, forcing the semi trailer upward. LaDeau and Manning lurch upward as the semi trailer lurches upward, as if its riders were on a bucking horse at a rodeo. For a moment, LaDeau's bottom obtains some relief from his overweight upper trunk of a body. But again, order is restored as gravity does its job and LaDeau's weight is restored with the full affect on his butt. There is a slight groan from both LaDeau and Manning, but it is not heard over the loud noise of the semi truck.

The slam of the truck door signals that Akhmed's assistant driver has joined him in the cab and they are ready to take off toward the warehouse. The rumbling of the engine again begins to increase in volume as Ahkmed begins to accelerate and the semi truck lurches forward.

Dad burn it. That knuckle head can't drive, LaDeau thinks to himself.

The semi trailer rocks up and down as if the race horse is in a small trot heading toward the warehouse. There are no paved roads here on Camp Trigger, and the road is rocky as the semi heads toward the warehouse. Upon arrival, the semi truck comes to a halt. Akhmed has positioned the truck so that it is ready to back up through the warehouse doors. He waits for hand signals from the soldiers, who are quick to get him backed into the warehouse. The engine growls as it is accelerated, and Akhmed backs up the semi trailer through the large door opening of the warehouse. Akhmed watches in his mirrors as the soldiers signal him through the doors. The semi makes its long crawl through the doors, and it is not long before the truck is in position and stops.

Screech! Again, the air brakes signal their stop; and Sergeant Hazard motions to Akhmed by moving his hand across his throat as if it was a knife cutting it, indicating to cut the engine. Akhmed kills the engine, for the semi is ready to be loaded. The soldiers make quick work to getting the doors open without being told. Sergeant Hazard signals one of the soldiers to board the forklift by pointing to the soldier and to the forklift. The soldier responds immediately and quickly boards the forklift and starts it up. The forklift moves forward as if it is a lumbering crab with its claws extended, ready to grab up what it perceives as food on an ocean beach. The lift inserts into the opened end of the wooden pallet, and the forklift moves forward until the pallet swallows up the forks on the end the forklift. The forklift pushes against the pallet, causing it to lurch forward enough to signal the driver that he should raise the forks on the lift; and he does so on key. The pallet and its container contents are then lifted just enough to clear the ground. A ramp has been positioned on the door entrance of the semi trailer, and the forklift begins to travel up the ramp and enters the semi trailer.

The sound of the forklift wheels are moving across the floor of the semi trailer, echoing a low rumble as the forklift makes it across the floor of the semi trailer and positions the pallet close up to the wall of the concealed room. LaDeau and Manning feel the vibration of the forklift. Each one has one hand against the concealed wall as if they are waiting for it to collapse. The forklift lowers the pallet to the floor of the semi trailer, and there is a loud noise as the pallet comes to rest on the semi floor. Once on the floor, the driver backs up the forklift back down the ramp and proceeds to the next container. The odor of sweat in the concealed room begins to become a little pungent. Manning knows that LaDeau sweats like a pig and almost has the same odor. Manning is so excited with the entire caper that he is almost ready to piss his pants.

I hope no one notices LaDeau's body odor, he thinks to himself.

Through the light that makes it through the cracks in the semi trailer, one can see that Manning is wide-eyed, for this is the biggest caper in his little life. Like a captain of a whaler who has just harpooned a whale, LaDeau is thinking of what he will do with his catch and Manning's catch once this fishing expedition is over. His thoughts are disturbed by the thump of combat boots drifting across the warehouse floor and the forklift inserting its forks into the next pallet. *Whir!* goes the lift as the container is raised and the forklift moves forward. The forklift makes it up the ramp, and the low rumble sound of a distant thunder is heard as the wheels of the forklift make it across the floor of the semi trailer. The forklift positions the container up to the first container loaded and drops it in position onto the floor—*Thud! Whir!* The lift backs out and down the ramp.

The last container is finally loaded, and the soldiers remove the drive-up ramp. The soldiers close the semi trailer doors and begin to latch the doors. The sound of metal on metal can be heard as the sliding latches are moved into position and buckled. The soldiers wrestle the large metal buckles into place and latch the door. A lock is inserted and snapped shut. There's no turning back now for LaDeau and Manning.

"Okay. It's good to go," announces Sergeant Hazard.

"Guide him out the door and into position for the convoy out, Sergeant Purdue," commands Sergeant Hazard. Sergeant Purdue, quick to task, trots over to the front of the semi truck. Raising his hand above his head and pointing his finger skyward and in a circling motion, he signals Akhmed to start the engine. Akhmed obeys, and there is a low rattle as the diesel engine growls then finally emits a low roar as Akhmed throttles the accelerator. The long stream of black smoke exits the smoke stack, filling the air with the acrid smell of spent diesel fuel. Sergeant Purdue changes the hand signals, and Akhmed responds by shifting the semi truck into gear. This event is announced with a grinding of metal on metal rattle of the transmission.

"We're moving," announces Manning loud enough that LaDeau could hear him. Before he can make another sound, a hand comes out of the darkness and covers his mouth. The hand is held in place with another hand on the back of his head. This announcement goes unnoticed on the outside of the semi truck as Akhmed is slowly having the vehicle crawl forward, ever-watching Sergeant Purdue's hand signals as Sergeant Purdue guides the semi out of the warehouse. The large, whale-like semi trailer begins to exit the warehouse. Meanwhile, LaDeau slowly releases his hand off from Manning's mouth. Yes, this captain is not going to let this whale of a mother load get away due to a stupid mistake by a wannabe criminal. Manning gets the message and understands that he should be quiet, not another peep. Outside the warehouse, Sergeant Purdue positions the semi truck into position and signals Akhmed to stop the vehicle. Once stopped, he walks past Akhmed toward the end of the semi trailer and signals the drivers of other military vehicles into position. He then walks back toward Akhmed, his military boots crunching on the rocks below loud enough for Manning and LaDeau to hear. When he's in the front of the semi truck, he signals the remaining military vehicles into position. Once the convoy is configured and all vehicles are ready to go, he signals the drivers, Akhmed included, for a safety brief before they hit the highway.

Akhmed cuts the engine off and exits the semi truck, slamming the door behind him. The drivers and assistant drivers gather around Sergeant Hazard in a semicircle for a safety brief, a typical military briefing on road conditions, weather, and what to watch for before the convoy rolls out.

The brief is quick and to the point. "Are there any questions?" asks Sergeant Hazard.

With no response comes the next command.

"Okay. Mount up."

The drivers break away from the briefing and head toward their vehicles. Akhmed boards his semi truck and buckles up his seatbelt. With a few motions of placing the transmission into gear, he starts the engine. The rattling of metal on metal announces the engine starting up. Inside the concealed room of the semi trailer, LaDeau and Manning wait silently until the semi truck begins to move. LaDeau puts his face close up to one of the holes in the semi trailer and takes in the view from outside to gain a bearing as to where they are. He sees that the convoy has exited the warehouse area and is heading toward the gate when the vehicles come to a stop.

Typical and right on cue, he thinks to himself. *These dumb knuckle heads are waiting on the checkpoint*, he thinks.

But this wait seems to be taking a little longer than expected. Over the sound of the semi truck engine, he can hear soldiers approaching the semi trailer. Again and almost instinctively, LaDeau covers the mouth of Manning with his hand. The soldiers chat for a moment and are checking the outside of the vehicle.

"I guess it's okay," one soldier announces as he points to the undercarriage of the semi trailer. "I thought it was loose, but I guess it's okay."

The other four soldiers nod in agreement and walk away. It is not long, and the semi truck begins to accelerate, announcing the next movement. It is then that LaDeau removes his hand from Manning's mouth. The convoy begins to exit the checkpoint and is on its way to the major highway that connects the dirt road of Camp Trigger. The convoy enters the highway and is on the road when the camp lantern light is switched on in the concealed room of the semi trailer.

"Hell, Country boy. I thought you were going to strangle me back there!" yells Manning, knowing that he is safe and no one can hear the conversation.

"Well, Yank, I would not want ya to give us away, now would I?" replies LaDeau.

THE ROAD TRIP

The small battery camp lantern illuminates the concealed room area, and Manning takes in the view of the room. It is clear to see that metal latches were attached to the wall of the semi trailer and the concealed wall hold the wall in place. The stack of duffle bags lies on the floor. On top the duffle bags, there is a role of wire banding metal that will hold the containers of money in place, including the giant metal clippers used to cut the banding material and a box of assorted stuff. In addition to bottles of water and sandwiches wrapped in clear, plastic food wrap compliment the duo's tool set.

LaDeau, Manning thinks to himself. *That country boy thinks of everything,* Manning thinks and then finally announces, "Hell, country boy. You even brought us boxed lunches. Man you think of everything!"

LaDeau is busy unlatching the concealed room.

"Come on, Yank. We ain't got time to waste," replies LaDeau. "Save your bull for later."

With that response, Manning begins to unlatch the other side of the concealed wall. Now, Manning is not very strong. He begins to wrestle with the metal latch, which is noticed by LaDeau. In two strides, LaDeau clears his side of the semi trailer and grabs the latch with his huge, hairy paw. With one movement, the latch is unsnapped. It is clear to see that LaDeau has performed manual labor in his past and is quite comfortable performing these manual tasks.

LaDeau continues to unlatch the remaining metal latches when Manning states, "Hey. I coulda gotten it." LaDeau ignores him.

LaDeau continues until all the latches have been removed. The configuration of the concealed wall is such that the wall is erected in two pieces, with the top half of the wall resting on the bottom half. This configuration is announced by the top half of the wall begins to lean toward Manning and LaDeau as each latch has been unsnapped. When the last latch is unsnapped, the top half of the wall begins to lower right on top of Manning and LaDeau, who slowly hoist the wall down. This is a bit of a juggling act since the semi trailer floor is shifting underneath their feet as the convoy moves down the major highway toward Kuwait.

As the wall is slowly lowered, the light filters through the remaining part of the semi trailer, revealing the three motionless containers. LaDeau and Manning lower the top half of the wall, and the light filters into where the containers are positioned. It is clear to see the containers are attached to the wooden pallets, as LaDeau had promised. LaDeau reaches down and grabs the wire banding material and the metal banding wire clippers and throws them over, where they land on top of the closest money container. He then grabs the duffle bags and throws them over onto the floor just on the opposite side of the now-exposed concealed room. With the top half of the concealed wall removed, the dynamic duo only need to step over the bottom half of the wall to reach the mother load. Manning has cleared the lower half of the wall, and LaDeau bends down to grab the electronic, battery-operated money counters and passes them to him. He then reaches down, grabs the camp lantern, passes that to Manning, and steps over the lower half the concealed wall.

LaDeau takes control. "Okay. This is how it plays out. We will start on de container closest to the doors and work our way back to here." They do not waste time and grab the wire banding material along with the wire banding clippers and head toward the container. LaDeau reaches out with the wire banding clipper and, with both hands on each leg of the clipper, compresses the legs inward. *Thunk!* There was a loud popping sound of the metal breaking and snapping backward, opposite of where LaDeau was standing. The metal almost hit Manning.

"Watch it Bowe! You almost got me!" LaDeau starts working on the next wire banding material, not paying attention to Manning. *Thunk!* There is another loud popping sound. This time, Manning is smart enough to move out of the way. The container reaches up and above LaDeau's waistline from the floor and is almost at chest level with Manning. It is not long before LaDeau has clipped all the wired banding material that was holding the metal container in place. He then lifts the top of the container; and as he does, the aroma of money fills the semi trailer. The light from the lantern that is now positioned on top of the adjacent container reveals the smirk of the Franklins. A smirk that almost implies, "What took you so long?"

Like two long-lost gold miners who had worked their claim for ten years and have finally stumbled upon gold, it is a moment of discovery. LaDeau's piercing eyes begin to shine and widen just a little while Manning's eyes are almost bugging out of his head.

"We're rich! We are rich!" And with that comes that middle-school giggle that only Manning can produce.

"Dat we are, Yank. Dat we are." And LaDeau does not waste time. "Yank, hand me a duffle bag, and you grab one as well. Now fill 'em up to the top, being careful to stuff 'em as full as you can."

And Manning chirps in. "Aren't we going to count it first?"

And LaDeau replies, "We need a place to put de money, and we will run it through de counter before we place it in the duffle bag. Yank, you will be running the counter."

And with that said, Manning grabs the counter and starts it up. The minute he hits the start button, the red lights on the display begin to twinkle and then roll up all zeros, as if one had hit the jackpot on a coin machine in a Las Vegas casino. LaDeau passes the money to Manning, who feeds it into the input hopper of the money counter and hits the start button. The money slaps through the counter mechanism, with a series of sharp claps as if an audience is applauding this moment. The aroma of money is intoxicating as it is fanned through the counter. When the applaud stops, LaDeau grabs the money in his hairy paw and stuffs it in the duffle bag. As he stuffs the money, Manning is loading the hopper and hitting the start button on the second money counter that they brought with them. Another series of sharp claps as the counter applauds yet another revealed discovery for our gold miners.

"We did it, Bowe! We're rich!" And again, the Manning middle-school laugh is heard above the roar of the semi as it travels down the highway toward Kuwait.

It is not long before all the money has been removed from the container and the duffel bags have been stuffed with money.

"Yank, let's leave it here'n and fetch the false bottom."

And they both head toward the concealed room area. Manning clears the lower wall quite quickly and hands the small, wooden pallets and the false plastic bottom of the container to LaDeau. Manning jumps over the lower wall and heads toward the doors on the semi trailer. They both walk like drunken sailors as the semi wobbles back and forth as it heads down the highway. LaDeau pulls out notepad, pencil, and a small calculator from his pocket. His big, thick finger punches a few buttons on the calculator as he begins to record the numbers. After punching in both numbers from the counters, he presses the equal sign on the handheld calculator and comes up with hundred and twenty-five million. LaDeau records the numbers on his small notepad.

He clears the calculator and punches in the numbers again and presses the equal sign and hundred and twenty-five million rolls up again.

"One more time, jest to be sure," announces LaDeau as he repeats the process. "Yep. A hundred and twenty-five million. Okay. Clear de counters, and we will install the false bottom."

Manning hands LaDeau the miniature wooden pallets, and LaDeau places the pallets strategically on the floor of the large, plastic container.

"False bottom," commands LaDeau. Manning hands him the false bottom. With the precision of a skilled surgeon, LaDeau maneuvers the false bottom until it is picture perfect. "Lantern," commands LaDeau. Manning hands him the battery-powered lantern.

LaDeau inspects the bottom for any flaws as if he was inspecting a fine diamond. LaDeau had spent time on measuring the supply containers, and he knows exactly how far to raise the false bottom from the floor of the container. Yes, LaDeau has done his homework on this one.

"Okay. Now let's count de money."

LaDeau hands the lantern back to Manning, who places the lantern back on the adjacent container. Manning clears the money counters by pressing a reset button. Again, zeros roll up in the eyes of the electronic money counter. Zeros and that blank stare as if to say, "Throw me a bone"; and a bone is exactly what it received as Manning reaches down into the duffle bag and removes a stack of Franklins. He loads the hopper; and in no time, applause of the money processing through the input hopper again is heard. Right behind Manning is LaDeau, loading his counter input hopper. The smell of money is aromatic and intoxicating but not enough to keep these gold miners from losing sight of the task at hand.

"What are you going to do with your money, Bowe?"

"Oh… I haven't figured that far ahead."

Manning has a vision of grandeur like a kid on Christmas Eve envisioning his new toy. "I'm going to buy me a Maserati. Yes, I will be the talk of the town back in Boston."

These conversations of Manning's grandeur continue until the box is filled to the top and the remaining four duffle bags are stuffed with hundred-dollar bills.

Without missing a beat, LaDeau gathers up the banding material that was cut.

"Let's gather this up and place it back dere in the concealed room," announces LaDeau. Manning follows through with the assist.

They store the cut banding material and return to the container they were working on. LaDeau records the numbers from the money counter onto his notepad and again punches in the numbers into his calculator.

"A hundred and twenty-five million," announces LaDeau. "Let me double-check." Again, he clears his calculator and recomputes with the large, stubby fingers punching in the numbers. "Same number: a hundred and twenty-five million," LaDeau says as he clears the calculator for yet another computation.

"We're good," cries Manning who is getting impatient. LaDeau raises his hand as if to scold a middle-school student who has disrupted his class.

"One more check and we're good." LaDeau returns to his calculator.

The semi trailer rocks back and forth, side to side, as it rolls down the highway toward Kuwait. A small breeze can be felt as the wind finds its way through some of the cracks in the semi trailer walls. The smell of diesel fuel can be detected, and the roar of the engine is heard as if rambles down the highway.

"Okay. A hundred and twenty-five million it is. . We need to clear the money counters and pull out money from the duffle bags. We will use one money counter to count the money. We need three hundred thousand."

With that, Manning clears the money counter and begins to extract the money. He loads the hopper on the money counter and hits the start button. The counter whirls through, and the counter rolls up the numbers.

"You count, and I will store the money," commands LaDeau.

"Okay. Here is the first count," replies Manning as he hands LaDeau the money.

Now the container is quite full, and so LaDeau has to stuff the money in the sides of the container to make the adjustment. He grunts and groans as Manning loads the hopper on the money counter and hits the start button.

"Hundred thousand." Manning counts off the money already counted and retrieves the money from the output hopper and passes it to LaDeau. LaDeau grabs the money, and here come the grunts and groans again. Manning loads the hopper and hits the start button.

This process is repeated until Manning finally announces, "Three hundred thousand," and passes the last of the stack to LaDeau.

LaDeau grabs the money and again crams the money into the side of the container. "Okay. Now we'll just place the container on top and not quite strap it down. Let's move on to the next container."

And the process repeats itself. Yes, the process repeats itself with Manning's visions of grandeur and how he will buy up all of Boston and find himself in the richest part of the city. The money counters are working overtime; and so are Manning and LaDeau, who have built up quite a sweat and an odor to match. The breeze blowing through the cracks of the semi trailer is enough to fan them, but not cool enough to keep them from perspiring. In another forty-five minutes, they complete the second container and move on to the third container. LaDeau is monitoring his watch, for he knows that he has to finish the job before he reaches Kuwait. During the count and loading of the second container, Manning begins to whine about not having the cash on hand and having to wait until the money arrives in the States for the split.

"When is the money going to get to the States?"

The questions push LaDeau closer to becoming annoyed with the little twit.

I guess I can give him some details. De little twit won't live long enough to tell anyone, LaDeau thinks to himself.

LaDeau gives more details of the operation to Manning, who stops during the operation when he hears that besides Smith, who will smuggle the money to the States, he has to put up with his brother-in law for a fourth cut.

"What do you mean your brother-in-law? How many more people do we have in on this deal, Bowe?"

LaDeau tells him that's it, but that does not stop Manning from questioning.

"Look. Let's stay focused and count the remainder of de money," commands LaDeau. "We will have plenty of time to discuss the details and the split when de work is done." This buys LaDeau some relief from the nagging little twit.

Once the third container has been counted, the false bottom is in place, and the container is filled, the crew begins to button up the containers with the wire banding material. They snake the wire banding material through the bottom of the wooden pallets and on top of the big, large, plastic containers that house the money. They use the tool that comes with the banding material to secure the banding material and tighten it up using a lever in ratchet-like motions. All three containers have been secured and the duffle bags returned to the other side of the concealed room. LaDeau makes one more pass around the money containers to ensure that he has not left anything in view. Both LaDeau and Manning return to the other side of the concealed room and begin to hoist the top panel in place. During this process, Manning is complaining about LaDeau's brother-in-law getting a cut.

"Why does he have a cut? We are the ones taking most of the risk."

LaDeau has completed latching his side of the concealed wall and returns to assist Manning. "Here, Yank. Hold that latch against the wall."

At that moment, LaDeau reaches down to grab a knife that he had strapped to his leg, housed in its sheath. As Manning Latches the final latch and turns to complain some more, he stops dead in his tracks, as if he has been electrocuted. "Ugh." And he takes his last breath, for LaDeau's knife is wedged into his sternum and straight through his heart. Manning is paralyzed and cannot move. His pupils become enlarged, his jaw drops as his body goes into shock, and he makes a gurgling sound as blood rushes into his lungs.

"Dere's your share, Yank," says LaDeau as Manning begins to slump forward and falls to the floor. "Dere's your damn share, you whinny little twit."

There is no honor among thieves. LaDeau is prepared for this moment. He reaches into the box he brought with him and pulls out towels and bottled water to clean the blood from his hands. He even brought a change of shirt and removed the pullover, sand-colored t-shirt known as the "been there done that t-shirt" containing the Iraqi Freedom logo with the outline of an Iraq map and all of its major cities. He reaches down and pulls over a solid blue T shirt with a pocket, and the T shirt barely fits over his pot belly. Again, he reaches down and pulls out two large, plastic bags. He begins to enclose Manning's body within the bags and secures it with duck tape. He hoists Manning's body into a spare duffle bag and secures the duffle bag. LaDeau figures that Manning's body will stay in the concealed room until the semi leaves Kuwait the next day. Once the semi is returned to Camp Trigger, he will remove the body and store it at the makeshift on-base mortuary where they store the bodies of insurgents and dead Iraqis that soldiers have came across during their combat missions, a temporary mortuary used as a staging area before the bodies are shipped out to the mortuary at Baghdad. LaDeau desk checks his work as the semi rolls down the highway. *Eight duffle bags,* he counts to himself, *two money counters...*

As the semi rolls down the highway toward Kuwait, the convoy begins to slow down.

ARRIVING AT AL JAHRA, KUWAIT

This is a scheduled stop where the highway comes to a T in the road, where it will make a right turn and head toward Kuwait. Currently, it stops for fifteen minutes to await another convoy to clear the turn lane that it needs to make. LaDeau opens the trap door to prepare for his next move and shuts off the camp lantern. Once again, the light from the trap door floods the concealed room as LaDeau prepares for his next move. As the semi comes to a complete stop, LaDeau squeezes his body through the trap door and onto the road. He closes the trap door behind him and crawls to the passenger side of the semi trailer. Moving quite quickly, LaDeau steps up on the step side of the truck and opens the passenger side of the semi truck.

Akhmed is in shock. "Boss, where did you come from?"

LaDeau responds, "Never mind." He motions to Akhmed's assistant driver to jump in the back of the sleep side of the semi truck, a small room behind the driver and passenger side of the vehicle that drivers use to take naps. In the States, these are frequently used. However, in Iraq they are not practical.

Akhmed suspects that something is not right but is afraid to ask, for it would mean his job. LaDeau would not hesitate to fire him for a lot less than his curiosity. But still, Akhmed knows something is not right.

"This is a scheduled stop, boss," Akhmed says in an attempt to distract his distrust from what he knows is strange.

LaDeau is lost in thought, rerunning the scheme through his mind. *Boy, that Louisiana brother of mine is going to crap in his pants when he sees all of this money,* LaDeau thinks to himself.

As LaDeau is lost in thought, Akhmed can't help feel that is truly strange that LaDeau is just showing up in the middle of a highway and popping into the passenger side. LaDeau has fired local nationals for a lot less and is a dictator when it comes to what he wants and is similar to a dictator much like the one that is at large, Saddam Hussein. Although he does not have henchmen working for him like Saddam did, he is ruthless when it comes to getting what he wants. Any questioning of his requests can be taken as objection, and that means getting fired. Getting fired in Iraq, where there are no jobs, can be threatening for one's day-to-day survival. No, Akhmed is not going to question this little Hitler and is going to keep his mouth shut when he notices what appears to be blood on the pants leg of LaDeau.

Should I bring it to his attention? Akhmed thinks to himself. *No. Better not.* Akhmed's survival instinct for keeping his job has protected him so far. Why not just shut up and ask no questions?

The scheduled stop is over. Farther down the highway, where it comes to a T, the traffic has cleared. The escort vehicle in front of the semi truck begins to slowly move forward. Although they are quite safe and quite a distance from any neighboring town or major city, this does not stop the soldier who has his hands on the fifty-caliber machine gun from scanning his sector of fire, looking for any threat. Soldiers on these missions stay focused, and they are well-aware of the danger.

Akhmed moves the shifting lever into gear, and the grinding sound of the gears meshing together announces with a rattling sound; and the semi slowly lurches forward, crawling ever so slowly as the engine accelerates. The acceleration is then followed by yet another change of gears as Akhmed manipulates the shifting lever, finding the next advanced gear; and the ever-so-slow semi again crawls forward. Meanwhile, in the concealed dark room of the semi trailer, the light filters through the few cracks in the semi trailer body enough for the vague outline of the duffle bags to be seen lurching up and down as the semi changes gears. In one such bag, the lifeless body of Manning bounces up and down along with the duffle bags of money that are piled on top of his body. The odor of a fresh cut beef steak to emanate from the bag, for this is the odor of blood that is just beginning to filter through from Manning's wounds to the small, concealed room. Back in the semi truck, with Akhmed busy changing gears and shifting the vehicle into the higher gears, the semi is gaining speed. LaDeau pays no attention to Akhmed as he is rifling through his master plan.

Once we get into Kuwait, I'll link up with Bubba, and we can move de money when it just starts getting dark, he thinks to himself. *Bubba should store the money and prepare it for shipment back to the States,* LaDeau thinks to himself. He reaches into his pocket and pulls out a packet of cigarettes. Tapping the back of the pack a few times as if he was adjusting the ammunition rounds in an M4 magazine assault rifle, LaDeau removes the cellophane from the pack and throws it on the floorboard of the semi.

Akhmed takes note of where it falls, for he has to pick it up when he parks the truck; and this is another reason for Akhmed hating LaDeau. *He treats us like crap,* Akhmed thinks to himself. *The lazy monkey boy does not have sense enough to hold it until we find a trash barrel at Camp Kuwait.* Akhmed's hate swelters. *I hate this son of a donkey.* Ahkemd continues to monitor the road, pretending not pay attention LaDeau's litter habits.

But LaDeau is unaware of Akhmed's hate and couldn't care less, for today, Akhmed is the last thing on his mind. LaDeau opens the top of the Camel cigarettes and removes the aluminum foil. The cigarettes are standing shoulder to shoulder as if they were soldiers in a formation, silent and not moving. The strong smell of tobacco almost having a raisin smell fills the cab of the truck. LaDeau reaches in with his strong, stubby fingers picking the tip of one of the cigarettes, nurturing it out of its package, and stuffs it underneath the bushy mustache that is his lips. He closes the box and reaches into his right, front hip pocket of his blue jeans and pulls out a clear, yellow, gas lighter and strikes the ignition pedal. A long, blue flame with a yellow tip comes to life. He places the blue flame at the end of the cigarette and inhales deeply. His lungs fill with the almost narcotic blue smoke which welcomes the nicotine. The end of the cigarette turns a bright orange. He releases the ignition pedal on the lighter, and the blue flame disappears. The bright orange coal of the cigarette grows brighter and begins its slow climb toward LaDeau's mouth as if it was lava crawling down the side of a volcano toward level ground. LaDeau exhales a thick plume of smoke inside the cab of the truck, not paying any attention to the nonsmoker, Akhmed.

Akhmed adjusts his window slightly open, allowing the smoke to be sucked out of the window and across his field of vision. *Rotten son of a donkey,* Akhmed thinks to himself. *He knows we are not supposed to smoke in the truck. At least, that is what he tells us,* Akhmed thinks to himself. *Rotten butt head.*

But again, LaDeau is lost in own thoughts and couldn't care less about Akhmed.

Meanwhile, pondering his scheme. *Once the money is moved, Bubba can pack it up in de coffins and ship it out. He should then use the base phones to call Duke.* LaDeau almost appears to grin to himself. LaDeau knows that this technique of using coffins work to ship contraband and it was used on another one of his schemes to ship diamonds out of Afghanistan. *Yep. Duke will be glad to get that call, and Bubba will give him the list of soldiers whose coffins contain de money.* LaDeau continues with his slight grin and rewards himself with another long drag off the cigarette. They pass a sign that indicates they are about ten miles outside of Kuwait. The convoy begins to slow down; and the once-familiar city can be seen from a distance, a desert city with a few modern buildings but the ever-so-desert-tan color of the buildings. The convoy skirts the city and inches its way about five miles from Camp Kuwait. The familiar camp is no new news to LaDeau or Akhmed, for they both have made many supply runs to Camp Kuwait. The convoy moves along, bringing with it familiar terrain that LaDeau recognizes: the small shops; cafes; and occasional vendors selling goods like fruits, CDs, radios, and even cell telephones. These vendor shops pop up close to the base camp in hopes of catching the eyes of passing soldiers that might spend their dollars. It is not long before the front gates of Camp Kuwait appear and the convoy begins to slow until it comes to a complete stop. To enter the base camps, one needs a pass card; and both Akhmed and LaDeau whip out their pass cards in preparation for the security guard to check their identification. Akhmed barks a command to his Iraqi assistant driver, who had been riding in the back of the sleep cab. He pops his head out, holding his badge just below his chin, flashing a big, wide smile showing perfectly straight teeth as if they were a ridge of snow-covered, white hills spreading across the wide grin. The security guard is an American contractor who works for BCKR, and he is toting an automatic weapon similar to the M16A2 weapons that soldiers carry. The broad, dark sunglasses hide his eyes, along with the facial expression that shows he means business. The guard steps up on the steps built into the cab of the truck and used by the driver to step into the high cab of the truck, a complacent move that could have cost him his life if this was a terrorist had he not caught the hand wave from LaDeau, whom he recognized.

"What's up, hoss?" asks the security guard as he pokes his head into the driver's side of the window of the truck.

"Same stuff, different day," answers LaDeau.

And they both break out into a loud chuckle. Small talk ensues that centers around shop talk of who got promoted within BCKR and who is taking charge of one of the many functions. It's common BCKR news that BCKR employees follow in the e-mails they receive from their employer, keeping them abreast of the movement within the organization.

"You take care, Bubba, and watch yourself up there in the Box," warns the BCKR security guard, referring to the combat zone acronym as he steps down from the side of the truck cab and continues to the next vehicle in the convoy.

A minute has passed, and the convoy commander begins to slowly move forward and is waved through the Camp Kuwait gate by the BCKR security guards. The convoy crawls through the small streets of Camp Kuwait, making its way over to the warehouse that is adjacent to the motor pool, and comes to a complete stop. The convoy commander walks to each vehicle in the convoy, checking the names of the manifest of names that he knew joined the convoy. He steps up on the step side of the cab, pokes his head in, and checks on Akhmed and the assistant driver. He looks at his roster and views the pass cards that are resting on the chests of both Akhmed and LaDeau.

The convoy commander glances down at his clipboard. "I am not finding your name on my manifest, Mr. LaDeau."

Akhmed is silent and is thinking to himself, *Yes, you son without a father. What are you going to do now?* He waits to hear LaDeau's response.

"I have been here all along, Sergeant, and you probably have seen me around Camp Trigger since I am the head supervisor for all the local nationals," responds a Louisiana accent in a compliant manner. LaDeau attempts to cover his tracks. LaDeau has worked hard at pistol-whipping the local nationals into keeping their mouths shut when he is talking and knows that neither Akhmed nor the assistant driver will say a word.

The sergeant scratches the side of his head with his pencil as he peers over the manifest and finally says, "Well, I'll just add you, Mr. LaDeau, but it is Camp Trigger's policy that you check in with the convoy commander before you ride with a convoy. Just be sure that you follow that policy in the future."

"Yes, Sergeant. I will be sure to do that," responds LaDeau. The sergeant steps down from the cab.

UNLOADING
THE CASH

It is not long before another armed soldier walks up some thirty feet from the semi truck and motions for Akhmed to steer his truck toward him. Using hand signals, the soldier signals Ahkemd to steer his truck into a position where the semi truck can be backed though the warehouse doors. Once in position, the soldiers walk to the back of the semi and, upon approaching the end of the semi trailer, start the hand signals to motion the truck to back up through the warehouse doors and into the warehouse. Akhmed follows the directions, pushing and releasing the gas pedal, which gently nudges the semi trailer backward. The thick, black, acrid smell of diesel fuel fills the air as if the door to a coal furnace has just been opened as Akhmed works the throttle backing the slow-moving dragon backward and into its cave. Akhmed shifts into reverse and jockeys with the steering wheel, left and then right, all the while backing the long semi trailer into the warehouse. Once in, the soldier performs a hand signal drawing his hand across his throat, which means to kill the engine; and Akhmed obliges. Just like Camp

Trigger, both inside and outside of the warehouse, the area is heavily guarded with armed soldiers standing at the ready. The table setup is similar with the three tables and the center table containing BCKR electronic money counters and two BCKR employees standing behind the money counters.

LaDeau spots the BCKR employees and thinks to himself, *they'll know the actual count. I'll just stop over and chat with them after the count is done.*

These BCKR employees are unaware of LaDeau's scheme and do recognize him as he exits the semi cab. They wave, and LaDeau walks over to greet them, stretching his hand across the table, and is joined by a handshake from each.

An army captain walks over to LaDeau. "Sir, I'm sorry, but you will need to stand by the front of the truck as we count the money," directs the captain.

LaDeau complies. "Yes, sir." LaDeau grabs the bill of his hat in a friendly sort of gesture common among cowboys and he walks over to join Akhmed. LaDeau can tell from Ahkemd's glare that Akhmed knows that he lied, and LaDeau figures he will wait until he gets back to Camp Trigger and fire both Akhmed and the assistant driver.

Sort of a safety precaution, he thinks to himself. *No need in keeping a loose mouth around,* as LaDeau stands a few feet away from Akhmed.

The captain walks out of the warehouse and is then greeted by the convoy commander, who renders a salute. "Mission accomplished, sir."

The Captain replies, "Good work, Sergeant. Go ahead and park the remainder of your convoy and have your men grab some chow. Check in with the billeting office for a bunk and a place to stay so you can get ready for convoy back the next day."

"Yes, sir," replies the sergeant. He then salutes, steps backward, performs a right-face, and walks away toward his convoy team, motioning them over to convey the command.

The captain walks back into the warehouse and is greeted by Lieutenant Armstrong, who was one of the convoy team members who drove down from Camp Trigger. Armstrong is holding a clipboard where he had recorded the count of money that departed Camp Trigger. Standing next to him is Sergeant First Class Hazard and Sergeant Purdue. There are several soldiers standing to the right of the tables and armed soldiers, rifles in hand, standing at the ready behind them.

"Listen up." In a loud, commanding voice, the captain begins to bark the needed instructions. "We have three containers in the semi that contain money captured from one of Saddam's caches. We have BCKR employees that will operate the money counters and the forklift to unload the containers." He points in the general direction of the BCKR employees standing behind the electronic money counters and the BCKR employee sitting on the forklift. The captain continues. "The money containers will be positioned to the right of the tables, just about where you are standing." He points to the soldiers. "The containers are secured with wire banding material, and BCKR will remove that for us and remember"—he glances to the BCKR employee on the forklift and his soldiers—"safety first. I do not want that wire banding material snapping and putting someone's eye out."

The soldiers all nod in agreement and reply, "Hooah, sir."

The captain continues. "We will place the money on the table to the right of the money counters where BCKR will remove it, place it in the counter's hopper, and start the count."

The BCKR employees behind the money counters nod in approval.

"At no time will BCKR reset the counters. We have Lieutenant Armstrong, who will be monitoring the count at all times.

When the count is complete, he will compare the count with the count of money that he conducted back at Camp Trigger."

LaDeau's heart begins to beat just a little faster, and the sweat rings around his armpits begin to show themselves. *Stay calm, hoss,* LaDeau comforts himself. *These dumb knuckle heads are not going to catch on,* LaDeau thinks to himself. Yes, LaDeau knows how to work the system.

Lieutenant Armstrong raises his hand in acknowledgement so that the team of soldiers and BCKR recognize who he is as the captain continues to instruct the team. "Follow Sergeant First Class Hazard's instructions when removing the money from the container and placing it on the input table to the right."

Sergeant Hazard raises his hand in acknowledgement.

"Follow Sergeant Purdue's instructions when you repack the money in the container."

And Sergeant Purdue steps forward and raises his hand in acknowledgement.

"Are there any questions?" asks the captain. "If not, I will turn it over to Sergeant First Class Hazard."

And Sergeant Hazard steps forward and instructs a few of the soldiers to unlock the semi and other soldiers to remove the ramp from underneath the semi trailer where it is stored. Once the doors are unlocked and the ramp is attached to the back of the trailer and the opposite end on the ground, the BCKR employee starts the little propane-powered forklift and accelerates the lift driving up the ramp. The ramp groans under the weight of the forklift across its back as the forklift rumbles across the floor of the semi to its target, the pallet. A rattling sound can be heard as the forklift forks are inserted inside of the pallet that the first container is resting upon. The forklift slams into the container with a bang and is fully locked in. The forklift strains under the weight of the container and the electric motors operating the lift begin to whine until they reach their attained height and come to a complete stop. The BCKR employee cautiously backs the lift down the ramp ever so slowly until he clears the ramp and then maneuvers the container to the position that was first instructed by the captain. The BCKR employee dismounts the forklift and cuts the banding material which makes a loud popping sound. And, as promised, it snaps back, whipping through the air and slapping the ground. The remaining banding material is cut, and the BCKR employee steps off the forklift and to the side. Sergeant Hazard wastes no time in instructing the soldiers to remove the lid. Once the lid is removed, the soldiers are greeted with the many receding hairlines the Franklin picture on the hundred-dollar bills. The odor of money begins to permeate the air, and the soldiers all have a wide-eyed stare.

"Man, will you look at that cash!" exclaims one soldier.

"There must be millions!" says yet another soldier.

"Never mind what it looks like," commands Sergeant Hazard. "Save the comments for later. We need to remove it. Pile it on the table."

The soldiers immediately follow instructions. The soldiers begin to load the table with the money, piling it close to the money counter. It is grabbed up almost immediately by the BCKR employees manning the money counters and loaded into the hopper. The BCKR employee hits the count button. The odor of money fills the air once again from this fanning process. The red lights on the counter begin to twinkle, and the numbers begin to role. Lieutenant Armstrong is on the job, watching the red lights display roll numbers across the hopper, as are the BCKR employees who remove the money from the output tray and place it on the table on the left. The hopper is quickly loaded. The red lights begin to spin again, almost as if they were the one-armed bandit coin machines found in Las Vegas. The sound is such a sweet sound to LaDeau, for it is that sound that is making him rich. By now, the table on the right is full of money and some soldiers who have piles of cash in their hands while other soldiers are empty-handed. This catches Sergeant Hazard's eye, and he glances inside of the container and finds it empty.

"Sergeant Purdue." He calls Sergeant Purdue over.

"This emptied quite fast," exclaims Sergeant Hazard. Sergeant Purdue looks in the container.

Meanwhile, LaDeau's sweat rings are beginning to permeate down from his armpit and are gaining ground. *Easy, hoss,* LaDeau thinks to himself. *You've got it covered.* He remains quiet.

"That's the false bottom that Mr. LaDeau told us about," Sergeant Purdue explains.

"Yes, I remember, but I am surprised we emptied it so quickly," exclaims Sergeant Hazard.

"Well. Okay."

And they walk away from the container.

Good. Walk away, you dumb knuckle heads, LaDeau thinks to himself as he reaches into his pocket to fetch a cigarette.

The last of the money from the container has been placed on the table, and the BCKR employees are making quick work of removing it and placing it into the hopper. It is not long before Lieutenant Armstrong, who had been watching the counters, glances up and notices that the soldiers are standing around.

"Sergeant Hazard, why aren't those soldiers emptying the container?" he asks.

"Sir, the container is empty," replies Sergeant Hazard.

"What? That can't be!" states Armstrong; and he walks over to check out the container. As he glances into the container, he sees the false bottom and begins to scratch his chin as if lost in deep thought. He walks back to his position by the counters, all the while scratching his chin.

Stay calm. Have him check the final count once all de money is counted, LaDeau thinks to himself.

LaDeau reassures himself as the sweat rings are beginning to gain ground around the armpits of his shirt. Minutes pass, and Armstrong is eyeing the counter lights. LaDeau has finished one cigarette and reaches into his pocket for a second one. Akhmed takes notice of this event and from past experience knows that LaDeau only performs this practice when he runs across a problem. But Akhmed does not say a word, for he knows that it would be his job. Minutes pass, and the last stack of money is finally loaded into the hopper. The counter rolls up the last figures for the container. Lieutenant Armstrong steps forward to review the figures on the money counter, comparing it to what he has on his clipboard. He then walks over to the table on the left where all the money is stacked and glances across all the stacks. Armstrong walks back to the container and glances inside of the container.

"We place a false bottom at de bottom of each container, sir," pipes up LaDeau. "It's common practice when shipping supplies, and it's used to keep produce off the bottom in case the container leaks and fills with water, sir," explains LaDeau.

"Yes, Mr. LaDeau. I know that," responds Armstrong. "But I seem to recall that we had much more money than what I am seeing here," explains Armstrong.

"What does de counters read, sir?" asks LaDeau.

"Well, the counters are right on," explains Armstrong.

With that comes a relief and a boost of confidence for . But he has said enough and knows not to ramble on.

"Okay, Sergeant Purdue. You can box it up," commands Lieutenant Armstrong.

With that comes an internal sigh of relief that LaDeau keeps hidden. *One down, two to go,* LaDeau thinks to himself.

Sergeant Purdue is quick to get the container refilled, and the BCKR employee secures the container to the pallet using the wire banding material. Once secured, the BCKR employee moves the container to the side and again travels up the ramp to the semi. As the forklift travels across the floor of the semi trailer, the sound is similar to the bowling ball traveling across the floor of a bowling alley; and that sound is stopped short as the forks on the lift rattle as if a bowling ball had struck its pins. The forklift connects to the pallet with a bang. The electric forklift motors strain with a whirl sound as the lift raises the pallet from the floor. Again, the sound of the bowling ball rolling across the wooden floor can be heard as the forklift backs out of the semi trailer. The forklift clears the ramp, and the BCKR employee positions the container where the previous container had once stood. The wire banding material is removed, and the BCKR employee steps back as the soldiers make quick work at removing the lid. Once again, the Franklins are smirking standing shoulder to shoulder in their Radio City Music Hall Rockette stance. Yes, there is nothing like the view of hundred-dollar bills. It is almost as great as the pretty legs of the chorus girls. The soldiers pause to savor the moment and then jump to the task at hand. Once again, the money is stacked on the table, and the two BCKR employees quickly gather up a stack and load it into the two money counters. *Slap! Slap! Slap!* go the money counters; and again, the smell of money permeates the warehouse. It is not long before the container is emptied; and once again, Lieutenant Armstrong is scratching his chin as he walks over to the container and reviews the counter figures with his clipboard and reviews the stack of money on the table, shaking his head from side to side.

"Okay. Load it back up," commands Lieutenant Armstrong.

Two down and one to go, thinks LaDeau; and this calls for a reward as he reaches into his pocket to fetch another cigarette. It is clear that he has been sweating as he wipes his forehead with a red bandana that he pulls from his back pocket. He wipes his forehead and returns the bandana to the usual position in his back pocket, where it is hanging half way out of his pocket as if ready to perform its next task. Out comes the lighter and a long blue flame appears, and LaDeau lights up another cigarette. By now, there are a few cigarettes butts on the ground where LaDeau has been standing.

Akhmed takes note of this chain-smoking event. *Yes, something is bothering the boss man.*

And LaDeau is well aware that Akhmed is eye-balling him, yet he pays him no mind and continues to smoke his cigarette. The second container has been bundled up, and the forklift makes its way up the ramp to retrieve the last container. The sound of the bowling ball moving across the hardwood floor of a bowling alley can be heard once again as the forklift makes its way across the floor of the semi trailer to retrieve the last container. The rattling of the forks as they find their way between the wooden pallets makes the sound of the bowling ball hitting the pins as the fork-lift slams into the wooden pallet. The forklift backs out slowly and down the ramp, where the container is placed once again in its load position. The wire banding material is removed, and the third and final container lid is popped open; and the count continues. The chain-smoking continues as well with LaDeau, as does the perspiration. By now, his shirt sweat rings have reached halfway on his shirt and they have appeared on the center of his back and on the front of his shirt.

What a pig, Akhmed thinks to himself.

The counters make a slapping sound, and that fine aroma of money fills the air as if someone has stumbled into the garden of Eden. Minutes pass that almost feel like days to LaDeau—the soldiers filling the table with the loads of cash, the money counts being loaded, the sound of the money being counted, the money being removed and placed on the table to the left... Finally, the count is complete. Lieutenant Armstrong steps forward to review the count. Again, he walks over the container and reviews the money on the table that had just been counted.

"Okay. Load it back up," commands Lieutenant Armstrong. He walks over to the captain, and a private discussion ensues.

The soldiers make quick work of packing up the cash, and BCKR secures the container once again to its wooden pallet. It is clear that Lieutenant Armstrong and the captain are in deep conversation, and the lieutenant waves over Sergeant Hazard. There is a nodding of Sergeant Hazard's head as if he is given instructions, and then he breaks contact with Lieutenant Armstrong and turns to the soldiers.

"Listen up. We will pull guard until the military police replaces us, which should be in an hour or so," commands Sergeant Hazard.

"Button up this semi, and if BCKR could remove it from the warehouse," asks Sergeant Hazard glancing over in LaDeau's position.

LaDeau nods and says, "Akhmed, I'll show ya where to park at de back end of the motor pool, and you and your side kick assistant driver go and fetch some food at the dining facility." LaDeau reaches into his pocket and pulls out a twenty-dollar bill and hands it to Akhmed. "Here is your lunch money and your billeting money," commands LaDeau and hands the money over to Akhmed, who takes the cash.

Akhmed speaks some Iraqi to his assistant driver, and they exchange conversation, turning and departing the building. Akhmed climbs into the driver seat and is joined by LaDeau on the passenger side. Akhmed hits a few switches, toggles the shifting lever, and hits the starter ignition. The rattling of the transmission and the diesel engine can be heard; and then it turns over, accompanied by the long, black plume of acrid diesel smoke. The rattling of gears can be heard as Akhmed searches for the proper gear. Once found, the truck lurches forward.

BACK TO THE MOTOR POOL

Once the semi has cleared the warehouse, LaDeau speaks up. "Guide 'er right and down to the far end of de pool," instructs LaDeau; and Akhmed follows the instructions.

The semi lumbers along at a walking pace until they reach their destination.

"Okay. Stop here, and I'll ground-guide you in," instructs LaDeau. There's a glint of confidence in Akhmed's eyes and perhaps all the months of taking LaDeau's bad mouthing has almost came to the point of Akhmed ensuring that LaDeau has an accident. But Ahkemd is no fool and knows that he would be arrested and held in a detention camp, and that is the last place he would want to be. LaDeau begins the hand gestures, and Akhmed follows his instructions. After a series of hand waving and the semi lurching forward, LaDeau finally gets the semi into position and motions for Akhmed to back it up. Once the semi is backed into position, LaDeau motions to Akhmed to kill the engine; and Ahkemd follows through by shutting the engine off, placing the hand break on, and stepping out of the driver side of the cab.

"Remove de cab from de trailer and have it serviced for de trip back tomorrow. When it's serviced and fueled up, go ahead and park it with the other semi cabs," instructs LaDeau.

Akhmed follows through with LaDeau providing little or no assistance other than watching Akhmed. Akhmed disconnects the vacuum hoses and lowers the foot pedals of the semi trailer that allow the trailer to stand on its own and jumps back into the truck and starts it up. There is the familiar rattling as Akhmed searches to find the gears. Once found, Akhmed accelerates and the truck lurches forward, disconnecting from the trailer. LaDeau watches Akhmed drive away, and he smiles to himself as he whips out his cell phone and places a call to Bill Smith.

The phone on the other end rings a couple of times. The person answering gives a, "Hello," in a long, Southern, Louisiana drawl.

It's Bill Smith; and LaDeau announces, "Hey, brother. I'm in camp and leaving the motor pool heading over to the dinning facility."

"I'll meet you there in ten minutes." Then LaDeau hangs up.

LaDeau meets Smith at the dining facility, and they stand in the long lunch line to pay for their meal. The line is composed of civilians and military personnel, and so both LaDeau and Smith know they should not discuss the diabolical mission they have both undertaken. They make their way through the lunch line to the counters, where they order their food, and find their way over to one of the few empty tables. At their table, they get to the business of eating. Smith starts the conversation with a topic that is more in line for the company they work for.

"I hear BCKR is going to reduce our pay for every day we spend out of de combat zone."

LaDeau understands where the conversation is going and joins in. "That sounds about right, de big company trying to keep the little man down."

"Hallelujah, brother," responds Smith.

They finish their meal quickly and waste no time in leaving the dinning facility. They exit the dinning facility and head toward the motor pool, where LaDeau had Akhmed park the semi.

"Bubba, we need to move de money tonight," said LaDeau with a slight sense-of-urgency.

"I'm scheduled to have the semi back at Camp Trigger tomorrow, and I need to dump that body," explains LaDeau.

"You mean you followed through—."

And before Smith could finish LaDeau jumps in. "Of course I followed though!" LaDeau said in an almost argumentative response.

"I had to, Bill. He would of bragged, and that would a cost us our fortune." LaDeau attempts to win Smith's confidence.

"Look, Bubba. It only happens once in your life, and de mother load has just dropped into our laps." LaDeau tries to win over Smith.

"This is it, three hundred and twenty-five million dollars! This is the mother load." LaDeau shows his warmest side to show. "What's it going to be, Bubba?" asks LaDeau.

"And you are sure you can ditch de body where it can't be found?" asks Smith. "Look. We were both correctional officers at one time." Smith attempts to explain his concern. "How many cons had spilled their sad stories on how they got caught? Huh? And it was always de same story on how they should of and would of and could of if they had a second chance," explains Smith.

At that point, LaDeau stops walking and faces Smith. "Look, Bubba. This is Iraq. There is no law. And even if it is an American contractor found dead, no one is going to care," explains LaDeau with an air of confidence.

"Okay, okay," agrees Smith.

"Do you have a vehicle that can hold eight duffle bags?" asks LaDeau.

"I have a van, and it will just about hold eight duffle bags," answers Smith. "I removed the seats in the back, but even with the seats removed, it might be a tight fit."

"Okay. It's going to be dark soon," remarks Smith.

"Let's beat feet over to where the van is parked," commands Smith. The duo head off to the BCKR parking area.

It is just about twilight as the sun is setting over the horizon. The sky takes on a pinkish hue, and the two lumbering images of LaDeau and Smith cast shadows across the ground as they walk across the motor pool. The shadows take on a primal image of men on the hunt. LaDeau maintains a -bellied frame that casts an eerie shadow across the ground, making his hands almost look like they are dragging across the ground. LaDeau's arms are so long that they almost hang down to his knees from the bulk of a torso that he sports. Thick, hairy arms and huge hands that should belong to a common laborer who has dug ditches most of his life are a façade for the lazy person that he is. Smith is a bit shorter and sports a six-foot frame carrying a two-hundred-pound body with powerful shoulders and arms from the constant, day-to-day weight lifting that Smith attends to. Contrary to LaDeau, Smith works out almost every day. The shadow sprawling across exaggerates this frame to an almost caveman appearance. Yes, the hunter-gatherers from long ago are on the hunt for the largest wooly mammoth of them all.

Smith guides LaDeau to the location of the van, and they board it with Smith at the helm of the steering wheel. He inserts the key into the ignition. After a number of turns from the starter, the engine starts up. It is twilight now, and Smith turns on his parking lights and drives across the motor pool to the semi trailer. Once there, LaDeau jumps out and makes his way at a quickened pace over to and underneath the semi trailer. He quickly opens the trap door. As the minimal light seeps in, he barely can make out the images of the duffle bags. He reaches up with his arm to feel around for the lantern and, after a number of attempts, finds it. He turns the lantern on. The light floods the concealed room, revealing the stacked duffle bags. LaDeau squeezes his large frame through the trap door, only stopping to suck in the pot belly as best as he can, and then hoists himself up and into the concealed room. He reaches down to stack of duffle bags that are almost as tall as him and finds the one that contains Manning's body at the bottom. With little or no effort, he grabs the duffle bag, extracts it from the pile and throws it to his side on the floor. *Ka-thunk!* Manning's body makes a lifeless sound, a body cold and without feeling as it strikes the floor. LaDeau wastes no time in grabbing the next duffle bag containing the money, and his hands travel all over the bag just to ensure that he has the correct bag. Yes, it is money, stacks of hundred-dollar bills. As LaDeau caresses the stacks through the duffle bag, you can almost hear Franklin's giggle as if they were tickled from his touch. He carries the bag over to the trap door with little effort and, in a loud enough whisper, says, "Here comes number one." He pushes the duffle bag through the opening until it falls on the ground.

Smith, who is outside of the semi trailer, wastes no time in moving it out of the way for the next duffle bag to drop.

LaDeau reaches for the next bag. "Here comes number two."

Again, Smith removes it from underneath the trailer and carries both bags over to the van and loads them to the back of the van. Smith took care in removing the dome light of the van, for he does not want to draw any more attention than needed. By the time he returns to the semi, he finds that two more duffle bags are lying on the ground. He scoops them up and carries them back to the van to store them. This process repeats itself until all the bags have been unloaded. Inside the semi trailer, LaDeau then picks up Manning's body and throws it where the previous duffle bags have been laying. Inside the duffle bag, Manning's eyes are wide open and fixed, with the jaw dropped open, as if this little Bostonian got the surprise of his life. LaDeau pulls his pants up, as they were falling around his butt showing his cheeks. This is common practice with LaDeau and is a day-to-day needed operation to protect the public. LaDeau takes a seat next to the trap door and begins to lower his legs through it. As his feet touch the ground, LaDeau works his pot belly through the trap door and squeezes his way through the door. Once out, he reaches up and shuts off the camp lantern and then closes the trap door. He crawls out from underneath the semi trailer and is greeted by Smith, who has a wide grin showing all his perfectly straight teeth.

"Okay, Bubba. I stored it. Let's go," directs Smith. They both board the van.

THE MORGUE

Smith winds through the short streets of the base until he makes his way up to sandstone building that has three garage-type entrances. Smith presses a button on the side of his door console, and his window rolls down slowly. He reaches into his coat pocket, pulls out a small control, and sticks his hand out of the window. Smith waves his hand as if waving a magic wand, one of the garage doors opens.

"I had automatic garage door openers installed when I first built this building back in two thousand and one." Smith grins as if accomplishing a milestone in his life.

As the garage door rolls up and finally stops when it reaches the top, Smith pulls forward. Once inside the garage doors, they are greeted by what appears to be a receiving dock. Smith pulls up to the dock and cuts the motor and turns to LaDeau.

"Wait here. I am sure there is no one here, but I cannot take a chance that one of de soldiers I work with has returned after lunch."

LaDeau responds quickly by grabbing his arm and almost menacingly saying, "Do not screw this up, Billy."

Not even surprised at this response, Smith reassures LaDeau. "Relax, Bubba. Dis Cajun has it all planned out. Ain't nothing but a thang," followed by a wink from Smith relaxes LaDeau; and he releases Smith's arm.

"Okay, Bubba. But could you close the garage door?"

Smith obliges. Smith walks up a small staircase on the far side of the loading dock and opens a door to a wide hallway with gurneys residing at the far end of the hallway, butted up against one of the walls. The walls have large window openings where some contain fluorescent lighting with only one light turned on, a signature that the work day has ended and the workers have departed for the day. In one such window opening, a fluorescent light hangs over what appears to be an examining table. In the back of the room are a number of caskets with one side of the wall lined with what appears to be freezer doors where the bodies are kept. The indirect lighting from the fluorescent lighting reveals these cold, blunt, lifeless images.

The cold, bright, white light illuminates the examination table directly below it, revealing every cut and scratch mark in the table. The table is painted a dull, greenish brown. It is the faded color commonly found in a field of plants that are dying or have been parched without water, like plants that are lifeless and are in the preliminary stages of decomposing. Yes, the table is a fine representation of the lifeless body that will rest upon it. Smith walks past a few of these examination rooms until he reaches the gurneys at the far end of the hallway. He grabs one gurney and pushes it while pulling another gurney. He reverses his direction, heading back in the direction he just came from.

When he arrives at the door from which he entered, he opens it and yells to LaDeau, "Lend a hand."

LaDeau responds, quickly closing the distance from the van and up the short staircase to the door. Smith has never seen LaDeau move so quickly and is quite surprised. LaDeau grabs the gurney without being asked what to do and immediately rolls the gurney across the receiving dock and over to the position where the van is parked directly below the dock. Smith follows directly behind him, and LaDeau jumps down to the ground below.

"I'll pass it up to ya," commands LaDeau. He opens the van's double doors and grabs one of the duffle bags.

He tosses the bag up to Smith, who positions it on one of the gurneys. They continue with this process with LaDeau pitching the duffle bags to his catcher, Smith, much like their own baseball team.

It's not long before Smith has all the duffle bags piled on each gurney and LaDeau has closed the van doors and beat feet up the short staircase and closed the distance between Smith and the gurneys. Smith heads back through the entrance door to the hallway with LaDeau right behind him.

"Got it?" asks Smith as he holds the door open for LaDeau, who pushes the gurney through the doorway.

"I'm good," responds LaDeau. He returns to grab the remaining gurney.

"Down this way," directs Smith as he grabs the gurney and begins to head toward one of the examination rooms.

Upon arriving at the double doors of the examination room, Smith holds the door open again for LaDeau as LaDeau pushes the gurney though the doorway and into the examination room. Again, LaDeau returns to grab the remaining gurney and rolls up to the next gurney. Smith enters the examination room and immediately walks across the wide room over to where there are eight caskets residing on top of a gurney. He rolls one of the gurneys containing the casket over to the side of the examination table and opens the lid of the casket. The casket is barren and does not contain the silk padding you typically find in a casket.

"Place one of the duffle bags on the examination table," commands Smith. LaDeau responds quickly. "Open it up and pass me the bills."

LaDeau is on it before Smith can finish his sentence, almost as if LaDeau could read Smith's mind. Yes, the Cajun brothers are marching to the same drum beat; greed. It takes Smith's both hands to grab the stack that LaDeau has passed. The sight is spellbinding for Smith as he stops to review the facial expressions from the Franklins if to say, "I told you so." The dark, Cajun eyes begin to widen as if he was an elementary school kid being given his first puppy. Yes, it is truly love at first sight. "Bubba, you got plenty of time to check it out later, but now we need to pack it up," directs LaDeau.

"Oh sure. It kind of takes your breath away!"

They both chuckle, and LaDeau agrees and joins in, "Yes suh!" as Smith gets to work stacking the bills at the bottom of the casket.

Smith gets to work stacking the bills across the floor of the casket. Stack after stack is positioned across the bottom of the casket; and again, the Franklins are stacked side by side as if they were the Vienna Boys Choir getting ready to perform a children's opera. . "Yes suh. I am going to get me one of them expensive villas over in Greece," sings LaDeau as both Smith and LaDeau chime in with what they will do with their fortune.

They are about a third of the way through the duffle bag, and the bottom of the casket is layered with Franklins. Smith reaches down underneath the examination table, grabs a thin sheet of plywood, and places it over the bills at the bottom of the casket. He then walks over and retrieves a padded, white, silk bottom that he places over the bills at the bottom of the casket. He uses a glue gun to seal the silk lining to the sides of the casket and, once this is completed, turns the casket onto its side with the assistance of LaDeau. Smith then begins to lay the hundred-dollar bills across the side of the casket side by side. The chorus of Franklins begins to appear on stage with the same facial expression, standing side by side, getting ready to sing their next number as Smith continues to lay the stacks of Franklins across the inside of the coffin. With every stack of bills laid down, Smith's eyes widen in awe. A smile extends across his face. LaDeau is enjoying this vision as well, and they both cackle in excitement. Although they are enjoying the moment, they waste no time in filling one casket after another until finally starting on the last one. As they are working, Smith speaks up.

"In the morning, I will be loading them up for shipment." Smith reviews the plan with LaDeau. "We always ship the caskets out minimum eight at a time. With all the insurgent activity in Iraq, we are guaranteed to ship about ten caskets a month," Smith explains with the sparkle in his eyes and the smile on his face from the money he just stashed away.

"The US Army has a mortician team that handles the preparation of the bodies, and we place the bodies in the casket," explains Smith. "We ship the caskets over to the base airport, where they are loaded on an Air Force C17 Globe master. The C17 stops in Germany to pick up additional cargo, and then it is sent to the US. It should land at Dover Air Force Base in Maryland, where they are unloaded and rolled over to the airport hangar." Smith is not even getting winded during the conversation; and, almost like a duet singing on stage with each having their stanza of song to sing, LaDeau chimes in with, "And that is where my brother in-law, Duke, will pick them up and ship them to his mortuary."

Smith reminds LaDeau that this process might take a couple of weeks and that he will keep LaDeau informed of all the events via a cell phone call.

Smith sounds like an elementary school kid opening up his Christmas presents. "We're rich, Bowe!"

"We are not rich yet. We will be rich when the money is in Duke's morgue," replies LaDeau. A reply followed by a wink and a smirk that only a felon like LaDeau could dream up.

LaDeau and Smith exchange a handshake, and they make their way out of the room with Smith locking the door behind him. They walk down the hallway, exchanging ideas of what they always dreamed of and what they will do with their money. Unexpectedly, a soldier enters the hallway from the far end of the hallway and makes her way quickly up the hallway.

Smith turns to LaDeau and says, "I will handle this"; and as the soldier approaches and gets within ten feet, Smith intervenes with, "Good evening Sarge."

The soldier, stone-faced, responds with, "Good evening," and goes about her business.

Both LaDeau and Smith work their way over to the receiving dock and board the van. Smith reaches in his pocket, grabs his electronic garage door opener, and waves it at the garage door as if he is waving a magic wand and the door begins to open. Smith backs the vehicle out of the receiving dock area and drives out of the motor pool. Off at a distance, a figure is watching their exit as if studying the scene. The figure is a bearded male Iraqi sporting a BCKR uniform. It's Akhmed.

Why in hell is that lazy butt head working this late? Akhmed thinks to himself. *That son of a donkey does not work late if his life depends on it. .*

BACK TO IRAQ

The next day, LaDeau stops over at the shipping area where he will load the semi truck containing Manning's body with supplies. LaDeau plans on loading the semi with supplies and then linking up with a combat patrol going back to Camp Trigger that afternoon. He meets up with Akhmed and barks his usual intimidating instructions for that day.

"Load 'er up with supplies. And, boy, be careful when you are loading the pallets," commands LaDeau. "I don't want that back wall scratched any more than it has been," commands LaDeau while reaching into his pocket to fetch a cigarette. "If I find one scratch on that back wall, I will take the cost of the repairs out of your salary." With that, LaDeau knows he has made his point, for that last statement made Akhmed blink. *Yes, you can always tell when you make your point when they blink,* LaDeau thinks to himself as he lights his cigarette and heads back over to BCKR office.

As LaDeau walks away, Akhmed walks over to the motor pool to obtain the semi truck containing Manning's body. After he hooks up the trailer, he drives over to the fuel pumps to fill the truck up. Before he leaves and after it is filled, he heads over to the BCKR supply warehouse to pick up the much-needed supplies. He enters the BCKR supply warehouse and places his order at the desk and then exits the building to drive the semi over to the loading dock. He backs the semi up to the loading dock with much precision and shuts the truck off. The BCKR employees working the docks are local nationals, and Akhmed stops to exchange much-warmed greetings; and the latches on the semi trailer are unlatched, and the loading of supplies starts. As the trailer is fully loaded, the BCKR employees noticed that not all of the supplies fit on the truck, and they bring it to Akhmed's attention. Akhmed is puzzled and is unable to figure it out. Pressed for time, Akhmed reports back to the order desk where he placed his order and makes the needed corrections to remove supplies that will not fit. The supply clerk prints a new receipt and hands it to Akhmed for his signature, which Akhmed signs. Akhmed exits the building and is still puzzled why the truck could not contain the usual load and steps into the cab to the driver's seat. Before he starts the truck, he stops to ponder why the trailer would not take the usual load again. Puzzled, he starts the truck and drives over to meet with LaDeau.

Akhmed drives over to where they will exit the base and positions the semi truck into position of the convoy, leaving the engine running. As soon as the semi is in position, a Hummer with an air guard standing through the roof of the Hummer who has his hands on the M240B machine gun pulls up behind the semi trailer. It is not long before the convoy commander, a US Army sergeant first class, walks down the length of the convoy, motioning to the drivers to attend his briefing. The drivers huddle around the sergeant, and he opens with his discussion. Back at the semi trailer, the engine is running. It cannot be heard from the occupant within the concealed room. That surprised look in the eyes with the jaw dropped open stares off into the darkness of the duffle bag that is home. Within the concealed room, a slight, noticeable odor begins to form, as Manning had soiled himself once he was stabbed. The bacteria that were feeding on the contents of his stomach intestines have begun to feed on the intestines themselves. Manning's skinny little body begins to take on a slight bloated appearance as the natural progress of decomposition takes place. Meanwhile, the convoy commander has completed his brief and the semicircle of drivers breaks contact and returns to their vehicles. Akhmed steps up into the cab and finds LaDeau sitting on the passenger side.

"Boss, where's Muhammad?" asks Akhmed. At that time, Muhammad sticks his head out of the rear sleep cabin of the cab.

"I'm here, Akhmed."

They both laugh and exchange greetings in their native Iraqi language as Akhmed buckles up his seatbelt in preparation for the long journey back.

The convoy begins to slowly move, and Ahkemd shifts the gears. The transmission rattles as he searches for the proper gear. Akhmed feathers the accelerator, easing ever so slowly forward. The semi barely crawls forward as Ahkemd searches for the next gear, completing the shift to the next higher gear. The convoy maneuvers quite slowly through the base camp until it reaches the exit and then begins to pick up speed. The convoy begins to skirt the outskirts of the city, finding its way to the main highway, where it begins to pick up a steady speed. Akhmed chats with Muhammad in his native Iraqi tongue as they roll down the highway. LaDeau ignores this conversation.

This is an A and B conversation and I will C my way out of it, he thinks to himself.

It is not long before Akhmed and Muhammad's conversation is nothing more than background noise as LaDeau drifts off in his planning process.

When we get to Camp Trigger, I'll position the semi trailer at de far end of the motor pool next ta the mortuary affairs building where we keep the rest of them dead Iraqis. Yeah. Then I won't have far to carry that little twit. LaDeau thinks to himself. The mortuary affairs building contains freezers to keep the body temperature low enough to slow down the decomposition process. Some bodies lay on the floor, awaiting shelf space, as some are stacked on shelves. This is a recent BCKR contract where a temporary storage location was created for mortuary services and is run by the local nationals on Camp Trigger. The bodies are stored here and then shipped to Baghdad, where they are identified as best as possible and processed through the local national's mortuary process.

That little twit does not weight much. LaDeau is thinking of Manning's body weight. *Hmm. Now he can't be wearing American clothes.* A problem that LaDeau did not think about until now. *Where can I get Iraqi clothes?* LaDeau thinks to himself. *Hmm. Maybe I could ask one of de locals to purchase me the clothes,* LaDeau thinks to himself as he continues to spar with the problem. *Nah. That's what that idiot at Angola did when he attempted to disguise de body of his dead wife.*

LaDeau is thinking of the convict he used to guard when Smith and him were corrections officers at Angola state prison back home in Louisiana. Meanwhile, Akhmed and Muhammad's conversation is dropping off and is beginning to cease almost entirely as the mundane trip begins to set in and time seems to drag on. However, LaDeau continues to wrestle with where to get the clothes to disguise Manning's body.

Hmm. That's it! LaDeau has a eureka moment while lost in his thoughts. *I'll just take of a shirt from one dead Iraqi and pants from another dead Iraqi and dress Manning up to look like one of 'em!* LaDeau thinks. A truly cleaver LaDeau thought by a thoughtless person, for LaDeau couldn't care less about the dead, especially an Iraqi. *Yeah. I could grab a shoe off from one and a shoe of another 'un… heck, I could dress that little twit up right!* That LaDeau smirk begins to widen across his face but goes unnoticed by Akhmed, who is lost in the long drive back. *Yes, suh. That is how to deal with that little twit,* a get-even thought that LaDeau is savoring as if it was a large, thick steak at his favorite steakhouse. *Hmm. What did de cons teach me back at Angola?*

LaDeau is thinking to be methodical in his approach to disguise Manning's body. LaDeau has sat in on a number of convict review boards and has heard just how every criminal had been caught when they were asked how they came to Angola state prison.

LaDeau thinks through his devious plan. *Oh yes. I will have to disfigure his face so he won't be recognized. I'll pick up a hatchet for that at our BCKR shed, and I'll need pliers to pull his teeth out. Yes. I'd like to stop this truck and go back there now and pull his teeth out, that little twit,* LaDeau thinks as he hatches a plan to hide Manning's body. *Yes, suh. That'll work here in Iraq. Back home, it would never fly. Yep. Iraq is de perfect place to commit a murder.* A congratulatory thought and a pat on his own back brings a smile to LaDeau's face. LaDeau continues with that wide-spread grin and rewards himself by reaching into his pocket to fetch a cigarette.

LaDeau whips out his cigarette lighter and brings the gas blue flame to life by depressing the strike pedal. He touches it to the end of the cigarette and begins that long, signature inhale of his lighting the cigarette when Akhmed speaks up.

"Boss, will Manning be helping us when we unload the supplies?"

LaDeau's small, rat-like eyes begin to widen. Yes, the adrenalin is kicking in as his pupils begin to expand and he immediately begins to choke. As he chokes, the blue wave of smoke exits his mouth like the smoke from the barrel of gun and bumps up against the window. The choking episode continues as he grasps for an excuse.

Don't want to sound paranoid. Don't ask why he is asking about Manning, he thinks as he runs down his avenues of exit. By now, his face is beet red and he begins to catch his breath.

"You okay, boss?" asks Akhmed, who couldn't care less and was actually enjoying watching him choke. Even below the beard, Akhmed's grin of satisfaction watching LaDeau choke could almost be seen.

"Yeah. I'm okay. If we don't get Manning, we find another one of the crew," responds LaDeau. *Good response,* LaDeau thinks to himself.

Don't look paranoid. That would be a giveaway. A calming thought LaDeau would practice as a kid when he would steal cigarettes from one of his father's drunk buddies who had stopped over from a night out and fell asleep on the couch. LaDeau recalls the time he almost got caught sneaking cigarettes from the slob's pack.

"Did you find any of my cigarettes?" the slob would ask.

"No. I'm a kid. Kids don't smoke," answered LaDeau. *A pretty good response for a twelve-year-old,* LaDeau thinks to himself.

"Huh. I must have dropped them at the bar." The slob rolls up the empty pack and tosses it, placing it on the cheap lamp table by the couch.

LaDeau snaps back to reality.

"How much farther, Akhmed?"

Akhmed responds, "We are 'bout thirty minutes from Camp Trigger, boss."

The convoy begins to slow down to take the needed exit to the feeder road to Camp Trigger and snakes its way off from the main highway and makes a sharp right to an auxiliary road to the base camp. The sand kicks up across the dirt road as it makes its way across the rough dirt road adorned with rock and patches of scrub grass. It is about a five-minute drive and the checkpoint of the base camp appears. The convoy slows and comes to a complete stop as the security guards approach the convoy commander and exchange conversation. With the conversation complete, the security guards wave the convoy through. It begins its slow crawl through the base camp and over to the motor pool, where it comes to a complete halt. The convoy commander immediately goes to each vehicle, checking the names of his manifest; and after LaDeau, Akhmed, and Muhammad are checked off, LaDeau fires the instructions.

"Go ahead and break convoy and head on over to the BCKR supply warehouse so we can unload this crap."

Akhmed follows the instructions and works his way across the camp to the BCKR warehouse. The semi crawls through the small streets until it finds the warehouse and pulls up to a position where it can be backed up to the loading dock, and LaDeau jumps out of the semi and walks around the back end of the semi trailer and over to the driver's side. LaDeau begins a number of hand signals to which Ahkemd begins slowly backing up the trailer. Muhammad has moved from the sleep cab over to the passenger side of the cab and begins speaking in his native Iraqi tongue. Let's listen in on this conversation.

"Now's your chance, Akhmed. Now's your chance," remarks Muhammad gleefully. "Run over that son without a father."

Akhmed begins to laugh and tries to hide it with a big grin.

"Quit it, Muhammad. If this son without a father sees me laughing, he will fire me." Akhmed laughs.

"Run over his monkey butt. Clothesline that monkey boy."

Akhmed has all he has to do from stopping and going into a complete roll on the floor and laughing. LaDeau finally signals to stop and draws his hand across his throat to kill the engine, and Akhmed complies. LaDeau reaches into his pocket and whips out the cell phone and calls his office. After a short chat with his secretary, he requests that she notify the other local nationals and ask them to drop by to assist with the unloading of the semi.

Akhmed exits the truck and walks into the small office that acts as a service desk for truckers that are either dropping a load or picking up a load. He hands over his supply receipt to the local national behind the desk, who exchanges instructions on where the supplies are to be stored. Akhmed exits the service office and meets up with some of his local national comrades, who exchange greetings. Muhammad has already opened up the doors of the semi cab to reveal pallets of supplies that are held together with shrink-wrap cellophane to keep them from falling off the pallet. One of the attendees shows up with a forklift and they begin to unload the semi. The forklift moves one of the pallets to the center of the warehouse, where the local nationals remove the cellophane and start inventorying the contents of the pallet. Once completely inventoried, they remove the contents and place them on the proper storage shelves within the warehouse. LaDeau is near the trailer when he sees the last pallet removed, he barks another instruction.

"Akhmed, jump into the truck. We need to park it."

Akhmed follows the instruction by jumping off the loading dock and into the semi cab. LaDeau joins him in the passenger side. The engine starts up, and then comes the next instruction.

"Head to de back side of the motor pool."

Akhmed navigates in the general direction. Akhmed thinks this is unusual from where they normally park but follows the instructions. As they arrive at the back side of the warehouse, LaDeau barks the next instruction.

"Pull up to the freezing unit."

LaDeau points to the large freezing unit that is under a cover of a makeshift roof to prevent it from getting wet and appears almost like a large, walk-in freezer that you would find in a supermarket back in the States. This is exactly what it is. Akhmed is superstitious and does not like to disturb the souls that he thinks hang around the bodies until the body is properly prepared for burial. Akhmed pulls up the freezing unit and awaits instructions from LaDeau, who jumps out of the passenger side and walks to the back of the semi trailer and begins a series of hand signals that Akhmed follows. LaDeau parks the semi truck so that the semi trailer is close to the freezer and hides any movement from the view of the warehouse, a cleverly concealed position that favors his work effort when he dumps Manning's body. Once the semi trailer has parked, Akhmed cuts the engine, which is typically what you would expect when you dump the trailer.

"Don't cut it off. Did you see me signal you to cut it off?" LaDeau jumps up on the side step and gets right in Akhmed's face. "Did ya?" asks LaDeau in the most arrogant that he can muster and a manner that immediately gets Akhmed's attention.

"No, boss. Sorry. I didn't." Akhmed tries to calm this outburst.

"Your problem is you don't listen! You need to start listening, boy!" LaDeau yells in a Louisiana accent that sends its message quite well. LaDeau's eyes are squinting in their rat-like appearance, and they reveal that long prejudicial hate that has been around the Deep South for some time. "Are you listening, boy?" The hate in his face is clear. If it was legal, LaDeau would have killed Akhmed right here and now.

Akhmed has seen that hate plenty of times in the past, in the small town he grew up and in the face of the Saddam's thugs that use to visit his neighborhood.

"Sorry, boss. I need to pull my head out of my butt, but I tell you, being near this freezer scares me, boss." Akhmed is being honest about his fear.

"You people are all alike! Now start the engine, boy!" LaDeau raises his eyebrows in an attempt to affirm his request.

Akhmed wastes no time and fires up the engine.

"Now disconnect it from the trailer and park it at the opposite side of the motor pool." LaDeau steps down from the cab.

That son of a donkey, Akhmed whispers to himself as he jumps out of the cab and begins to disconnect all the hoses that connect the semi truck to the trailer, providing the control for the lights and brakes on the trailer. He lowers the metallic feet that allow the trailer to stand on its own and then jumps back in the cab to drive forward and disconnect the truck from the trailer. Akhmed drives off, leaving LaDeau, who walks away from the trailer, watching Akhmed pull out of the motor pool.

Yes, suh. I'll be getting rid of your little butt this evening. He laughs to himself as he walks out of the motor pool.

MANNING AND THE MORTUARY

LaDeau left the motor pool and made his way over to the dining facility at Camp Trigger. He falls to the end of the line of personnel that is reminiscent of a line that you would find at a ticket booth for a football game. The personnel who are made up of soldiers and American contractors shuffle their way to the desk where a BCKR employee, a local national, has them write their name and where they work on the base. Soldiers do not have pay for their meal, but BCKR employees do. Most BCKR employees agree with this; and if the soldiers had to pay but did not have the money, BCKR employees probably would take the money out of their own pockets to pay for the soldiers' food. This is the kind of patriots that work for BCKR and they are respected by all. However, LaDeau does not agree with the process and thinks the soldiers are getting preferential treatment. This is the bitter attitude within LaDeau that has its roots within his childhood.

When LaDeau was a kid growing up in Louisiana and was dirt poor, and his mother ensured that they filled out all of the paperwork required to receive government surplus food. Instead of food stamps, government surplus food was given in its place. It was the same canned good government surplus served to prisoners and even US soldiers. LaDeau remembers standing in line and watching larger families obtain their portion of food, which was always larger than what LaDeau's family would receive.

His father would mutter to his mother, "They are getting more because their black. If dat was a white family, they would not get as much." LaDeau grew up with this hatred most of his life. And grew up with the beatings his father used to dish out whenever he was drunk and wanted to take out his anger on someone. Anger rooted in the reason LaDeau's dad was a failure all his life. Yes, that is where it all started for LaDeau and his father, Bowe Senior. It all started growing up dirt poor with an abusive father.

LaDeau formulates his plan as he sits at the far end of a cafeteria-sized table, minding his own. *I'll wait until it just starts getting dark,* he thinks to himself. *Yes, suh. Just when there is barely enough light to see, he thinks.* The look of confidence begins to appear in those piercing LaDeau eyes, followed by the smirk of a grin as he chews his food.

Hmm. I need to make that little twit look like one of the locals. How to do that? he asks himself as he ponders the question. *Mutric acid will destroy the fingertips. It's used in concrete work, and anyone who gets it on their skin knows what that feels like! Yes, suh. I'll have to disguise his skin color. Hmm. Shoe polish?* He asks himself and another eureka thought as LaDeau smirks once again. *I'll darken that little*

twit up so he'll look like one of Aunt Jemima's own chil'in! Yes, suh.
And he actually chuckles to himself at this thought.

LaDeau is pondering over this effort during his lunch when
a soldier sits down beside him, an expected event in the dining
facility since it is organized as a cafeteria with table after table
lined up in neat, uniformed rows.

"How's it going?" a chipper young voice asks LaDeau.

"Not bad," answers LaDeau. A respectful response for
LaDeau knows what would happen if it was disrespectful. It
would not take long before the news would travel along the
soldier community and eventually would land on the ears of
higher management at BCKR. One thing he did not want was
his butt in BCKR management gun sights. He did not want to
attract negative attention during a time when he is attempting to smuggle three hundred and twenty-five million dollars
off this lousy continent. No. Negative attention is dealt with
quickly and usually followed up with a quick ticket out of Iraq.
For now, he needs Iraq. Both the soldier and he have exchanged
greetings, and it is not before long then the discussion goes
quickly to football and who in the NFL is likely to be at the
Super Bowl. One thing about soldiers is they like their country,
and NFL football is represents that quite well.

LaDeau finishes the conversation. "Have a good one," he says
as he departs the table.

LaDeau heads back to his room in the cormac. He obtains a few
tools; pliers; brown shoe polish, a paste type; a hatchet, and rubber
gloves and places them in a plastic bag, which he carries with him.
He leaves his cormac and stops by a utility shed where tools and
chemicals are used in some of the construction activities around
the camp. He picks up a gallon bottle of mutric acid, an acid used
in finishing concrete. He leaves the shed and heads toward the
motor pool on foot. As he enters the motor pool, he heads over to
the semi trailer and crawls under the trailer, opening the trap door

to the concealed room. He reaches in through the door and feels around until he finds the battery-powered camp lantern and hits the switch. Once again, the room is illuminated, revealing some of the tools that both Manning and LaDeau had used to construct the false bottom for the money containers and the lone duffle bag containing Manning's body. The remainder of the room is barren. LaDeau squeezes his body through the trap door.

"Ugh. Crap. Ugh," he mutters as he squeezes his pot belly through the trap door.

After some grunts and groans, he has hoisted himself within the room and stands up. The odor of death is beginning to show itself, and the gasses from Manning's body give the slight smell of a rotted meat that has been lying around. LaDeau grabs the tools and tosses them through the trap door and onto the ground. He grabs the duffle bag that contains Manning's body and tosses that onto the ground and begins to lower his legs through the trap door. As he steps down on Manning's body, he gives it a couple of kicks to get it out of the way.

"Ugh. Crap. Uggh." Again, he works his pot belly through the trap door. "Glad I won't have to do this very many more times," he mumbles.

He places the tools in the plastic bag he had been carrying and peeps through the trap door one more time to ensure that he has not left anything behind. After a once-around look and a good visual check, he grabs the camp lantern and shuts it off and ducks out of the trap door hole and back into the twilight. He pauses until his vision has corrected itself and then reaches up to close the trap door. He places the lantern into the plastic bag and crawls out from under the semi trailer, dragging the duffle bag containing Manning's body, the plastic bag, and the bottle of mutric acid. LaDeau walks over to the entrance of the adjacent mortuary affairs building.

The mortuary is a large building created from cormacs that are snapped together like LEGOS. The building is enclosed with an overhead roof, a drive-up loading dock with huge, garage-like doors and is run by mortuary affairs, a US Army unit. The cormacs that make up the building have been converted to walk-in meat freezers, similar to what you would find in a US supermarket, slow the decomposition process. Most of the soldiers and local nationals who work the area are gone for the day, and LaDeau walks up the short staircase on the side of the loading dock.

No one will bother me. They'll just think I'm checking on my business, he thinks to himself. . LaDeau walks up the steps, all the while looking around just to make sure.

He walks across the loading dock and walks up to one of the cormacs that has a tumbler lock. He works the cipher wheel between his big, thick, hairy fingers and rolls up the cipher to unlock the door. He yanks down on the lock and, *Click!* the lock comes apart. He removes the lock, opens the cormac door, and is greeted by a cold blast of air. He reaches over and feels around for the light switch and hits the light. The light is powerful and illuminates the entire room, revealing a grisly sight. Dead Iraqis are stacked on shelves, with some lying on the floor. There is no sparkle to the eyes that are open, only a blank, lifeless stair. Most of the bodies are dead women and children.

"Crap," he mutters to himself and realizes this cormac is of no use. He closes the door and locks it and walks across the loading dock to the next cormac door, dragging the duffle bag containing Manning's body. He works the tumblers on the lock and, *Click!* unlocks the lock and removes it and pulls the door open. After hitting the light switch, another grisly sight is revealed; and this time, the dead bodies are all Iraqi men. LaDeau wastes no time and begins to remove a shirt from one body and pants from another.

"No one will notice," he mutters.

He removes the shoes from one dead Iraqi and now has all the clothes he needs to dress up Manning. He steps outside the cormac and grabs the duffle bag containing Manning's body, all the while looking around in all directions, checking to see if anyone is watching.

"Nah. I'm good," he mutters and carries the duffle bag into the cormac. He quickly opens the bag and removes Manning's body that has been wrapped in plastic. Manning's head can be seen through the plastic bag, and LaDeau wastes no time in removing the plastic from the body; and there, staring off into nothing, no sparkle to the eyes at all, is Manning with his jaw dropped open. LaDeau grabs up the plastic bag and stuffs it back into the duffle bag.

"I'll drop this off at the nearest dumpster," he mutters. He wastes no time in removing Manning's clothes. "Ugh," he groans as he removes his pants. Manning did not wear underwear, and his penis is revealed. "Huh. I am surprised this punk had a penis," LaDeau says aloud. LaDeau has completed removing all of Manning's clothes; rubbed him down with brown shoe polish paste and prepares to dress him in the Iraqi clothes that he just scavenged. The clothes do not fit on Manning and are quite baggy; and once he has Manning all dressed, he reviews his work.

"Screw it. Baggy or not, it will do. No one will notice when I'm done," he mutters aloud.

LaDeau gathers up Manning's clothes and stuffs them into the plastic bag he had been carrying. He glances outside the cormac door and reaches down to grab the mutric acid and looks around. There is no one in sight, and LaDeau wastes no time to step back in continue his grisly work. He reaches down and grabs the pliers and gets to work on Manning's teeth. "Ugh," LaDeau groans as he begins to pull his teeth. Pulling teeth can take some effort, and the ones that do not come out are broken and chipped off using the pliers. "Ugh," he groans as he completed with the upper jaw and has started on the lower jaw. "Ugh," groans LaDeau as he pulls the teeth out, one after another. When he has completed pulling out all the teeth except for a few of the large molars in the back, he reviews his work. Manning's jaw is dropped open and toothless, a sad sight to a man who once had a great smile. This disfigurement a human face does not slow down LaDeau. He whips out the hatchet and starts on the face—*Kathunk!*—as if he was a butcher working on a side of beef. The cut disfigures the face, for it is dead center of the forehead and through the center of the face. LaDeau continues until there is nothing there that would remind a person of a human face. He places the hatchet back in the plastic bag and takes the cover off the mutric acid. He begins to poor mutric acid all over Manning's hands and fingers. The acid has a strong odor that requires that LaDeau cover his face as he is performing the process. Some of the acid falls on the floor and is soaked up by Manning's new baggy clothes. "Ugh," groans LaDeau; and he stands up and steps back to review his work while he keeps his face covered. There, lying on the floor, is a human body in baggy clothes that clearly do not fit with a severely disfigured human face.

"Good enough for government work," mutters LaDeau as he puts the cap back on the mutric acid. He gathers up all the tools that he took with him, including the mutric acid, and places it on the plastic bag and carries it outside of the cormac and next to the door. He mops up some of the mutric acid that has spilled on the floor with some of the clothing still attached to an Iraqi that is adjacent to Manning's body. He then exits the cormac, closing the door behind him. LaDeau gathers up the duffle bags, plastic bag, and bottle of mutric acid and is on his way. There is no emotion in LaDeau. The entire morbid work that he just performed did not even faze him one bit and was more a matter of survival in LaDeau's mind.

"That takes care of that whiny little twit," mutters LaDeau.

He shuts the light off in the cormac and walks across the loading dock to the small staircase. LaDeau makes his way down the staircase and onto the ground of the motor pool. He pauses to take one more look around. The sky is clear and full of stars with very little lighting except for some of the base lighting that can be seen that illuminates some of the walkways between the buildings.

LaDeau exits the motor pool and heads for his cormac to rest for the evening. As he exits the motor pool, off in the distance, we see two shadowy figures watching LaDeau as he leaves.

"What time is it?" asks one of the figures.

The other figure hits a button on his watch and the dial illuminates the person's face. The faint, green light of the watch dial illuminates enough so we catch the glimpse of the person's face, a face with concern manifesting in the eyes and a hardened look that probably came from combat.

"Its twenty-three hundred hours, sir," answers a quiet but assertive response.

There is a pause, and the figures walk away. It is clear in the starlight that lights the landscape that they are carrying automatic weapons.

LaDeau makes his way back to his cormac and turns in for the evening. He is dog tired from the laborious day and falls asleep quickly. There are no bad dreams from the vile acts that he committed earlier, and it is clear that he is a man with no conscience. The next day, he awakes and performs his daily hygiene and gets fully dressed and heads over to the dining facility for his morning breakfast. During his breakfast, he reviews where he is within his planning and what tasks he needs to follow through on. LaDeau knows he has to remove that concealed room and he needs to follow through with the firing of Akhmed and Muhammad.

That butt head was eyeballing me back here when de money was being counted, he thinks to himself. *Yes suh. No need in keeping him around.*

He continues with his breakfast, making quick work of the meal in front of him. After morning breakfast, he stops by the shop office to give the local nationals their instructions for the day, and Akhmed is an attendee. The locals gather around LaDeau, who is bellowing off the instructions and closes with, "Are there any questions?"

Akhmed raises his hand.

"Boss, should we load the semi trailer truck up for another shipment back to Kuwait?" asks Akhmed.

LaDeau responds, "No." He is thinking, *Not until I dismantle the concealed room.* LaDeau terminates the meeting and heads over to BCKR upper management office for the monthly brief. *Time to let 'em know that Manning has quit,* LaDeau thinks to himself.

BACK IN KUWAIT

Meanwhile, back in Kuwait, Smith prepares the last four caskets for shipment. He obtains one of the money-laden caskets and, with the assistance of a local national, Rishad, places the casket on a stretcher to be rolled over to the adjacent room. With Smith on one end and Rishad on the other, Smith gives the command.

"Lift."

Rishad and Smith groan but finally get the casket up and onto the stretcher.

"I must be getting old. This casket appears heavier," remarks Rishad.

Smith's jerks his head in Rishad's direction. He knows the money added additional weight and needs a quick response. "Yeah. You are getting old, ya old goat."

And Rishad chuckles.

But Smith knows he needs to dispel the weight of the other caskets and conjures up a response that a consultant of caskets might give but is an outright lie that Smith had just made up, and it even surprised himself. "Some of the metal in these caskets have been made with a denser metallic ore that makes them heavier. It is an American standard sometimes used."

Rishad just nods his head in acceptance as they wheel the casket out of the room to the next adjacent room where they will load the body of the soldier for shipment.

As they enter the adjacent room, they see that four soldiers are laid out on the tables. The soldiers have their uniforms on, and some have their legs missing. They are dressed up in their battle dress uniform or BDUs, to include their rank with patches and their name tag. It is burial with dignity in the US Army and other US services as well. For the soldiers that are missing their limbs, the pants legs are rolled up to whatever part of the leg is remaining. When an arm is missing, the uniform is left as is. In the case where the body has been badly burned or is in a number of pieces, the uniform is folded up and placed at the top of the casket with the remains below it. Today, the four soldiers only have either a missing leg or an arm.

Smith rolls the casket up to one of the tables where the US mortuary affairs soldiers are standing by. The soldiers take the position a soldier positioned at the head and another at the feet. They raise the soldier. On the opposite side of the casket are two other soldiers with their hands stretched out, waiting to slip their hands underneath the body and lower it into the casket.

"Easy," says the sergeant in charge. "We do not want to cause any more damage on this soldier. There has been enough done already."

The soldiers respond almost in a choir, "Hooah, Sarge," as they lower the body into the casket and make last-minute adjustments to the uniform the dead soldier is wearing and to the positioning of the body.

One of the soldiers notices that the casket lining does not have the same texture as previous caskets he has worked on. The soldier speaks up.

"This casket lining does not seem as soft as the previous linings."

And at that moment, Smith's eyes begin to widen, for the fear is setting in. Yes, the fight or flee response is intense as the brain begins to race to figure out the next move. *Great. I knew we were going to get caught,* Smith thinks to himself. *Wait a minute, can't think of any negative outcome now. No. I need an answer.* Smith's mind races to find a solution. In an almost unsteady voice that has a bit of a shake to it, as if he was sitting in a massage chair that vibrates when the chair's settings are set at full speed, Smith attempts to speak; but the adrenalin shot is so intense that he is unable to regulate the volume of his voice, and when he speaks, the volume is just above an octave or two above a whisper. Smith begins to speak.

"Yes, we received feedback from our stateside supplier that some of the shipment would contain a casket lining that would be a lot firmer than usual. Something to do with de way they process the cotton." Smith begins to weave his web of lies, for Smith has become accustomed to soldiers accepting his lies.

"It is a lot firmer," claims one soldier. The other soldiers begin to join in on the inspection.

"Sure is lot firmer. Almost like rock," claims another soldier.

"This is only a temporary shipment, but it has the same long-lasting quality," answers Smith in an attempt to cover up the problem and distract the soldiers. "I'm sure it's okay and there is nothing to worry about."

"Okay, Mr. Smith." says the sergeant. "Okay, team. You heard him. Let's get on with it," barks the sergeant.

Man, that was close, Smith thinks to himself as his heart stops racing and his blood pressure returns to normal. The relief is intense and almost as if a great weight has been removed from his shoulders.

When they have completed the last adjustments, the sergeant in charge, in a commanding voice, announces, "Attention," and the soldiers snap to attention and stare straight ahead as if mesmerized. The next command breaks the silence by saying, "Present arms," The sergeant's next announcement is, "Oh heavenly father, take this soldier's soul by your side. Amen."

The remaining soldiers respond, "Amen."

There is a pause, and the sergeant's next command is announced. "Order." There's a three-second pause, and then "Arms." The soldiers slap their arms down sharply, recovering from the posture of the salute.

Smith is untouched by the experience and is just recovering from the adrenalin rush he just received. Rishad is always touched by this ceremony and respects the US soldiers for their courage. He once saw an American soldier risk his life under fire by running from cover to scoop up an Iraqi child who had ran across the street, stumbled, and fell. This did not stop the insurgents from firing, but the young US Marine was not going to let the Iraqi kid die. He braved the gunfire by running out into the street. The marine retrieved the Iraqi kid and did acquire some wounds in the process, but nothing severe. That day, Rishad realized what a real soldier was made of; and that was the difference between the US soldiers and Saddam's force: the willingness to commit regardless of the consequences.

The sergeant bellows the next command, "At ease," and the soldiers relax.

Smith and Rashid step forward and lift the lid that belongs to the casket and place it on top, snapping the latches along the side of the casket, ensuring that it is secured. The lid of the casket has a shipping order taped to the outside and is enclosed in clear cellophane. The transmittal form has the name of the soldier, his or her rank, and the shipping from and shipping to addresses. The casket is wheeled away by Smith and Rashid, back into the room from which it came; and the process is repeated until all four caskets have been loaded with the American soldiers for their long trip home. Smith and Rashid roll the caskets out of the room to the loading docks, where they are placed in the semi trailer truck awaiting transport to the US military airport in Kuwait and from there to an intermediate stop in Germany.

Smith and Rishad arrive at the loading docks, where six soldiers are standing around. "Good morning, sir," greets the African American female and sergeant in charge.

"Good morning, Sergeant," responds Smith.

"We got it from here." The sergeant steps forward, taking the handles that Smith had been holding. "Okay, detail. Take up your positions."

The soldiers each grab a handle on the metallic casket.

"On my command of lift," barks the sergeant. "Lift," she commands. The casket rises off the gurney as if it was levitated. "Now listen up," barks the sergeant. "Six steps forward." The sergeant pauses and then says, "March."

The soldiers walk the casket away from the gurney until it's cleared.

"Okay, detail. Guide it round and onto the trailer," barks the sergeant; and the soldiers follow the command. "All the way to the back," instructs the sergeant as she steers the soldiers over to the destination. Once they arrive at the back of the semi the sergeant barks the next command. "Detail, halt. Now let's ease it to the floor and let's not drop it. Remember, keep your back straight and bend your knees. I don't want any back injuries," commands the sergeant. The soldiers follow the instructions.

One of the soldiers returns and obtains a clipboard that has a roster of the caskets loaded. The casket has the name of the dead soldier, to include their rank and social security number. Smith signs off next to the dead soldier's name and turns to assist Rishad with pushing the stretcher back to the room to obtain the next body. This process is repeated until all of the caskets have been loaded and Smith has signed off on the last casket.

"Okay. Button her up," barks the sergeant. The soldiers latch the semi trailer shut and move out to their awaiting vehicles.

Two of the soldiers jump into the cab of the semi, and it is not long before the growl of the diesel engine can be heard and the engine turns over. The semi trailer eases away from the loading dock and out of the area, on its way to the Kuwait airport.

Smith returns to his office, where he calls LaDeau to inform him of the success. Smith types out the phone number on the office phone, and it rings a number of times before LaDeau answers.

"Yeah," responds LaDeau at the other end.

"Bowe, its Billy. De shipment just left," announces Smith, who elaborates. "It will stop in Germany to pick up additional soldiers who have been wounded, and then it should leave for de States and arrive sometime on Wednesday." But Smith is not happy with just presenting the news and has been nervous during the entire scam. Smith does not want to get caught and needs some reassurance from LaDeau that his relative will follow through. "What about your relative, Bowe? How are we going to know that he has received the shipment?" asks Smith.

"Ugh," LaDeau groans but continues on with the explanation. "You need to send me de list of the shipment so I can e-mail it to my brother-in-law," answers LaDeau.

Smith almost chokes.

"What?" He knows of one and only one brother-in-law that LaDeau has ever had, and that has to be Duke. "Duke? We have Duke handling this? Ah crap, Bowe!" Smith responds almost as if he has received an electric shock from a Taser.

LaDeau groans again. "Ugh. Yes, it's Duke. Billy, you are worrying over nothing."

"Bowe, Duke has always been an idiot, and I can't believe we are letting him handle something like this!"

"Look, Billy. He needs the money, and when money is involved, he pays attention. Look. You are worrying over nothing."

"I hope you're right, Bowe. For god's sake, I hope you're right," remarks Smith, whose voice loses volume toward the end of the sentence.

"Relax, Billy. There is no way we can screw this up. Now, do you have the list?"

"Sure, Bowe. Do you want me to e-mail it to you?"

"No. Go ahead and give me the names, and I will call Duke." Smith gives him the list of soldiers.

After numerous questions from LaDeau asking if he spelled the names correctly, LaDeau finally has recorded all the names.

"Okay, Billy. We're good," responds LaDeau, more confidently now that he has the list of soldiers. "I will call Duke and give him the info, and once the call is complete, I will call you back, Billy."

Smith has calmed down somewhat and responds with, "Okay, Bowe."

LaDeau and Smith terminate the call, and they return to their work.

STATESIDE MORGUE

Back in the States, Duke is driving down the highway and headed over to Dover Air Force Base to in-process the next caskets that are due in from the previous day. The easy listening radio station is playing a soothing instrumental melody as Duke makes his way down the highway that sports the most recent shave from the snow plows that have removed snow from the previous night's storm. Snow plows can be seen in the opposite lane of the two-lane freeway, plowing through the snow as if they were Gillette razors removing the most recent stubble and the shaving cream that goes along with it. Duke is on the south side of forty and has a bald strip directly down the center of his head that he tries to hide by combing his hair from the left side of his head over in a really feeble attempt to make him younger than his years. At five-feet-four-inches, he is short in stature compared to most males and is obviously overweight. Duke's mouth droops down at the corners. Just above a long pointed nose are eyes with circles underneath set in hollow sockets. Augmenting this appearance is a sunken chest that causes him to have a slightly stooped posture.

Together with a poorly tailored suit, you have a mortician with a sloppy appearance.

Duke met LaDeau's sister, Mary Sue, at a high school football game and did not actually play football himself. Duke was a below-average student who really was nobody in school and hung around with his buds of the same scholastic stature. Duke had been eyeballing Mary Sue all during the middle school years. This was his last year in high school, as it was Mary Sue's.

"Go ahead. Ask her out," prompted his bud, Tony Barrett, who was standing close enough to Mary Sue and knew she could hear every word.

Mary Sue, who was looking straight ahead as if focused on the game and, with a side glance, was obviously looking in Duke's direction with the typical high-school glance that students would give when another classmate was doing something mischievous. Skin that was milk white with dark black hair and dark blue eyes was housed on a frame that was overweight even for her five-foot-five-inch height. Without a doubt, if Mary Sue could have dropped about forty pounds, she would have been a knockout. A man could fall into the dark blue eyes so easily with eyebrows that were architected as if they were a cathedral archway for those perfectly round eyes. Eyes that were lonely and wanting augmented by a perfectly shaped pert nose as if it were a supporting column between two archways. With the right shade of eye shadow and rouge on those high cheek bones, the combined color affect was what you might find in an expensive stained glass lighting up with the morning sun that had been filtered thru clouds. The lighting effect providing a soft rainbow of colors that one would find in a garden of many colored flowers. Yes, stained glass windows right below the cathedral archways capturing the warmth of the morning sunlight that was soothing and comforting. Below that perfectly shaped nose, were full lips with just the right amount of lipstick. Combined in total, features containing that animal attraction that called out to you and say "Kiss me, I am yours." Eye catching, colorful, and bright, this girl would definitely catch your eye, as did it catch Duke's eye. Duke was drunk enough to ask her out and, after the fourth date, made it with Mary Sue in the backseat of his Dad's 1963 Rambler Classic. Mary Sue turned up pregnant. After graduation from high school, they were married. Duke traveled into Alexander and worked as a driver for a mortuary service. Duke's macabre facial features, with the double chin and small mouth that always has a hint of drool dripping from one corner of it, fits the bill for a slob. His overweight appearance and purchased shirts that were too small were always riding up out of his pants. Duke was weak and always admired a stronger person, like Bowe LaDeau. LaDeau was known to have won a few fights he had never picked. During high school, he played as a fullback on the high school football team. However, LaDeau was never a hot head and was quite calm when someone was attempting to pick a fight. Then, at an unexpected moment, LaDeau would swing that left hook. Yes, fighting a lefty is tough enough, especially if you are right-handed. LaDeau, being an opportunist, knew this. It was LaDeau's illegal activities that acquired the money to fund Duke's mortuary and even paid for Duke's mortuary schooling. It was LaDeau who had his ear to the ground on upcoming BCKR contract acquisitions, and it was LaDeau who sold Duke on the purchase of the mortuary. The BCKR contract was sweet in that all mortuary prep work was performed by the mortuary services in Kuwait and the there was minimal work required in the States other than transferring the body from a military shipping container to a common casket and shipping the soldier and the casket to the soldier's home of record. Duke owed Bowe everything. Duke will transfer the bodies to his morgue, where they will be shipped to the soldier's home town. Duke owns his own business and was successful in obtaining the bid because his brother-in-law, LaDeau, had provided him with knowledge of this BCKR acquisition. Therefore, Duke was able to underbid the competition, and it is just one more underhanded activity that LaDeau can add to his long list of fraudulent activities.

Duke is heading down the highway driving a black Cadillac that is trailing a convoy of four black hearses. The trailing Cadillac and the leading hearses give the appearance of a stagecoach being pulled along by four black stallions as they traverse the hills and curves over to the air force base. The hearses have a fresh coat of wax that had been buffed up with such a bright finish so that our four black stallions almost appear to have worked up a sweat from the gallop down the highway. With Duke driving the Cadillac stagecoach, dressed in black, double chinned, and drool hanging from the corner of the mouth, and eyes that almost appear hawkish, he gives the macabre appearance of death's own driver. As the convoy arrives at the air force base, they work their way over to the airplane hangar to where they expect the caskets to be unloaded from the Boeing C17 Globe master military transport that will land nearby. The macabre convoy drives along the front of the air hangar and parks. Duke lights up a cigarette and waits for the C17 to role in. This is not Duke's first smuggling caper, and LaDeau and Duke have smuggled drugs out of Afghanistan using caskets before. While LaDeau was stationed in Afghanistan, Duke was able to smuggle out close to a thousand pounds of heroin that he got dirt cheap; and they were able to distribute it in New York City. However, due to the low death rate on US soldiers in Afghanistan, they could not bring in the real quantity that they would want to bring in using the existing casket smuggling scheme. It is not long before the image of the C17 breaks through the gray, low over-cast. Like a blue whale breaking the rippling surface currents of an ocean, the lumbering C17 drifts through the sky. Although the big transport is traveling at about 290 knots, its length and size give the slow movement appearance of a blimp. The C17 lumbers through the sky, dipping lower and lower and growing in size as it approaches the airstrip for the landing. As it touches down, the tires make the sudden braking sound like you would expect a vehicle to make as it breaks to prevent a sudden accident. The engines bellow out in acceleration as reverse thrusters strain to stop the beached whale from sliding off the runway. The engines do their job, and the behemoth slows to a crawl.

There is a crowd of people off in the distance, some of whom motion toward their eyes as if they are drying them from the rain—tears most likely, and they probably are relatives of the deceased soldiers. The C17 lumbers up to its parked position and comes to a complete stop. A moment or two passes; and finally, the back ramp begins to ascend ever so slowly. Like a boa constrictor unhinging its jaws, the cabin area of the C17 begins to lift up, revealing the ramp used for loading and unloading supplies. The C17 contains wounded soldiers as well as the deceased, and the caskets are unloaded first. The caskets are draped with the American flag, and the ceremony begins. The caskets are rolled down the ramp with US soldiers acting as pallbearers guiding the stretcher down the ramp. At the end of the ramp are US soldiers from each branch; and when the casket guides pass them, they render a salute. The pallbearers roll the casket over to the hangar, where it is greeted by soldiers who roll it inside the hangar; and the US soldier pallbearers return to the C17 to obtain the remaining caskets. This process is repeated for each casket that is rolled out of the C17. Duke is closely monitoring this process carefully and is almost counting the dollars as each casket rolls by. His eyes have the look of confidence, and an occasional smirk appears.

Could they really have skimmed three hundred and twenty-five million dollar? he thinks to himself.

Duke can hardly wait to get the bodies back to the morgue, where he will remove the remains from the transfer cases and place them in the conventional caskets. From there, another trip back to Dover Air Force Base, where they are returned to the hanger for shipment to their home of record, a military term for where you consider your home address. The last casket is rolled by, number eight; and this should be the last casket for transport. Meanwhile, the drivers are in a football huddle, smoking cigarettes and sharing their escapades from the night before.

"And we went back to my place after the lap dance," brags one of the drivers.

"You are so full of crap," remarks Bert. "There ain't no way a dancer in any of the night clubs is going back to your place after a lap dance." All the drivers break out in laughter.

"You got that right," remarks one of the drivers.

"Hey, why do you suppose the boss is coming along on this trip?" asks Bert.

"He never goes anywhere where there is heavy lifting," says another driver. They all agree, shaking their heads.

"What is different about this load?" asks Bert. All the drivers lift their hands as if stumped with the question.

Duke walks over to the lead vehicle in the convoy and motions all the drivers to his location.

"Okay. Looks like the big boss is going to put us to work," remarks Bert. The drivers break up the huddle and walk over to the lead vehicle.

"Okay, boys. Follow me to de hangar, and I will give ya your assignments," instructs Duke in a monotone voice.

The drivers are thinking this is not rocket science and they could have figured it out themselves. Duke is their boss, and they will go along with the decision. They walk in the hangar, and Duke meets with the soldiers who are standing guard near the caskets. Duke is prior service himself and was given a general discharge due to the fact that he could not adapt to military service. Duke did a stint in the service in the early nineties but never made it out of basic training. He boloed—a military term for failure—his marksmanship at the rifle range and could never pass a physical fitness test. In fact, Duke pretty much failed every event and spent more time in the hospital for injuries incurred during his training, which included a blanket party on a number of occasions from the soldiers in his own unit. After the last blanket party, the drill sergeants probably thought that it was best that they removed him from the unit before he ended up getting killed. Halfway through his training cycle, they removed him and recycled him through with a new cycle that was just starting. After failing that cycle, the army probably thought it was best that Duke depart the army; and so they discharged him.

Duke walks up to the sergeant in charge and presents his request. "Hi, Sarge. I'm here to pick up these caskets and process them for shipment to their home of record. Here's the documentation of the deceased."

The US Air Force sergeant sports a military haircut that is shaved on the sides and is short-cropped at the top. Judging by the size of his arms and shoulders, it is clear that this soldier works out. The sergeant peers over the paperwork and then up at Duke and back at the paperwork.

"It's okay. He's with us," remarks Bert.

The sergeant has done business with Bert in the past, and so this is routine procedure.

"Okay, sir. It looks good."

The Sergeant accepts Bert's authentication and allows Duke to proceed. Duke turns to his team of hearse drivers. "Bill, that one's yours. Dan, you have that one."

Duke gives each driver their assignment, and he heads back to his vehicle and waits as each driver loads the vehicle. Another thing that Duke does not like to do is physical labor, and the drivers are aware of this and pretty much help each other when loading the caskets. After each hearse is loaded, the next hearse pulls up to obtain its load. The drivers have loaded their caskets; and since there are eight caskets, another trip is needed. The last casket is finally loaded, and the hearse vehicles return to line up one behind one other in a convoy, with Duke this time leading.

Duke begins a slow drive out of the airport and heads toward the entrance to exit the base with the convoy of hearses right behind him. He exits the air force base and heads for the highway to his mortuary, about a forty-five-minute drive. Duke lights up a cigarette as he drives down the highway.

"I'll believe it when I see it. Three hundred and twenty-five million dollars, I don't think so. " Duke speaks out with no other audience other than himself in the vehicle. Duke takes a long drag from his cigarette and turns on the defroster, making some minor adjustments as he drives. "More like a hundred thousand in twenty-dollar bills." He tries to convince himself that some money exists. "Hmm. Where can we hide that much cash?" Duke thinks aloud. It's Duke's extrovert nature that requires him to work out details of a problem by speaking out aloud and is probably why he performed so miserably on high school exams.

"Hmm. Maybe I could store it in de South Branch mausoleum." He says to himself. "I would need a way to secure it though. Hmm." Duke ponders the problem all the way back to his morgue.

The convoy arrives at the mortuary and proceeds to the back of the building that contains double garage doors. He presses the button to roll down the window, reaches into his pocket, and pulls out an automatic control and sticks his hand out of the window and hits the switch much like a magician would wave a magic wand and chant the magical words. The garage doors begin to slowly rise; and he raises the window, shuts the car off, and exits. He enters the garage door, which opens to an expansive bay area room almost the size of basket ball court with eight tables that he had set up prior to the start of this endeavor. He got up earlier for this piece of work, 5:00 a.m. He never gets up that early but could hardly get to sleep the night before and was up most of the night, thinking about the money.

"More like a hundred thousand dollars in hundred-dollar bills," he mutters.

He hits a switch, and the fluorescent lights above flicker on. One sees a pile of caskets stacked one on top of the other against the wall. He has to return those to Dover to the rightful owners, the air force. Two of the convoy of hearses that is already backing up through the garage doors finally come to a complete stop. The driver and assistant driver get out of the hearse and open the back to roll out the casket. Both of these guys are not small by any means. Even though they are dressed in suits, it is obvious that they are not your typical office workers—more like your typical furniture movers who heard about this opportunity for making the same amount of money for less work and jumped on the job.

They grab hold of the handles on the side of the casket assisted by the other two drivers from the hearse that just backed in, who jump out of their vehicle to assist. As one grabs the handles on the end of the casket that protrudes from the hearse, they slowly back the hearse out. With the casket appearing almost levitated, as if gravity did not exist, the drivers stop and wait for the remaining drivers to move into place and grab the end of the casket that still rests in the back of the hearse. The driver reaches over and grabs the end of the casket and lifts. The hearse springs up six inches, like a farm animal that was relieved from a great load that was on its back. The casket is hand-carried over to the side of one of the tables, and Duke announces, "Stop. Put it on the floor next to the table."

The drivers acknowledge and maneuver to the side of the table and begin the slow descent. There are a number of groans— "Ugh. Ompf."—and the casket is set on the floor. The drivers maneuver to the other hearse and remove it as well, and the process is repeated.

Duke unlatches the first coffin while the drivers board their hearse in preparation for driving out of the building and for the next two hearses to pull in. Duke opens the lid. There he finds a soldier, with eyes that are closed and the corners of the mouth turned downward that one would interpret as a sad expression. .

As the drivers exit the hearse, he calls both of them over and asks, "Can you place that body on de table?" and Duke goes over to the next casket and begins to unlatch it.

The drivers are reluctant to pick up the body and so they do not jump at the task at hand right away.

"What's wrong?" bellows Duke. "Tell me you never seen a stiff." ask Duke as he ridicules him with absolutely no consideration for the deceased or the drivers' anguish.

One of the drivers speaks up. "Boss, it's just that we are not morticians," answers the driver with a sheepish explanation that angers Duke.

"Look, thar ain't no boogeyman, and thar ain't no such thing as ghosts, de Easter bunny..." By now, Duke is working up to one of his long, familiar, sarcastic speeches that the drivers have heard plenty of times before. "Thar ain't no Santa Claus, so pick de dead body up and place it on the table."

The drivers look at each other; shrug their shoulders with the palms of their hands upward, as if to say, *What can we do?* They pick the body up and place it on the table.

By now, Duke has the other casket lid off; Duke motions for the drivers to pick this one up as well. They go over to the casket and hoist the body up onto the table and then return to the hearse where the other two drivers are waiting. There is a discussion between them in whisper form, meant only for their ears and not Duke's. "This butt head wants us to do mortician work as well," one driver complains to the other.

Another driver pipes up with, "This guy is a complete idiot," while the other chimes in with, "How in heck did he ever become a mortician. He does not respect the dead," remarks one of the drivers in a statement that is witness to some of Duke's antics with dead bodies.

There is another bellow.

"What are ya doing? Get those rotten caskets unloaded!" bellows Duke. Another biting command echoes through the room.

This gets the attention of the drivers; and almost like a pack of wolves that perk up when they hear a deer or moose call, the drivers move toward the task of unloading the caskets. They repeat the process of unloading the caskets; and as before, Duke persuades them to remove the bodies from the caskets and place them on the table. They do so and, like the other drivers, question why they should be removing the bodies when they are only drivers.

And once again, "What is it with you people?" Duke starts his familiar sarcastic speech that ends up with the drivers grudgingly removing the bodies and placing them on the table. As the drivers begin to leave, Duke yells, "And go back and pick up de other caskets!"

A driver acknowledges with a tip of his hat.

"And don't forget de paperwork!" yells Duke.

The driver yells back, "I'm on it!" and jumps into the hearse and drives off.

Duke exits the building to make sure the convoy of hearses have departed and returns to the building and closes the garage doors.

Duke's full attention is now on the caskets. Like a rat that has just noticed a bread crumb on the floor, Duke moves toward the first casket. He is thinking that he has plenty of time and starts to work on removing the facade of satin sides and bottom of the casket. He pries the first side open to reveal the number 100 on the face bill of the stacks with the stacks lined up one after another across the side of the casket. Almost immediately, his eyes widen and begin to sparkle. His jaw does the slow descent downward, as if in awe.

"Holy Jesus! He did it!" yells Duke in a loud bellow, like a joyous kid at Christmas time who has just opened the first Christmas present and has seven more presents to open.

The stacks of bills are held in place by strips of cloth that were taped to the side of the casket. Duke pops the tape off from the side of the casket and the stacks of bills that were held in place to the side of the casket tumble to the bottom with some of the Franklins looking up, staring up with that unmistakable smirk. Duke grabs a stack of the smirking Franklins and fans the stack. The smell of money makes it through the stench of the room, which contains some odors of embalming fluid left over from previous work that Duke has completed. As he fans the bills, the Franklins almost appear in motion, and they continue to smirk; and for a moment, he almost thinks they are smiling at him.

"He did it. That turkey did it!" shouts Duke in a joyous shout followed by laughter. "We're rich!" And there is more laughter.

This moment is forever as far as Duke is concerned. He wastes no time in snapping the remaining straps off, and the bills fall to the bottom of the casket, that unmistakable smirk of the Franklins with a look of confidence as if to say, "I made it." Yes, Duke has made it, and almost immediately, as the joy drifted down from the heavens like freshly fallen snow, so did the paranoia rise up from the ground like a broken water pipe that had burst within the building and spilled over the floor, crawling up Duke's pant legs as if it had a life of its own, covering his entire body. Yes, the fear of getting caught settles in. With Duke, this is a familiar fear that he has come to acknowledge with his previous capers with LaDeau. Even in Duke's feeble brain, he has a purpose now; and now is not the time to gloat over the money. He pops to his feet quickly and walks over to the stack of caskets on the opposite side of the room. Next to them resides a stack of nylon tote duffle bags similar to the nylon tote bags you would see in an airport. He picks up the stack from the floor, heads to the casket that he was working on, and throws them on the floor next to the casket.

Duke quickly unzips one of the tote bags and begins stuffing the money into the tote bag. He then begins to pop the silk facade of each side of the casket, which reveals the money. Placing the silk facades to one side, he removes the cloth straps, releasing the money, and starts to work in scooping up the money and placing it in the tote bag. With the silk sides removed, he starts on the false bottom and removes that as well, revealing a number of Franklins staring up at him, shoulder to shoulder, as if they are waiting for a street car in an underground subway station. "De're winking at me!" he gleefully shouts and begins stuffing the money in his tote bag. "That turkey did it! Bowe, you are da man!" he yells in praise of his brother-in-law's scamming abilities.

By now, the tote bag is stuffed full and he can barely zip it up. He is laughing as he works to zip it up. Duke then returns the silk facades to the casket and fastens them in place. He checks his watch. About fifteen minutes have expired, and it will take the drivers forty-five minutes to get to the air force base and another twenty to thirty minutes to load the caskets and another forty-five minutes to return. He has to move quickly, and so he starts on the next casket.

Meanwhile, the convoy of hearse vehicles has entered the air force base and moved toward the hangar to pick up the remaining caskets. They pull up to the hangar and two of the drivers exit and head toward the sergeant, who has been waiting for their return.

"We're here to pick up the remaining caskets," one of the drivers says.

"Yeah. We were with that fat little turd who signed for the other four caskets," says the other driver. The sergeant manages a smirk.

"Oh yes. I remember," responds the sergeant with a slight laughter.

After an exchange of paperwork, they start with the loading of the caskets onto the hearse.

"Are these caskets heavier?" asks one of the drivers.

"Yeah. I noticed that too," remarks the other driver.

"Even with some of the soldiers missing a leg," remarks the other driver.

"I really did not want to remove those bodies from the caskets," states one of the drivers. "I think I'll have nightmares for weeks," he groans.

"Yeah. That's mortuary work as far as I am concerned," said the other driver.

"If I'm going to do mortuary work, I want to get mortuary pay and not driver pay," says the other driver, who appears to be well versed on the wages in the mortuary service.

After the remaining caskets have been picked up, one of the drivers meets with the sergeant and signs off on a form. The sergeant tears off a copy and gives it to the driver.

"Here you go, sir," said the sergeant. "Hey. Thanks, man, and I think you guys are doing a great job." The driver compliments the sergeant. The driver jumps into his hearse and drives off with the remaining hearses following behind.

Near the entrance of the hangar is a black sedan with two men inside. The men are dressed in business attire, suits. As the last hearse leaves the gate, the one on the passenger side pulls out a cell phone from his coat pocket and punches in a few numbers and places the cell phone up to his ear.

After the phone rings a few times, it is finally answered; and the man announces, "This is Special Agent Williams."

A brief pause and, "They have left Dover Air Force Base." And another pause.

"Okay." A pause and then, "Yes. Okay." He finally hangs up.

Duke has completed obtaining the remaining money out of all of the caskets. One at a time, he picks up the tote bag and enters a side door that is an entrance to the remaining part of the mortuary. He travels down the silent hallways until he comes to an office and enters. The office is spacious; and behind the desk, in the corner, is another doorway. He walks over to the door, reaches into his pocket to pull out a key ring with a number of keys, and fumbles with the keys until he finds the correct one. He inserts it into the keyhole and turns the key—*Click!*—and opens it. He reaches inside and flicks a wall switch, which turns on a light. The room is small and narrow and has the appearance of a walk-in closet that you would find in a contemporary dwelling. He drops the tote bag at the rear of the room and exits. He closes the door behind him; he looks around in a very slow and cautious manner, as if he was a child in a store who is getting ready to steal candy out of glass jar when the attendant is not looking. With no one in sight, he locks the door—*Click!*—and heads back to the rear of the large, open-bay room to retrieve the remaining tote bags. One at a time, he grabs the tote bags and stores them in the walk-in closet. Once this task is completed, he returns to the back of the mortuary and waits on the drivers to return. He does not have to wait too long because there is a honk on a car horn.

"Wait up, for God's sake," complains Duke. "I'm getting it."

Duke opens the garage doors by depressing a button just to the side of one of the garage doors, and the doors begin their long crawl upward to the open position. The doors rattle and clank until they are finally open. Two of the hearses are positioned to back in through the doors and begin slowly backing up, entering the building and coming to a complete stop once inside. The drivers exit the hearses and open up the backs, and the process of unloading the hearse begins.

"Ugh," grunts one of the drivers as they strain under the weight of the casket.

"Umpgf," groans another.

"These things are heavy," complains one of the drivers; and this immediately catches Duke's attention. Duke, who has worked up a sweat from his previous work, glances nervously at one driver and then the next.

"Yeah. I don't understand how they could be so heavy when some of them have their legs missing," complains another driver as Duke can begin to almost hear his heart pounding as he nervously glances from one driver to the next.

They know. They know, Duke thinks to himself as his attention begins to focus on the facial features of the drivers, looking to see if they are looking in his direction, waiting, waiting for the next statement to be, "Why is the casket so heavy, Duke?" Yes, paranoia has set in.

One of the other drivers speaks up.

"These ain't any heavier than normal," announces Bert, the driver. "You guys are just lazy from all the beer drinking you did the night before."

All the drivers begin to laugh.

"Boss, I was with 'em last night, and they were guzzling the beers at the sports bar," Bert announces.

"Yeah. Must be de beer," remarks Duke nervously. Bert is a native of Newark, New Jersey, who occasional works his way into small-time scams and has a knack for reading people.

That fat boy is nervous, thinks Bert. *And my guess is he is hiding something, and I'm going to find out what,* Bert thinks as he reviews Duke's character.

The drivers carry the casket over to the next available table and place it by the table. The four bodies from the last visit to Dover Air Force Base are still laid out on the table, and one of the drivers shivers as if a cold breeze had just blown down his back. It is the shiver from fear, and he looks at the bodies in disgust.

"Boss, some of the drivers and I think we should be getting mortuary pay if we have to unload these bodies this way," complains Bert. Now, Bert is ready for a counter from Duke and will give in if he sees he is not making any headway.

Duke glances from one driver to the next and back to Bert and, with a raised eyebrow, "Not a problem. There is an extra hundred dollars in your weekly paychecks, men." announces Duke with all the confidence in knowing that he has the cash to afford it.

The drivers are immediately taken back and surprised that this Ebenezer Scrooge would ever give anyone a raise.

"Thanks, boss! You're the greatest!" says one driver and is joined in by a chorus from the remaining drivers.

Duke loves attention and, with his newfound fortune, can afford the small bonus. Duke unlatches the top and again instructs the drivers to pick up the body and place it on the table. Now that they are being paid for their effort, the drivers shrug off their fear of handling a dead body and pick up the bodies and set them on the assigned tables; and the drivers return to the vehicles.

"That hundred dollars is going to come in handy," remarks one of the drivers; and the others join in how lucky they are for their newfound fortune and how lucky they are to work for Duke.

But to Bert, this is a signal that his hunch is correct. *This fat boy is hiding something,* Bert thinks to himself. *But what?*

And before they enter the hearse Duke makes a request. "Men, go ahead and park the vehicles and then return here if you would."

"Sure, boss," answers one driver.

"Sure thing," answers another; and the drivers attend to their tasks.

ONE IS
MISSING

By now, all the caskets have been unloaded from their respective hearses and all the drivers have returned and assembled with Duke for further instructions.

"Empty the first four caskets and stack them at the far end of de room towards the wall," instructs Duke; and the drivers follow through. "Replace de caskets with those caskets at the opposite end of the room." Duke points to substandard caskets that he will charge the US government at expensive casket prices.

"How much do these caskets cost?" ask Bert.

"About the same cost that de soldiers were shipped in," lies Duke, one thing he learned from LaDeau. *Small businessmen do not give away their secrets,* Duke recalls LaDeau preaching in the many past conversations.

"We charge them fair market price, and we make a profit," teaches Duke, for Duke likes to think he is a professor and the drivers are his students, even though Duke was close to being a high school dropout. *Fair market price my butt. What the hell.*

Everybody does it, Duke thinks to himself in the knowledge that he is screwing the government.

"Place the caskets to the side of each of the bodies, and then go perform your monthly maintenance inspections on de vehicles, and when you are through that, go ahead and break for lunch," commands Duke while, all the time thinking, *That will get them out of my hair for at least de next couple of hours.*

The drivers shuffle off to their vehicles.

"Who's up for a burger?" yells a driver.

One of the other yells, "Pizza!" as they jump into their vehicles and drive off.

Duke walks around the back of the building, peering around the corner like a middle-school student peering around the corner of a stocked shelf in a grocery store, watching to see if a clerk will catch him while he is stealing a candy bar. He waits until the last vehicle has departed the driveway and is headed onto the main highway and down the road. This middle-school student runs back to the garage entrance. Since he is overweight and never exercises, along with the black suit and bow tie, he resembles a penguin waddling into the garage entrance. The garage doors are segmented panels that seal along their horizontal edge with rubber seals, therefore allowing each panel to independently move along the rail and traverse the curve at the top of the garage opening. Once in, he quickly hits the button to close the garage doors, which react immediately with a rattling sound as if they were box cars attached to a freight train that had just throttled, jolting the box cars with a loud banging sound coming from their couplings. The garage doors make their slow crawl downward, rattling all the way. Duke is rocking back and forth on his feet, peering under the door, peering all around as the door is being lowered, glancing from side to side, eyes wide open, resembling a chicken that has come to feed. *Bang!* The doors slam into the concrete floor, making a sound as if this freight train had come to a complete stop and all the box cars had slammed into each other. The sudden stop echoes across the remaining panels as they to come to a sudden stop, which is announced with a loud rattling sound.

Duke immediately gets to work on the inside of the caskets, popping the sides of the silk facades and retrieving the money; filling the tote bag; and, every once in a while, stopping to fan the bills, eyes glazed over with wonderment and greed, the drool continuing to flow from the corner of his mouth as always. Duke is like a kid on a Christmas day. Duke made it through three of the caskets and has the money loaded in the tote bags and starts on the last casket. When he pops the silk facade off the side of the casket, he does not find any money. Duke's expression changes with eyes widening, and the cold chill of fear fills his body. A moment of panic grips Duke.

"Where in hell is de money?" he mutters to himself.

He then pops the next facades from the remaining sides of the casket only to find no cash.

"What da hell?" he mutters and pops the false bottom of the casket off with the same result: no cash.

"Oh, man! Bowe must have got caught!" he franticly mutters. "He's caught! He's caught!" he yells and this continues for some time.

All the while, he is panting heavier and heavier until he reaches the point where he has difficulty catching his breath. He stumbles over to one of the tables he has cleared and lays across it. His heart pounding and totally confused, he stares off with his eyes half opened in an attempt to stop his head from spinning. The pounding of the heart begins to subside and the panting right along with it as he lies across the table with his feet still on the ground. He slowly pushes his top-heavy body off from the top of the table, and then he stops for a moment and composes himself.

"Wait a minute! Don't panic! I will call Bowe tonight! The shipment must have gotten screwed up. Bowe will figure it out. He always does," Duke mutters to himself in an attempt to convince himself.

He picks up a tote bag and exits the room to the hallway that contains his office, where he has stashed all the money. Once again, he opens the walk-in closet and deposits the tote bag and returns to the back of the building to obtain the remaining tote bags. "Whew." He wipes the sweat from his forehead with the used handkerchief he keeps in his pocket.

"This is too much like work." He laughs as the drool has worked its way down the corner of his mouth and onto his double chin. He does not wipe the drool away, for it has become a fixture that he has lived with so long that it goes unnoticed unless someone brings it to his attention.

His shirt has risen up out of his pants in the front, as does his shirt tail in the back, as he fumbles around, pushing the shirt tails back into the pants that accent his pot belly. He looks all around the room while he reaches into his pocket to obtain the key to lock the closet door. He walks over to the entrance of his office and peers from side to side down the hallway.

"Well, back to work," he mutters. He heads back to the bay area room to complete the task.

Once all the tote bags have been locked in the walk-in closet, he returns to the next task of placing the bodies into the substandard coffins. There is no respect, for he blatantly pushes the bodies of the table into the coffins, where they hit with a thud. He then positions the body in the coffin and moves to the next one. "Whew." He stops to rest.

"Heck. We've got a boat load of money now. Who cares about that last casket," he mutters.

He continues this process until all eight bodies have been returned to the coffins. "Whew." He stops again to wipe the

sweat from his forehead. "There. All the stiffs have been positioned okay. I'll let de boys return them to Dover Air Base," he
mutters and checks his watch.

What would take a normal person forty-five minutes to perform this work took Duke right at an hour and a half, for Duke
does not like manual labor and depends on others to do the physical labor.

"Them lazy fools are probably finished by now," he mutters
and exits the bay area room. Duke leaves the back room and
heads toward the grieving room to summon the drivers. All the
drivers are present except Bert.

"Where de hell is Bert?" asks Duke.

"He said he had some business to take care of, boss," responds
one of the drivers.

"He should be back shortly," announces another driver, who is
trying to cover for his tardy companion.

Just then, Bert walks in.

"I'm here," he announces.

"Come on. We got some work to do," commands Duke.

As the drivers return to the back room, Duke announces,
"Now lets git de lids on these caskets and transport them back to
de base," as if the drivers do not know what to do.

But today, the drivers are not complaining like they typically
do. No sir. That extra hundred dollars in their paycheck has qui-
eted that complaining. They respond with a, "Yes, sir." The drivers have been through this process before, and so they start to
work. The lids are placed back on the coffins with more reverence
then Duke showed when he first deposited the bodies into the
coffins. Meanwhile, two of the drivers break away and fetch the
hearse that will transport the bodies to the base. One of the drivers is Bert.

"Wow, Bert. I am sure glad you asked for mortuary pay," compliments the driver accompanying Bert.

"Yeah. Well, I thought I'd give it a shot," replies Bert. But Bert is not letting on to the driver what he really thinks and starts reviewing the facts that he knows. *Why did the boss accompany us to Dover in the first place? This turkey never comes with us. And why did he give us that extra hundred dollars? He hasn't ever done this in the past, according to Dan, who has been working for him for the past five years.* Bert recalls asking Dan if he ever received a bonus from the boss before.

"Hey, Dan. Has the boss ever given you a bonus in the past?" Bert asks.

Dan recalls to himself, "Nah. Not since I have been working for him, and that's been five years. Must be business is good." Dan shrugged his shoulders, from what Bert could recall.

I ain't buying that 'business was good' crap, Bert thinks to himself as him and the other driver jump into the hearse to drive it back to the bay room area.

Meanwhile, the lids have been replaced on all the coffins. By that time, the two garage doors already have a hearse backing through their arches. The vehicles stop, and the drivers open up the back door. Once again, they lift the coffins and carry them over to the hearses to place them in the back.

One of the drivers announces, "I must be getting stronger or this coffin has gotten lighter." The statement immediately captures Dukes attention. Duke immediately darts his eyes from one driver to the next.

Could they have found out? Duke thinks to himself.

"Yeah. It does seem lighter," remarks another driver.

By now, it appears to Duke that each driver is looking directly at Duke as if to say, "Aha! You are up to no good." This is all in Duke's paranoid mind as he begins to sweat more profusely, eyes darting from one driver to the next.

They know we did it! They know, Duke thinks to himself as he continues to lick his lips as his mouth has gone dry. Then, out of the blue, Bert jumps in with, "It must be these replacement coffins that the boss has purchased." Yes, Bert has saved the day. This is loose change that Bert will keep in his pocket to spend at another time. All the drivers seem to agree as they continue to load the coffins.

"Yeah. It's the replacement coffins," remarks Duke breathing a sigh of relief as he continues to descend from the paranoia that never seems to go away but now hangs there in the background, like death itself.

It is not long before all the coffins are loaded and the drivers return to their vehicles and begin to convoy out of the parking area and onto the highway toward the airport. Duke stays behind; and his greed gets the better of him, and he revisits the closet where the money is stored. As he enters his office from the hallway, he glances to the right and then to the left, making sure he has not been seen, and locks the office door behind him. Duke pauses at the door, listening to see if someone has walked up the hallway, as if he was breaking into an apartment or an office that did not belong to him. Yes, paranoia has set in for Duke. He turns quickly and walks over to the walk-in closet behind his desk and opens the door, and before him are the seven tote bags laid end to end. He opens the tote bag and grabs a stack of bills. The Franklins are staring back with that silly little grin, as if to say, "What took you so long?" He fans the stack, and the scent of money fills the air like the sweet smell of a rose garden. Duke fans the bills again and looks at the Franklins in animation mode with the quality of the 1920s films. The Franklins appear almost as if they are winking at him.

Duke spends most of the day reviewing each stack of money in the tote bags, fanning the money as he goes. The sweet smell of money fills Duke's nostrils, providing an intoxicating odor, as if Duke had fallen into an opium den. Duke loads his opium pipe with each stack of hundred-dollar bills and lights his pipe by fanning the bills; and then the aroma of money is the drug that takes affect, carrying Duke away. Duke loads his hookah pipe with one stack of bills after another, constantly fanning each stack under his hook nose and taking a deep breath. Yes, the opiate smell of money has taken Duke far, far, far away. Duke's opiate dream is one of money, with him buying Mary Sue the largest diamond ring she has ever seen. Another fan of hundred-dollar bills, and the opiate smell of money brings another dream of a new car. Yes, a Maserati. Another hit of his hookah pipe, and this dream is one of a new house. Yes, 6500 square feet or greater. Duke snaps back to reality when he hears a knock at his office door. Duke's high is lost as he quickly zips up the tote bags and exits the walk-in closet, locking the door behind him.

"Ahem. Yes. Come in," responds Duke. He has forgotten he had locked the door. "One minute." He walks over to his office door and unlocks it and opens the door only to find the hallway empty. "Huh? What de hell?" He sticks his head out the door, glancing from side to side, finding no one in the hallway. "Hmm. Must be Sally," he mutters. He locks the office door and travels up the hallway.

Peering from a crack in the doorway from a cleaning closet, we see the faint image of someone's forehead. The image becomes clearer as the image moves from out of the darkness and into the light of the small crack of the doorway. It's Bert. Bert slowly opens the door and peers around the doorway, glancing up and down the hallway. Bert tiptoes over to Duke's office door and pulls out of his pocket a small instrument that Bert had stolen from the lock shop he had worked at in many of his prior jobs. Bert inserts the small tool into the lock and rotates it around until— *Kathunk!*—the locked door opens, and Bert peers in around the door. He quickly enters the office door, closing the door behind him and, like a ballet dancer, tiptoes across the floor to Duke's desk. Bert glances around the room, looking for a possible hidden safe. He moves from wall to wall, lifting up pictures and peering underneath as if in hope to find a wall safe.

"Crap. Nothing," mutters Bert as he lifts up one picture after another. He finally stops and moves toward Duke's desk and rifles through one desk drawer after another. He pays no attention to the small door to the walk-in closet that is adjacent to the desk. Little does Bert realize that within arm's reach is hundreds of millions of dollars. Bert truly is an amateur at burglary; and finally, the fear of getting caught is too much for Bert. He stops what he is doing and tiptoes again across the office floor to the door. He peers out of the office and looks up and down the hallway; and finding it clear, he moves into the hallway and locks the door behind him. Bert makes his way back toward the grieving room. Meanwhile, Duke is checking into the grieving room and finds that the drivers have taken a break and have not returned as of yet. Perhaps it's Sally, one of his sales consultants, who is the first face his clients see when they are negotiating funeral arrangements.

"Hmm. No. Sally is not here and is probably working with a client," he mutters.

His other assistant mortician is on vacation, so he is not expecting him in. Strange. He got the impression that someone was watching him.

"Ah. I am just getting paranoid," he mutters aloud in an attempt to explain away the sudden fear he was experiencing. "Must have been Sally," he mutters to himself.

He hears a car horn and, expecting the drivers he returns to the back of the building and raises the garage doors. The drivers returned to pick up the remaining four caskets, and so they back in two of the hearses into the building and continue with the loading of the remaining caskets.

"Here ya go, boss," announces one of the drivers as he hands Duke the paperwork. "We processed four caskets and have four more caskets to go." announces the driver.

"Okay. Once you have unloaded the caskets at Dover, go ahead and break for lunch," instructs Duke.

The afternoon is busy with new clients, and so the afternoon goes rather quickly. Duke realizes he has to stay up late in order to call Bowe due to the time difference between Iraq and the US.

Duke breaks for lunch and heads to a restaurant down the road. He has pocketed some of the hundred-dollar bills and will test them out on one of the more expensive restaurants.

Meanwhile, back in Iraq, LaDeau is just waking up. Waking up for LaDeau starts with a fart, and then he slowly rolls out of bed. LaDeau scratches himself a number of times and walks out of his cormac over to the latrine. . After his morning hygiene, LaDeau gets dressed and walks over to the dining facility for breakfast and appears to be pretty chipper. LaDeau exits the dining facility and is walking over to his office when his cell phone rings.

"Yeah," answers LaDeau as he continues to walk.

"Bowe, I thought you were kidding on de three twenty-five number. Wow."

"Great. So you received it all?" LaDeau asks anxiously.

"Bowe, seven were full, but one was empty." Duke attempts to explain the current situation.

"What do you mean one was empty?" LaDeau asks in panic that stops him right in his tracks. Truly, LaDeau is panicked, for he knows if the soldier's body is shipped to another mortuary and the casket is disassembled, the caper is up.

"Exactly what I said. One was empty." Duke attempts to recover with something like what kind of problem it could be. He is cut off by LaDeau.

"Crap! We are in trouble!" yells LaDeau, a clear response that indicates that he is about to go through the roof. LaDeau goes onto explain what a problem this could be if another mortuary opens the casket and tries to disassemble it. "We have to get the casket back!" yells LaDeau even before Duke can butt in on the conversation. "I need to call Smith!" yells LaDeau as he is looking for an answer. "Look. E-mail me de list of bodies you received, and I will get with the guy who shipped it and see if we can find the error," commands LaDeau. It is the only rapid solution that he can think of.

"Is that a good idea?" asks Duke, questioning the logic that LaDeau has drummed up.

"Look! I need de list, Duke!" yells LaDeau. LaDeau is yelling at this point loud enough so that everyone in Iraq could hear him.

"Okay, okay. I will send de list," remarks Duke in an attempt to quell LaDeau's temper tantrum.

"I will call you back when I have more information."

That ended the call as LaDeau hangs up. After hanging up, LaDeau immediately calls Smith.

"Bill, we've got a problem."

LaDeau goes into detail about all but one casket is missing the money. That is all Smith hears, that one of the caskets is missing. The rest of the conversation falls into background noise. Smith gets control and gets back to the call.

"Have your relative send you the list of personnel he has received."

And before he can get in another word, LaDeau pipes in with, "Already did that." LaDeau does not rest. "Bill, what went wrong?"

Smith recognizes the fear in LaDeau's tone and again tries to get control on the situation. "Let's not panic. Wait until your relative sends you de list, and I will compare it with my list. If there is a mix-up, we will get de air force involved, and they will track down the shipment. Look. Let's use the system. It will work."

This is a pretty good response, and LaDeau begins to calm down. "Okay. Okay," LaDeau finally accepts Smith's response, and the phone call is terminated.

Anxious for Duke's e-mail, LaDeau quickens his pace as he walks over to his office. LaDeau enters his office, which is a number of cormacs that have been joined together, creating a temporary building like a LEGO toy for adult construction projects. He turns on the fluorescent lights that flicker on, illuminating the room that contains a large, oak desk with a computer on it. LaDeau had the desk transported from Germany, where it originally came from. The desk appears to be an antique and is quite expensive but not a problem on LaDeau's salary, which is a six-digit figure and includes a handsome tax break to boot. One side of the room is lined with file cabinets. The other side contains bookshelves, many of which contain contracts from the past and current contracts as well, most in which LaDeau has performed some sort of illegal activity where he has overcharged the US government and which set the foundation for his advancement at BCKR by showing he can bring in some profitable contracts. LaDeau walks over to his desk and takes a seat in his plush leather chair. Almost immediately, he powers up his computer and waits for it to come up. Like a dog on a bone, he needs to obtain the list of deceased soldiers so he can forward the e-mail to Smith and they can resolve this once and for all. After logging in, he brings up his e-mail window and checks his incoming mail. Sure enough, no mail.

"Dad burn it," he mutters to himself aloud. "It will take forever before that idiot sends de e-mail. Well, I might as well start my rounds and come back in the next hour or so," he mutters.

Pissed off, LaDeau exits his office and walks over to the smoking area, where the local nationals like to meet for their morning coffee and cigarette.

As the locals enter the smoking area, they immediately light up a cigarette and start their morning chats. These locals have traveled down from Baghdad to work at the base and do not live in the neighboring Sunni towns, even though they are Sunni themselves. Fearing their own secular group would kill them for working with the Americans, they travel back to Baghdad at the end of a twelve-hour day in a bus provided by BCKR that links up with a combat patrol, probably the only thing that prevents this bus from being hit with an RPG as it travels the neighboring towns. Locals know there are Sunnis aboard. Word gets out. As the US soldiers continue to win hearts and minds, eventually, the neighboring towns will try to get work at the US base as well.

LaDeau is within shouting distance and yells, "Listen up," in a command voice as if he is a US soldier himself. He quickly rifles down the tasks for the day, some of which are the cleaning of restrooms or latrines in military jargon. "We need to get them latrines cleaned!" yells LaDeau as he continues down the list of tasks: servicing some of the civilian vehicles used by BCKR in their travels; construction of additional buildings around the base camp; and working in the dining facility as cooks, dishwashers, and anything else it takes to complete the work. The meeting adjourns with a, "Let's move it." LaDeau claps his hands as if he was an elementary school teacher motivating his first-grade class.

After traveling around the base camp and ensuring that all the assigned tasks are ongoing, a few hours have passed. LaDeau is back in his office at the computer. This time, he has received the e-mail. He reviews the e-mail and its contents and then forwards the e-mail to Smith, following it up with a cell phone call to Kuwait. Punching in Smith's telephone number with his crooked finger, which was broken on a number of occasions either by some of the prison inmates at Angola or during one of the burglaries he had committed as a kid, LaDeau raises the phone up to an ear that is small compared to the size of his head. The size of the ear and the profile of the broken noise that is greeted by the broad chin appears a profile that might belong to an aged boxer.

"Yeah!" Smith yells with enough volume to blow the wax out of anyone's ears. Smith is sitting in his office at the time of LaDeau's call.

"Billy, I just sent ya the e-mail. Now do your stuff. We can't blow this one, Billy!" warns LaDeau in a desperate reminder of the state of their scam.

"Okay. I will check my e-mail and get back with ya. And relax. This is a no-brainer. We will use the system and let the air force track down the casket for us," says Smith, confident in that he thinks everything is in control.

"To hell with getting back with me, I need to know now. Look. You have the list of caskets you sent, and you told me you could identify them by the soldier's name and social. Just check your list with the e-mail I sent you!" yells LaDeau in a reply that started off low in volume and that increased before the sentence was complete.

"Okay! Okay!" shouts Smith as if trying to ward off a dog that was about to bite him. "Give me a second, and I will check my e-mail."

Smith quickly rifles through his paperwork and comes to the list of deceased soldiers that had made it out on his last shipment. He opens his e-mail and begins to compare bodies shipped one for one.

"Hmm," he mutters into the cell phone.

LaDeau is quick to respond, "What is it?" asks LaDeau in a sharp, contentious request which brings Smith back to the conversation.

"Looks like a soldier from another base was shipped in place of what we received. Okay. I need to call the base at Ramstein, Germany and find out when the missing casket will ship. Either way, it should go through Dover. Now, this will take some time to call Ramstein, and so I will have to call you back. Look. We know which one is missing, and Ramstein will be able to track it." Again, a confident reply by Smith; and LaDeau pauses for a moment.

"Okay, but get on it before someone decides to swap the body with another casket and they decide to break it down," chimes LaDeau and terminates the call.

LaDeau now has to report to BCKR that Manning has left the country, a lie that he had been working on and that he knows will be accepted by BCKR since it is common for the corporation to lose employees. The twelve-hour days, seven days a week, with only a break every four months can wear on a person, and especially if the person is a civilian with no military training. Soldiers get rid of the stress through exercise, which is a common task for them on a daily basis. LaDeau then has to retrieve the money counter and destroy the electronics so that when it powers up, it appears to be damaged. He then has to disassemble the concealed room in the semi trailer truck. LaDeau will be pretty busy most of the day; and so he goes about executing the tasks, thinking the disassembly will have to wait.

The reporting of Manning leaving the country is accepted by BCKR, and he goes over to the BCKR supply warehouse to retrieve the electronic money counter. Upon entering the warehouse, he goes over to the shelf where the electronic money counters are stored.

"Hmm." LaDeau is puzzled when the electronic money counter he eyes appears to be in better condition. "The locals must have polished it up," he mutters. He opens up the bottom plate where the electronics are stored.

Once opened, it reveals the electronics, which are revealed as an electronic board with large, shiny, silver highways of soldered connections that connect all of the electronic parts together. LaDeau is no electronics expert, but he knows that if he takes a knife and breaks a few of these LAN's that it will destroy the electronic and the next time it is used, it will be reported as malfunctioning. It will be returned to the warehouse, where the warehouse personnel will turn it in on job order and send it out for repairs. LaDeau is skilled in this art and has performed purposeful destruction of other equipment in the past.

LaDeau moves onto the next task of disassembling the concealed room when he gets a call. "Yeah," he answers. It's Smith.

"Bowe, I found the other casket. It was held up in Ramstein to make room for additional wounded soldiers, and it looks like it will make it out on the next scheduled flight!" Smith said in an excited response and a proud one that he is able to track it down.

"Okay. So that means it should be in the US the next day."

Smith chimes in with, "That is what I figure."

"Whew! That was a close one. Good. Now that we know where it is, I can phone my kin folk and have them pick it up. You're a life-saver. Thanks, Billy."

"No problem, Bowe!" and the call is terminated.

Satisfied with the outcome, LaDeau exits the supply warehouse and heads over to the motor pool.

As he exits the warehouse, two BCKR employees enter the warehouse and head over to where the electronic money counter is located.

"This is the one."

One of them lifts it off the shelf, and they head over to the checkout counter to have the equipment checked out of the warehouse.

The two men carry the money counter with them through a number of small streets and alleyways on the base and come to command headquarters, where they enter and make their way over the provost marshals' desk. The provost marshal consists of a small group of soldiers that are essentially the base camp police. They ensure that soldiers are following all of the base camp rules. The two men are greeted by a US Army captain, who they follow into his office and close the door.

"Okay, Special Agent Adams. Let's see what we have."

The BCKR employee starts to disassemble the electronic money counter.

———————————

After lunch and later into the afternoon, LaDeau heads over to the motor pool. On his way over, he decides to place a call to his brother-in-law, Duke. It is around 3:00 p.m. in the afternoon, which is nine hours ahead of the US east coast. LaDeau couldn't care less and is thinking, "I'll wake up the useless turd," and punches in the number.

The phone rings about four times, and someone answers.

"Hello," a very sleepy, female, Southern voice responds; and LaDeau recognizes his sister's voice.

"Hi, Mary Sue," answers LaDeau in one of his better tones, if one existed.

"Hi, Bowe. How's it going over there?" asks Mary Sue in a slow, sleepy voice.

"Okay. Let me yak at your old man."

Mary Sue attempts to wake her husband up. In the background, we can hear her call his name several times. He finally wakes up and takes the call.

"Yeah. What's up?" a sleepy voice responds.

"They held one of the caskets back to load a few more wounded soldiers, and the casket will be shipped sometime this morning. You need to check with the air force base and find out when it is due in." The instructions come quick but clear. There's a pause that

LaDeau is familiar with and knows that it is taken time for the instructions to sink in.

After a few moments, "Okay. I will get on it when I get up." LaDeau executes another set of instructions. "Give me a call when you have picked it up and broken it down."

Again, a very slow pause.

"Okay. I'll call ya." replies Duke. LaDeau then hangs up and returns to going about his business.

Duke knows that his wife will be right on cue and, as always, begins to ask questions about the call.

"Just business, babe," replies Duke in a cavalier manner.

Mary Sue knows her brother can be tough and wily. Mary Sue is satisfied with Duke's explanation. She snuggles up to her husband and drifts off to sleep. Meanwhile, Duke is working out the details on how he will spend the money and explain it to Mary Sue. Duke is thinking that Bowe can help out in this arena on how they can hide the money from the taxman as well. Duke drifts off to sleep, dreaming of thoughts of a new home, new cars, and even opening up a new business.

TRIP TO MICHIGAN

Its morning. Duke awakens quite easily and quite chipper, knowing that the missing casket will arrive at the air force base today. After his daily morning hygiene and a quick breakfast with a cup of coffee, Duke heads to his mortuary to pick up his drivers. Duke pulls into the mortuary parking lot and finds that most of his drivers have arrived. He enters the front door of the mortuary and works his way through to the greeting room, where the executive assistant, Sally, is interviewing perspective clients. Sally is middle-aged, slightly overweight, and dressed in a blue pants suit of formal attire. Sally's age is well hidden, and she does not even look her years and possibly looks ten years younger. Duke greets the clients, but he knows he does not have the warm personality that Sally has and lets Sally do most of the talking. Like a hungry kid in cafeteria line with sad eyes that looks like he has not eaten in a couple of days, he waits for a pause in Sally's conversation to interject, as if the conversation was a tasty morsel for a starved kid.

"Sally what did you want yesterday when you stopped by my office?" asks Duke.

Sally blinks a few times as if Duke had shot a spit ball and it landed right between her eyes. "Not sure what you are talking about Duke," responds Sally with a perplexed look on her face.

"Yesterday, right around two p.m., you knocked on my office door. What did you need?" asks Duke.

Sally grins. "Wasn't me, Duke. It must have been one of the drivers." Duke pauses for a moment and raises his hand with his finger pointing upward.

"Yes. It must have been one of de drivers." Duke leaves the group with, "Sally will take care of all of your needs," as he walks away. "Nice meeting you!" yells Duke in a parting greeting. The clients wave in acknowledgement.

Duke returns to the grieving room, where he finds his drivers.

"Bill, you and Bob need to clean up hearse number three. It's a dirty mess." Duke assigns tasks. "Bert and Dan, you two head over to Dover and pick up de remaining stiff," Duke commands. "The rest of you can clean up around here and head over to the embalming station to empty de trash." But Before Bert and Dan can depart, "Hold up. I'm going to be traveling to Dover with ya." Duke joins Bert and Dan.

"Okay, boss. Glad to have ya aboard," responds Bert in his typical suck-up manner.

Dan glances out to the side of Duke as they are walking and then looks straight ahead, all the while thinking *That Bert, what a kiss-up.*

The drivers pile into the hearse, and Duke jumps into his car. They head out to Dover Air Force Base. As they arrive, Duke reports to the air force sergeant in charge.

"Good morning. I'm here to pick up the scheduled morning delivery of a casket," says Duke in an upbeat tone.

The sergeant checks his clipboard that he carries around with him and, using a pencil as a guide to each line item on the page, proceeds to scroll down through the list of inventories. "That was picked up at eight a.m., sir," the sergeant explains.

Duke's jaw drops, and it is clear to see that he is confused by the sergeant's response.

"What you mean picked up by eight a.m.? I have the contract for the processing of corpses being flown in," asks Duke in clearly an argumentative tone that is elevated in volume.

The sergeant has been in this situation plenty of times before, either in his basic training or dealing with the local nationals in the Balkans, Afghanistan, or Iraq, where he has previous deployments.

"Well, sir, I can tell you that it was picked up by Crayton and Walton mortuary service and the destination for the casket is Lansing, Michigan," answers the sergeant.

"How in the hell did they have the right to pick up the lousy casket?" Again, the volume is elevated and the question is argumentative.

Like a chess move, this question has not checkmated the sergeant, who knows he has the answer that might calm this ill-tempered civilian.

"Well, sir, in order for this company to even be able to pick up an inventoried item, they have to be on our list of approved contractors, which they are." The sergeant is checking his list of approved contractors.

"Can I see that list?" asks Duke in a question that is a little lower in volume but still argumentative. Duke's hands are held up in an almost come-get-some-wrestling gesture that in no way he could even think of whipping this Sergeant's butt . Sergeants in all branches of the US military are not weak, and clearly Duke would get a beating if he even tried something foolish.

"No, sir. The list is for our eyes only. Sorry sir," replies the sergeant with a confident look that the sergeant knows is respectful and that he knows is the correct response for this question.

In no way does the sergeant take Duke's posture as threatening, which is lucky for Duke. As the sergeant heads in another direction, he leaves Duke with the same pose, both hands still in the come-get-some pose. Duke finally drops his hands in defeat, and his jaw is still dropped with the mouth open.

Holy crap, he's thinking to himself. "Bowe is really going to be pissed.How in hell am I ever going to get this crap straight?" he mutters to himself. And even in muttering mode, Duke is wondering how he is going to get himself out of this predicament. He turns to walk away, and the drivers can see that he is flustered over the situation; and one of them speaks up.

"What's going on, boss?" Clearly, the driver was expecting Duke to motion him over after the discussion with the sergeant, which would have been a routine expectation.

Duke does not want to discuss the situation and responds with, "We are not picking one up today. Let's head back." Duke heads for his car.

Dan and Bert turn to head for the hearse; and Dan mutters loud enough so that Bert can hear. "Why in hell didn't he call first?"

"He's an idiot ," responds Bert and they both snicker.

Clearly, Duke does not have their respect since most of the time he issues instructions in an intimidating style. He is quite lazy. Along with those attributes, there is the overweight five-foot-four-inch frame that makes Duke appear like the slob that he is. As Duke gets in his car, he follows the hearse out of the air force base and not far from the entrance. As if waiting to turn with the directional lights on is a black sedan. It is the same black sedan with the two special agents who had been monitoring Duke and the drivers just a day earlier.

The special agent on the passenger side announces, "Okay. He must have heard that the casket was picked up earlier,"

The other special agent replies, "And now he probably places another call to his brother-in-law to discuss the next option."

The agents drive off and exit the air base.

On the way back to the mortuary, Duke knows he has to call Bowe. This is not going to go over well, and so Duke prepares himself for the conversation. It is 11:00 a.m. now; and so Duke does a computation and comes up with 7:00 p.m., a time that Duke knows that Bowe should be kicking around. Duke is driving down the highway and decides that now is just as good as time as any to call Bowe. He pulls out his cell phone from his pocket and punches in the number. After a lengthy pause, the phone begins to ring.

In Iraq, LaDeau is headed over to the semi trailer truck where he needs to disassemble the concealed room. LaDeau is expecting this to go quickly, and he will just leave the contents of the concealed room walls in the semi and have the local nationals remove it the next day. As he walks over to the motor pool, his cell phone rings. "Yeah!" yells LaDeau.

"Bowe, another mortuary picked up de casket."

The conversation stops LaDeau dead in his tracks. "What in hell are you talking about?" yells LaDeau in a confused tone.

Duke continues. "The sergeant at Dover told me that another mortuary picked up de casket, some Crayton and Walton mortuary out of Lansing, Michigan," answers Duke in a response that clearly stuns LaDeau.

There is a long pause, and Duke checks to see if the connection is still working.

"Bowe! Bowe!" yells Duke.

"Shut up for a moment! I'm thinking," yells LaDeau in the same contentious manner that is his signature response. LaDeau is reviewing his options. Option one: they can forget about the money since the money in the remaining seven caskets is more than enough for a three-way split. However, option one would not work since the mortuary that picked up the casket will probably follow protocol and remove the body and then the casket lining, revealing the money. More than likely, they will call the cops. An investigation might trace the theft back to Kuwait, and Smith will be in trouble. Although Smith and LaDeau were in on previous scams, LaDeau knows that there is no honor among thieves and Smith will give him up. That leaves only option two, where someone will have to go to Michigan and retrieve the casket. But that has to happen quickly, and the quickest route to Michigan is via the interstate. Looks like his stooge brother-in-law will need to make the trip. But in order to pick up the casket, he will need a fake transmittal that states that the casket was destined to his mortuary; and Smith has access to such transmittals.

"Listen. I will e-mail you the transmittal that states that the casket was destined to your mortuary. By the time you get back to the mortuary, I will have the e-mail sent to ya." LaDeau is speaking with confidence, thinking he is in control of the situation. "When you get to the mortuary, just print the transmittal and then beat feet to Michigan to the mortuary where the body was shipped and pick it up. The transmittal will show proof that the casket was destined for your mortuary and they should be able to release it."

Duke ponders over this plan. If Bowe feels confident, then he is confident. Duke knows that Bowe has always been right in the past, and this time should not be different.

"Okay, Bowe. I will get back and check my e-mail."

"Duke, I will talk with you later," and hangs up. As soon as he hangs up, LaDeau phones Smith and explains the situation. Smith says he will make up the fake transmittal and scan it into his computer to be attached to an e-mail that he will send. LaDeau gives him the e-mail address, and then LaDeau hangs up. LaDeau begins his stroll over to the motor pool to disassemble the concealed room within the semi trailer truck. Most of the local nationals have left for the day, and this leaves the motor pool empty of personnel. LaDeau makes his way to the semi, toward the front of the semi, where the trailer rests on the back of the truck, and ducks under the trailer and maneuvers under the trailer and opens the trap door. As the door opens, it illuminates the concealed room, which shows the faint images of the tools and banding material that was used to fasten the container to the wooden pallet it rested on. LaDeau hoists himself through the trapdoor; and again, he has to squeeze the pot belly through the door. Once inside the room, he turns on the small, battery-driven camp lantern that illuminates the walls and the latches that hold the walls in place. He notices the blood stain that must have belonged to Manning when he thrust the knife into his solar plexus. "Four-way split. Ha! Four-way split my butt ." he mutters, laughing to himself. LaDeau unlatches the wall and gives it a kick. It falls forward onto the floor of the semi, which is now illuminated throughout the trailer. The trailer is empty and barren except for the temporary wall that is lying on the floor. LaDeau unscrews the latches that were appended to the inside walls of the trailer and to the inside of the concealed wall, which latched to metal latches attached to the trailer wall. LaDeau unscrews all the latches and places them in small gym bag he used to carry his tools. Once all the latches have been removed, he gathers up the banding material and all the tools and drops them through the trap door in the floor. The only thing remaining is the temporary walls that once held the concealed room, and LaDeau does not seem worried about the walls.

LaDeau thinks to himself, *The locals will take care of this and just do what they are told. Otherwise, they get fired.*

The bigoted, rude, little voice within satisfies any fears that he might have. He squeezes through the trap door, grabs the lantern, and closes the trap door. LaDeau gathers up the gym bag and banding material, takes one look around to make sure he has everything, and begins his walk to exit the motor pool.

Meanwhile, back in the US, Duke has made it back to the mortuary and took care of some additional assignments with his drivers and other mortuary affairs. He checks his watch and realizes that two hours have passed since he last talked with LaDeau. He figures the e-mail must have been sent by now. He heads over to his office and logs into his computer to check his e-mail. Once logged in, he checks his e-mail. There in the inbox is an e-mail. He opens the e-mail, and there is no description other than an attached file. He double-clicks on the file and in what seems to take hours to an impatient Duke, the file opens, displaying the awaited transmittal. The transmittal has the department of defense logo and has all the formal transmittal information that identifies the casket inventory number: the deceased soldier's name and the mortuary destination, which is Duke's. Duke's spirits lift, and he knows he has to get on the road quickly. He gets on the intercom and calls his drivers into the office, explains the situation, and asks if anyone can accompany him to Michigan to pick up the casket. After a lengthy negotiation on meals and boarding accommodations, they agree on a price. He asks that they stay in the office, for he now has to explain to Mary Sue about the trip. He calls Mary Sue and begins to explain the situation. Mary Sue interrupts him a number of times with questions, which he answers and continues to explain the reasons until she is satisfied. Duke instructs three of the drivers to ride with him while the other two drivers will be riding in the hearse. Duke logs onto his computer and finds an online Internet tool to print a roadmap from the state of Delaware through Pennsylvania and Ohio and on to Michigan. Once the maps are printed, he highlights the route with a magic marker and gives one to the driver of the hearse while retaining the other.

The drivers pile into their assigned vehicles with one of them driving Duke's car, two in the backseat of Duke's car, and Duke riding shotgun. Duke is clearly the aviator from the start, and instructions begin pouring out as they head down the highway. Duke continues to adjust the review mirror to see if the hearse is following him, an adjustment the driver finds annoying but knows better than to comment on. After many turns and merging into traffic from entrance ramps, they end up on US Highway 76, the Pennsylvania Turnpike. From here, it is a 335-mile trip to Cleveland, Ohio.

"Boss." The driver in the back seat of Duke's car gets Duke's attention. "Why are we traveling all the way to Michigan to pick up the casket?" asks the driver and a question that Duke was prepared for.

"It's in our contract," answers Duke in a firm but informative response. "It's in our contract, and by not following it to the letter, we could lose the contract," Duke says in a response that he was proud of. For a moment, he could picture himself giving lectures at some university on the contractual agreements between parties. But this delirium passes as Duke glances over to the driver in the backseat. The driver nods as in agreement with the answer.

As they travel over US Highway 76 through Pennsylvania, the route is filled with rolling hills that, as the hearse transcends a snow-covered hill, opens up to a small valley with once-rich fields of corn, wheat, and rye that are now populated with the last corn harvest's wilted stocks sticking out of the snow. This scene is augmented by large silos towering like large, silver bullets pointing toward the sky that are filled with the last corn and silage harvest that did not make it to market and are used as winter feed that are accompanied by long, large, red milking barns that house the large, black-and-white-patched Holstein cows. The Holstein is the top milker of its breed and the farmer's choice on a dairy farm. Hardwood trees that had lost their leaves stand out against the snow-covered landscape like large, many-fingered skeleton hands reaching toward the sky. The white birch trees with white bark still have their orange and yellow leaves, along with the pine and fir trees that frequent the landscape. The drivers strike up a conversation that is invariably about last night's hockey game and what the players should have and should not have done. Duke is not even listening and is thinking of all the money that he removed from the closet and stored in the safe of his morgue. A quick calculation, and he is thinking that a four-way split will bring two duffle bags a piece—not a bad score. LaDeau first informed Duke of a four-way split and did not update him on the most recent change, the murder of Manning, which would reduce the split to a three-way split.

Ten minutes outside of Pittsburgh, they exit the highway onto a feeder road that has a number of fast food shops. They park Duke's car and wait on the hearse to park before they enter to place their order. It's not long before they pick up their order and go to their table to chow down. Once the meal is complete, out of the blue, one of the drivers speaks up.

"Remember that Lufthansa heist at the Newark Airport? I knew a guy whose second cousin was in on that heist."

All of a sudden, the tension is thick enough that it could be cut with the knife. It must be the animal sense in us all that picks up on this vibe; and the drivers, like a pack of wolves, look at each other as if they were acknowledging a fresh kill. One of the drivers speaks up.

"Did he get wacked by his own crew?" asks a driver. The tension breaks and all the drivers chuckle. During this conversation, Duke is not laughing. This does not go unnoticed by one of the drivers, Bert. Bert was involved with enough small-time scams and was lucky enough never to get caught. Pure luck, that was

Bert. Bert is perceptive and notices whenever there was a chuckle from some stupid joke, that Duke would join in on the laughter. Duke was not laughing at this one; and Bert began to suspect that there was something going on. Duke trails the laughter by saying, "Okay. If anyone needs to take a dump, there is the restroom and you need to go now."

The drivers follow the instruction and head for the restroom. Bert does not let this go and keeps this as a deposit in his extortion savings account that he might be able to withdraw from in the near future, should he find it worth his while.

The drivers pack it up and head back onto the entrance ramp of US Highway 76, heading west to the Ohio border. Bert knows that Duke tries to be one of the boys, and so he baits him with a proposition that he had championed on a past scam. Bert had a relative who passed away some time ago, and some of Bert's relatives wanted to bury the deceased on his farm in northern Pennsylvania. Now, Bert's relatives are as shifty as Bert. One of them happened to be in the house-moving business and had moved a couple of mausoleums for a company that made them. The company went bankrupt and they owed Bert's relative the money for the movement. The company worked something out and paid Bert's relative in mausoleums. This happened to work out for Bert, and his deceased relative got the mausoleum; but the relative in the house-moving business ended up with a couple, and they had a terrible time trying to unload them. Bert thinks he can sell Duke one of the mausoleums, and so Bert applies the bait.

"You know, I have a relative that you could say is in the mortuary business," announces Bert in a New Jersey accent. "I guess you could say it's the mausoleum business." Bert starts to spin the tale. The story continues. Finally, like a pro bass fisherman casts his fly spinning rod across one of the Great Lakes, he casts the lure. "I could probably get one of the mausoleums for about half the normal price." He glances over to Duke to see if any expression has taken place and, to Bert's surprise, there is nothing. "But for you, Duke, I could probably get for, let's say, one third the price." His eyebrows raise, and he expects Duke to turn around and bite for it.

"Not interested," replies Duke. Duke does not turn around to discuss it further.

This caught Bert by surprise. Having been a driver for morticians over the past eight years and listening to them complain about rising utility bills and the cost to run the operation, he knows that Duke has another plan. Bert is wily enough to know that he must press on. So he says, "You know, most morticians would have jumped at this offer, Duke, and it is a good deal."

The other two drivers in Duke's car agree, and the driver behind the wheel speaks up, "Sounds like a good one," replies the driver like a member in a Southern Baptist choir chiming in at the appropriate time. The driver sitting opposite Duke in the backseat speaks up. "That is a good deal," replies the driver as if he was a member of a corporate board making a decision.

"Boys, I am not interested, and I have my own plans."

Now Duke has taken the bait as far as Bert is concerned. Bert will make Duke another offer when none of the boys are around, and it might not be related with mausoleums.

Traveling down Highway 76, they pass outside of Cleveland and are traveling along the coast of the Lake Erie, one of the great lakes. The highway snakes along the coast, traveling through townships that cater to the sportsman who is eager to get out on the lake and make the big catch. Bait houses with engravings of oversized wali fish carved out of plywood adorned with the gray green colors are attached to the building. The engraving is known for hanging over the entrance of the bait house, beckoning the sportsman to drop in and buy the bait that can make the big catch. After a few hours, they are on the outskirts of Toledo and have crossed the border into Michigan. About an hour away from the mortuary where Duke is suppose to pick up the casket, it dawns on Duke that he might want to call the Crayton and Walton mortuary. Duke reaches into pocket and pulls out his cell phone to make the call. Now, Duke is not that much of a planner. One would think that Duke might have called when he was back in Dover, prior to taking the trip. But all the delirious daydreaming of the money he has scammed and what he is going to do with it has gotten in the way of his common sense. After entering the numbers, Duke holds the cell phone up to his ear and hears the distance ring. The phone continues to ring until an apologetic answering service comes online.

"Hello, and thanks for calling Crayton and Walton. Currently, we are busy…" It is clear that Duke is getting angry, and he mutters a few cuss words. When it comes time to leave a message on the answering system, he leaves his name, the morgue he represents, and why he called with his call-back number. It is not long before the team is entering Lansing and Duke navigates the driver to the location of the mortuary. As they arrive at the mortuary, they are greeted by a much larger parking lot with a covered drive-through at the front door, something that Duke always wanted for his mortuary. The covered overhead has Roman pillars that support it, giving it a gates-of-God look that is truly magnificent.

No matter how bad you have been all your life, the appeal is that it almost seems like God has forgiven you, Duke is thinking to himself as he continues his review of the building, which contains large double doors with floor-to-ceiling windows that follow the doors along their sides to a window that forms an archway at the top of the door.

Gates of gold, Duke thinks.

"Look at that, boss," one of the drivers speaks up. Duke can almost feel the envy in advance of what the driver is about to say.

"This is one hell of mortuary!"

The choir within the car begins to chime in.

"Check out the entrance!" a driver in the back exclaims.

Bert attempts to needle Duke with the following statement. "I bet you sure wish this was yours, Huh Boss."

Duke pauses and replies, "Well, boys, someday, I might have a place like this." It is a confident reply from a person who, it appears, can predict the future. This reply supports Bert's deep, intuitive thought that Duke was up to no good; and he wanted to be part of it.

His place is a dump , and there is no way he could afford a place like this unless he is coming into some money, Bert thinks to himself, *and I am going to find out about that money,* another greedy little thought; and Bert begins to hatch a plan where he can find a time when both him and Duke are alone.

LANDING IN LANSING

"Park under the drive-through. This shouldn't take long," instructs Duke. As the car pulls up underneath the drive-through, the hearse that had been following them on the trip follows suit. "Wait here," and Duke jumps out of his car and heads for the large double doors. He opens the door and enters the greeting area that has large, vaulted ceilings with a glass-enclosed atrium containing a small garden of assorted flowers with statues of what appears to be Adam and Eve. *The garden of Eden,* Duke thinks to himself. "What a layout," he says in an envious mutter.

"Can I help you?" A voice echoes from a corridor where a suited, well-dressed, middle-aged man, accompanied by a much younger man who is suited as well, are approaching in his direction.

"Hi. I'm Duke Pearson from Pearson and LaDeau's Mortuary Service, and I have come to pick up a package that was given to you by mistake."

Duke fumbles in his coat pocket for a while and pulls out the Department of Defense transmittal that details the casket by its inventory number and the deceased and that it is to be turned over immediately to Pearson and LaDeau's Mortuary Service and hands the transmittal over to the middle-aged man before the duo can even be introduced. The middle-aged man looks over the transmittal, and it is clear that he is all business. The expensive, dark blue suit; white shirt; and metallic blue, silk neck tie that holds in place the white shirt contain the weathered features of skin that has seen many sunny days, which sort of surprises Duke.

How could a mortician be that weathered? Oh well, Duke thinks to himself. As long as he gets what he wants, who cares what this old codger looks like. The dark blue eyes continue to scan the transmittal, and a slight grin can be seen forming at the corners of his mouth. .

"My name is Bob Garrison and this is Todd Williams. We are assistant managers of Crayton and Walton's Mortuary Service and currently, Mr. Walton and Mr. Crayton are out on the road on business. We honor this transmittal but cannot release the casket until either Mr. Crayton or Mr. Walton signs the transmittal," replies Garrison. A response that might as well have been to a teen who has been told by his parents he or she is not allowed to go out with their friends. "But I have to be back at my mortuary tomorrow morning, and I have to be out on the road tonight," begs Duke in a response where he is not skilled enough to work his way around the problem.

"I am sorry, Mr. Pearson, but again, I am unable."

Duke really does not hear the rest of the conversation as he spins down the whirlpool of rejection. After Garrison concludes his response, there is a long pause. Garrison again apologizes.

"We are truly sorry for this inconvenience. Perhaps you could leave us with a telephone number so that we could call you when either Mr. Crayton or Mr. Walton returns."

Duke finally snaps out of it. "Okay. I guess that will have to do." Duke gives Garrison his telephone number but concludes the conversation with, "Call me when he returns, regardless of de time, and leave a message on my answering service if I do not answer the phone." Duke turns and walks back through the double doors to the carport, where his drivers are standing around, having a cigarette and making small talk.

"Listen up," commands Duke. "We will have to spend the night here, so who wants to book the rooms?" asks Duke.

"I will, boss." A proposal that Bert jumps at as he whips out his cell phone and punches in the number. "We saw that Motel 8 just up the road from here. I will call directory assistance for the number and see if they can book us all there," remarks Bert; and that pleases Duke.

"Good work, Bert!" applauds Duke as he addresses the other drivers, " That is what I call team work."

And the other drivers clearly do not like what they think is competition and statements like, "Kiss-butt," and, "Brown-noser," can be heard.

"I need to make a call, and Bert needs to setup the rooms at de hotel. Probably while I am done making the call, the sleeping arrangements will have been made." Duke walks away from the carport and into the well-lit parking lot. It is close to 8:00 p.m. and, by Duke's calculations, is about 7:00 a.m. Iraq time. He knows that Bowe will be up and running around the base camp, so he places the call.

What the hell, he thinks to himself. *We've got a boat load of money.* The phone charges are of no concern. Besides, Bowe was looking out for his brother-in-law and had written into the contract with the mortuary service that phone calls to overseas would be paid by the US government if it was addressing mortuary business. *All part of working the system,* Duke thinks to himself as he whips out the cell phone and punches in the telephone numbers and waits.

In Iraq, LaDeau has been awake and has eaten breakfast and briefed the local nationals on the day's work. He is walking over to the supply warehouse when his cell phone rings to the tune of, "Good ol Boys," a ring tone with Waylon Jennings at the helm of lyrics. By the time it gets to, "Never meaning no harm," LaDeau has the phone open and yells. "What is it?" It is not a warm greeting, but it is in typical LaDeau fashion.

"Bowe, I am at the mortuary, and it seems like we might have to wait until the next day to pick up the casket."

"Are they going to release de casket?" LaDeau asks in heightened anticipation of a positive response that Duke had better have.

"Yes, they said they'd honor it, so there's no problem dere."

And Bowe accepts this warm response. "Good. Just make sure we get it back."

"What are we going to do with all the duffle bags? How are we going to hide purchases from our income tax statements at the end of the year?" asks Duke. All the while, he is careful not to mention anything related with the money they scammed. Yes, this coded message was taught to Duke by LaDeau on many repetitive occasions.

"Don't worry about it, and let's not discuss it further until I am back in de States." A response that does not quiet Duke's questioning.

"But, Bowe, we need to—."

Before he can get another word out, Bowe says, "Listen. I have to get back to work. We can discuss this next month when I take a few weeks off from work and fly back to de States." LaDeau in an a warm, aggravated sort of response that indicates that he is pleased with the way things have gone so far. "Gotta go. I will talk with you later." LaDeau hangs up.

Duke was not happy with Bowe's abrupt response and mutters to himself as he heads back toward his team of drivers.

"Good news, boss," yells Bert. "We have all got rooms at the motel just a few miles from here, and they have a strip club just across the street." A response expected from a bass fisherman who just landed a prize catch.

And the other anglers chime in, "Titties, boss." They laugh and grin from ear to ear.

"Okay. Let's get down there before they all decide to get married," yells Duke; and They pile into Duke's car and the adjoining hearse and drive away.

Meanwhile, back inside the mortuary, both Bob Garrison and Todd Williams are reviewing the scene from one of the expansive windows inside the mortuary.

"Do you think the drivers are in on it?" Williams asks Garrison.

"No. Not according to the intel that has been picked up from electronic surveillance," Garrison responds. "But a lot can change between now and the time we pick them up."

They continue to monitor Duke and his drivers pull away.

Duke and his drivers check into the motel. To the drivers' surprise, they all get their own rooms; compliments of Duke. The drivers head to their rooms to check them out, and then they meet up with Duke and go out for a bite to eat. Duke takes them to one of the best restaurants in Lansing based upon a tip from the motel attendant who had checked them in. All the drivers were expecting something like drive-through, where burgers and soft drinks are sold, but instead were treated to steak, lobster, and wine compliments of Duke. At the restaurant, the drivers were shown to separate tables and Bert made it a point to be seated with Duke. At Duke's table, there is Bert and one other driver while the adjacent table has the remaining three drivers.

"Eat whatever you want, boys. It's on me." Duke looks through the menu.

"Does that include booze, boss?" asks one of the drivers at the adjacent table.

"Booze included. But be sure you are able to drive," warns Duke.

Now, Bert has not been working for Duke that long, and this extravagant behavior immediately catches his eye. This is not typical of most employers who watch every dime and nickel. It's almost as if Duke is celebrating something or he has received an inheritance.

A chunk of change, Bert thinks to himself. *This idiot has found himself a chunk of change.*

Duke and the drivers are scanning the menu, each asking the other what they think is a good meal. Since it's free, the drivers order the most expensive steak and lobster they can find.

"Did you run into a large inheritance?" asks Bert.

Duke pauses before he answers thinking of the lie that will shake Bert's suspicion. "As a matter of fact, yes, I did run into an inheritance." Duke is thinking that admitting to it appeases Bert's suspicion and that it will end the conversation.

But not Bert. No. Bert's eyebrows rise as if to say okay, but Bert fires another question. "Wow, boss. When did you run into that?" asks Bert with another penetrating question that removes Duke's focus from the menu to confront Bert's inquisitive stare.

"About two months ago, I was notified that my uncle had passed and he left me an inheritance. Now, if you don't mind,

I am reading de menu and would like to order." Duke says in a cantankerous statement that prompts a response from Bert.

"Okay, boss. Sorry about that. I was just curious." And Bert goes back to reading the menu but does not hide his wonder, for Bert is thinking to himself, *Two months ago my butt . No way in hell he would receive an inheritance that quick.*

Yes, Bert knows that was a really weak answer; and now he knows for a fact that Duke is wrapped up into some scam. The waitress comes to their table, and they place their order. It's a big meal with all the drivers ordering the most expensive dish on the menu, and they ordered common table wine. But as the waitress is taking down the order, Duke stops her and looks at the menu and points to the most expensive wine on the menu.

"Bring a couple bottles of this."

The waitress takes the order and walks away.

"Wow, boss. it must have been one hell of an inheritance. That's some expensive stuff.'

'Just how much was that inheritance, boss?" asks Bert. Duke is ready for this one, and has the perfect answer."Oh, it was about as much as my mortuary makes in three years." The response really does not reveal a figure but is good enough to answer the question, Duke thinks .

The wine finally shows up at the table, and the drinking starts. When the bottles empty, more bottles are ordered. The drinking continues. Everyone is socking down the sauce except Bert.

No. Bert is staying sober and is waiting for Duke's mouth to really run loose. When the wine bottles empty, Duke orders more wine. After they have eaten and made small talk, the waitress arrives with the check. The drivers are somewhat intimidated by the figure on the bill as they read it and pass it over to Duke. They begin to excuse themselves and tell Duke they will meet him outside. They all leave except for Bert, who hangs back to see how this bill will be paid. Duke reviews the bill and reaches into his pocket and pulls out a wad of bills large enough to choke a horse. He peels off about ten bills in hundred-dollar denominations and places it on the payment tray. All the while he is doing this, Bert's eyes begin to sparkle as if he had an epiphany.

Yes. Looks like my friend is in on a scam, he thinks to himself. For in Bert's mind, only people who are in on a scam would keep such a large amount of money on them at one time. Bert guess is that Duke must have had ten thousand dollars on him in that monster wad of bills that he just pulled out of his pocket.

Duke and Bert leave the restaurant and meet up with the other drivers outside and pile into the cars. As they leave the parking lot, Bert speaks up.

"Hey, let's check out the babes at that strip club."

The other drivers chime in with, "Titties! All right!"

Duke joins in, "Okay, boys. The babes is waiting for us."

With that response, Bert knows that Duke is getting loose. Now all he has to do is to get him to brag. They head over to the strip club, which is right across the highway from their motel. They enter the club and, like all strip clubs, it is quite dark and thick with smoke, with just enough lighting to find your way around. Duke and the drivers spend most of the night at the club with the team continuing to drink heavily. The drivers watch as Duke places one hundred dollar bills in the G string of the strippers.

The drivers have been drinking but are not drunk, and it is clear to them that Duke is drunk. Bert notices this as well, and he needs to protect this bank roll and at the same time obtain Duke's allegiance.

"Come on, boss. We got a big day tomorrow and a long drive. Let's spit this joint."

It takes some convincing by Bert. It finally ends with Duke, Bert, and the drivers leaving.

It's the next day, and Duke awakes to a splitting headache and to the courtesy call he asked for the night before. He lays there in bed for a moment to collect his thoughts. The phone rings again, except this time it is Bert.

"Rise and shine, boss." It's the morning songbird, Bert.

"Oh my aching head," complains Duke. "I need a cup of coffee."

"I'll have one sent up to you, boss, along with juice and some breakfast." Bert hangs up.

Duke crawls out of bed and heads to the bathroom, where he crawls into the shower. The hot water is somewhat punishing as it hits his skin like tiny little knifes. It is effective though. He starts to come around and makes his way through the hangover. He finishes cleaning up. When he is out of the shower and drying off, he hears a knock on the door. Covering himself, he goes to the door. Its Bert with a tray with a number of plates and a carafe of coffee.

"Good morning, boss." Bert makes his way over to the desk and places the tray on it. "Me and the boys have had breakfast and are ready to roll." Duke waddles over to the tray and grabs the cup of coffee that Bert has already poured for him. Bert reaches into his pocket and pulls out of a bottle of aspirins and places them on the tray. "Here, boss. This ought to take care of that five-hundred-pound gorilla that is sitting on your head."

Bert manages a quiet chuckle and says, "Boss, that is quite a wad of bills you flashed last night. Where did you get such a chunk of change?" asks Bert.

Duke, although his head is hurting, manages to say, "From my inheritance."

But Bert does not settle for this. "Hmm. Excuse me, boss, but the only people I know who keep that chunk of change on them are bookies or drug dealers." Although curious, Bert does not want to piss off Duke. "And both of which I know you are not."

This shows some respect to Duke, who always wanted respect from the time he was growing up. Duke was always picked on in high school and, of course, did not obtain respect in his short stint in the service, where he flunked every basic soldier skill presented to him. If he had not been removed from his basic training unit, the soldiers in his platoon would have probably killed him.

"Well, we will talk about it someday, but not right now. My head is killing me." He reaches for the aspirin bottle, opens it, and pours out about four aspirins.

Bert has landed the twenty-pound bass that all fly fisherman wish they could have landed and is pleased with this response. "Okay, boss. I will be downstairs, waiting on ya." He leaves the room.

About an hour later, Duke shows up and links up with his team of drivers. After good-morning greetings and some small talk, Duke pays the hotel bill and they climb into their vehicles and head over to the mortuary. They arrive at the mortuary and pull up to the same drive-through carport. Duke gets out of the car, accompanied by Bert, and walks up to the large double doors. Bert opens one of the doors; and Duke walks in, followed by Bert. They are greeted by Bob Garrison and Todd Williams, who happen to be just standing in the greeting area.

Garrison greets Duke. "Good morning, Mr. Pearson."

But Duke gets down to business. "I'm here to pick up the casket," announces Duke as he manages to get out the words from the breath that emanates the odor of alcohol and cigarettes from the night before.

"Oh, yes," Garrison replies. "It appears that our clients wanted the body buried quickly for burial today. Unfortunately, the family could not afford a contemporary casket and not even a pine box, and so we let them have the casket that the body was shipped in for burial out of respect for the soldier who perished. We thought it was the American thing to do in support of our troops."

This is like a cold bucket of water in Duke's face, and Bert speaks up.

"That's mighty nice of you, Bob, and what a great American thing to do," replies Bert. The sincere statement catches both Williams and Garrison by surprise as Bert reaches out his hand to shake Garrison's hand. Garrison is about to take Bert's hand when they are interrupted by Duke.

"Are you crazy?" asks Duke with his eyes wide open as his five-foot-four-inch frame begins to shake as if there is some sort of internal earthquake within. "You do not have the authority to do that, and that casket belongs to the US government."

This catches Bert completely by surprise. "But, boss. It's an ugly shipping container."

Before Bert can get a word out, "Shut up, you idiot," Duke stops him in his tracks. "That casket belongs to Pearson and LaDeau's Mortuary Service, and you were given a Department of Defense transmittal that clearly states so." Duke's face is bright red and eyes are bugging out of his head. "If we do not get that container back, we will be seeing you in court."

Garrison seems to brush off the threat. "Well, if it's a shipping container you want, I am sure we have a number of them around here from previous contracts with the government that we would be glad to give you."

Garrison is talking through a grin and Williams is carefully watching both Bert and Duke's every move.

"We want the container and the lousy body that was shipped in it." The explosive statement from Duke ricochets off the walls of the mortuary.

For a moment, there is a pause in this heated debate as Garrison continues to manage a small grin that almost appears as a smirk that adds to Duke's anger.

Before any of the two combatants can speak, Williams intervenes. "If you want the casket container back, you probably could negotiate some sort of transfer with the client."

Before Duke can say another word, Garrison speaks up. "If you want, since we owe you a casket container, we can give you one in our store room to use in the swap."

Another pause. In his previous negotiating history, Duke knows that this is the final ultimatum. He also knows that he must contact Bowe for advice.

"Well that's sweet and all, but I have to contact my business partner. Give me ten minutes and I will return." And Duke turns to exit the building with Bert right behind him.

"Boss, that sounds like a pretty good deal."

And before Bert can say any more, Duke says, "Look. Do not open your mouth when I'm negotiating business," and the sermon continues. "Don't write a check that your butt cannot cover. Understand?"

Duke is glaring at Bert with the I-am-going-to-whip-your-butt look that Bert shrugs off. "Okay, boss. Okay."

Bert knows that Duke would not be a match for him in any physical confrontation. Bert does not want to lose sight of his goal, which is to weasel his way into Duke's fortune for he knows that where there is one large roll of hundred-dollar bills, there must be another. So he licks his wounds from the butt-chewing he just received and focuses on the big picture.

"Wait here." Duke walks from out under the carport where the other drivers are lounging around, having a cigarette. He passes the drivers and walks onto the parking lot to where he thinks they will not be able to hear the conversation. He checks his watch. Its 9:00 a.m. and around 6:00 p.m. Iraqi time, and he knows that Bowe should be running around overseas, taking care of business.

He whips out his cell phone and punches in the overseas number for Iraq. LaDeau's phone rings with the same tune of Waylon Jenning's "Good O'l Boys." LaDeau is in his office and steps outside to take the call. "Yeah."

"Bowe, I'm in Lansing, and these butt heads are telling me that they gave our casket away to de family of the soldier that will be buried in it. Some sort of good Samaritan deal."

Before he can explain further, LaDeau screams, "You stupid idiot!"

Duke knows what is to come next. It's the same speech he has heard in the past where Bowe reminds him of who set him up in business and how if it wasn't for Bowe he would be on the unemployment line in Louisiana or on welfare, how Bowe backed him up in a number of bar fights, and how Bowe turned him on to the diamond scam where they both made around fifty grand apiece. Actually, Bowe had made a hundred and fifty grand; but when he pawned the diamonds, he told Duke they only made fifty each.

"Did they open de casket?" Bowe screams into the cell phone.

Duke searches his memory that is hung over from the night before and responds with, "I don't think so. They would not have time to prepare de body, come to think of it." LaDeau finds this response titillating.

"Then why are they just turning over the casket?" And it still has not registered to LaDeau , who is now riding a high of anger and fear.

"Like I said, Bowe, it's a good Samaritan deal. The family does not have the money to bury the trooper." Duke goes on to elaborate with, "They offered us a deal where we could swap caskets, but we have to negotiate it with de family that's burying the soldier."

And this opportunity halts Bowe's sermon.

"What casket?"

Duke goes on to explain the details of the swap. After the explanation is over with, there is a pause as the little squirrel cage within LaDeau 's brain begins to turn. LaDeau knows he needs to get the casket back out of fear of another mortician finding the money and therefore exposing their scam. However, the major reason is pure greed. It is greed that motivates LaDeau . By hook or by crook, he is going to get that money back. More like by crook as LaDeau begins to scheme. LaDeau knows that funerals are closed caskets simply out of the fact that most of the body is unrecognizable. That the only thing he needs now is to come up with is an excuse that Duke will need to convince the family that the swap is necessary.

"Okay. Tell the family this that de government wants their casket back." As LaDeau is talking, one can actually see his eyes glisten with the confidence in knowing that this explanation will convince them. So LaDeau continues. "Everyone knows de government are bunch of greedy bastards, and you might want to mention that if the government does not get their casket back that they will grab any tax refund that the family is expecting as a down payment on the casket and, at them payback rates, it could take seven years to pay de government back." It is a pure lie that LaDeau had just conjured up.

Even Duke is surprised and responds with, "Yeah. That ought to work. Everyone knows de government is out to screw us. Great idea, Bowe." Duke applauds this lowdown lie. For a moment, all the tension of the call has lifted.

"Okay. Make it happen." And he hangs up. Just as he deposits his cell phone in his pocket, he notices two US civilians walking toward him with MP's not far behind.

He continues to walk toward his office when he hears, "Bowe LaDeau, may we have a word with you?" asks one of the civilians who are within ten feet of Bowe.

Bowe stops in his tracks and nervously responds. "Can I help you?"

One of the civilians flashes a badge. "I am Special Agent Burton, and this is Special Agent Murphy. We would like to talk to you about a missing US civilian contractor by the name of Joe Manning."

For a moment, LaDeau almost had the feeling that the prison doors were about to close behind him. But all the training as a correctional officer in Angola state prison back in Louisiana came into play, and he corrected himself.

"Well, like I reported to BCKR management, Manning came to me and said that he quit and that he was going back to de US."

The agents do not seem to be surprised with this explanation, and special agent Burton speaks up.

"Can you follow us over to BCKR branch office?"

LaDeau walks off with the special agents and the MP's.

DIGGING UP
THE BODY

Duke is pleased with Bowe's explanation and heads back toward the carport, where his drivers are in a huddle, reminiscing about the night before. Duke heads for the double doors with Bert right behind him, opening the doors.

They enter the greeting area where Garrison and Williams are talking amongst themselves, and Williams breaks the conversation. "And what is your decision, Mr. Pearson?"

Duke immediately speaks up. "Looks like we will take you up on your offer." Through the hangover, Duke manages a pleasant sort of smile.

"Follow me."

Both Bert and Duke follow Williams down the corridor to the back room, where an inventory of caskets can be found.

Williams points to a casket. "You can have that one."

For a moment, Duke pauses to check out the casket. It seemed to be meet his expectations plus, and he pulls out the wad of bills in his pocket.

"Look. Sorry about the incident earlier. Let me pay for this one. Let's say it's about three thousand dollars." He peels off the bills, counting loudly as he goes, for Duke is in bragging mode now. He knows that this impresses Bert, and he wants Williams to think he is a successful mortician.

Duke hands Williams the money. Williams, with raised eyebrows comes back, "Yes. This will do, Mr. Pearson." He grabs the money without counting it and holds it in his hands. He explains to Duke and Bert that they can drive around the back and he will open the back garage door. From there, they can carry out the casket. Duke apologies again, and places a hundred-dollar bill in Williams's front suit pocket, and both Bert and Duke head back the way they had come. Williams fetches the bill from his suit pocket and places it on top of the stack that he has in his opposite hand, all the while watching the team leave the area.

Duke and Bert link up with the other drivers, and Duke instructs them to drive the hearse around the side of the building to the garage doors. They jump into the hearse. Duke and Bert jump into the other vehicle, along with the remaining drivers, and head to the side of the building. When they get there, the garage door is opening and the drivers stop the hearse just outside the view of the garage door so they have enough room to load the casket. They exit the vehicle, and Williams instructs them as to which casket to load. Duke and Bert did not exit their vehicle, and Williams goes over to their car. Duke rolls the window down.

"Mr. Pearson." He hands him a slip of paper. "This is the address of our client, and the casket is at this church. You probably can make the transfer right there."

Williams hands Duke a slip of paper and gives Bert some additional instructions on how to get to the address. By the time Williams is finished with the instructions, the casket is loaded into the hearse. They wave good-bye to Williams, and the vehicle pulls up to the side of the hearse, where Duke gives the driver instructions on how to follow him. Duke and his team depart the area.

Williams watches as the vehicles pull away, and he pulls out his cell phone and punches in a number. The phone rings. At the other end, Garrison answers, "Hello."

Special agent Williams begins to speak.

"Yes. They have taken the bait. We can tell electronic surveillance to monitor the electronic plant."

"Good," replies Garrison. Williams and Garrison continue their conversation on how they will make the bust.

Duke and his boys are heading over to the church where their payload is waiting. Lansing is not very big, and they find the church quite easily. They pull up to the address and park in front of the church.

"Wait here," instructs Duke. He heads into the church.

From the outside, it's about what you would expect from a Catholic church with a tall tower extruding above the pitch of the roof containing a shuttered window, hiding a bell used to call its parishioners. This is an old-style church compared to the contemporary church, that have enough room for a few hundred parishioners and not more. Duke enters the church; and for a Louisiana Baptist, this is an awkward moment. Duke is not aware of the Catholic's protocol, but he is here on business. That thought reassures him, so he walks down the center aisle where he spots the casket. As he continues toward the casket, a priest appears.

"Can I help you, my son?"

This interruption startles Duke. For a moment, he is speechless. "I'm from Pearson and LaDeau's Mortuary Service, and I came here to claim the casket that this poor soldier is about to be buried in." And Duke goes onto explain the mix up and the mistake that was made.

As Duke is explaining the situation, the pastor joins in with "Ohs" and "Ahs," and ends with a "Hmm."

As Duke completes the discussion, the pastor pauses and then says, "Well, my son, I am sorry but we are not able to do that at the moment, for the funeral is about to take place in about three hours."

This response catches Duke by surprise, and the pupils of his eye begin to widen as the fear sets in. Once again, his face seems to have lost its pinkish color and appears bleached white from the stressful moment and his shoulders appear to be hunched over more than usual as if they were carrying a large weight. Duke is stroking his chin as if he is trying to think his way though this, and then it comes to him. Yes, the biblical snake once again appears and begins to formulate its next plot.

"Pastor, we really need to return this casket to the government. If we don't, I am afraid the family will be billed by the government, and you know what the government will do if the family does not pay." Duke goes on to explain what Bowe had tutored him on how the government could grab the family's tax refund for the next seven years and how much of a burden this could be to a family that probably could not afford such a debt. The biblical snakes head drifts from side to side as if it was a cobra attempting to hypnotize its prey before it strikes.

For a moment, the priest pauses and then explains, "Well, we will just have to raise the money throughout the years to pay the government back. Maybe we could do this with our small parish cookie sales." As he goes on to explain how he would pay the money back, Duke is becoming increasingly agitated; and then a sudden thought. In a voice that beckons, the biblical snake continues to entice its prey with the forbidden fruit.

"Pastor , you don't have to worry about that." Duke pulls out the monster wad of bills from his pocket and hands the entire roll over to the priest. "Here you go, and if this is not enough to pay the government, then take my card and give me a call and I will wire you de cash. However, I do need to acquire that casket and return it to its rightful owner, de government. For if I don't, I could lose my contract with the government. You know, I do all of de mortician services for them." The biblical snake waves the forbidden fruit in front of its prey, beckoning the prey to take a bite.

There is a pause and the priest begins to explain to Duke why that is not possible in that the body of the soldier has undergone enough torture in this life and that he could not put it through more torture by moving it again. "The soldier will have to be buried in the casket he arrived in." The priest hands the money back to Duke. "Here, Mr. Pearson. Our poor little parish will have to make due."

Duke slowly raises his hand to take the money back. "Well... Pastor, do you know where he will be buried? I would like to pay my last respects."

The priest pauses for a moment and says, "Yes. He is being buried at Chapel Hill Cemetery off from Bolm Road."

The priest gives Duke the directions. Duke turns to walk away when he hears, "Bless you, my son, and may God always be by your side."

Duke returns the farewell by waving his hand and continues to walk out of the church slithering away like a biblical snake that almost had a prey that had gotten away. As Duke walks away, he is thinking, *Chapel Hill. Hmm. I will get the casket, and I will get it tonight.* Duke exits the church and walks over to his car and calls all the drivers out and they huddle around Duke.

"Okay, I need the rest of you to head back to Maryland, and you can take my car back. I will need Bert to stay behind to help me with returning de casket."

There is a moment where the drivers are scratching their chins with wrinkled-up foreheads, trying to understand the reason.

"Okay, boss. I'll stay behind." Bert is thinking that he has moved up a notch in the food chain of drivers, since he is now being trusted to stay behind with the boss and work things out.

The drivers agree; and the driver of the hearse passes the keys to Duke, who immediately passes the keys to the hearse to Bert.

"You're driving."

Both Bert and Duke jump into the hearse and drive away. As they pull out of the mortuary service parking lot, Bert asks, "Where we headed, boss?"

Duke responds, "Chapel Hill cemetery." And Duke proceeds to give directions.

They pass through some quaint homes and over across a railroad crossing and a baseball field, and not far up the road and to the left is the cemetery. The snow-covered cemetery hides most of the gravestones except for the exceptional monuments that rise up out of the snow in either the form of a tower or rectangular shape of a wall. Farther up the hill, one can see where a gravesite has been prepared and a fresh pile of dirt is lying on top of the snow.

"How do they dig that gravesite?" asks Bert. "You would think the ground would be frozen solid."

It is not long before Duke speaks up. "They pre-dig them in de summer. They save the dirt usually in a shed, and they build a wooden form that fits all the way into de grave just about eight inches below de ground and pile sod on top of it. That's how we run our cemetery for our mortuary service. Okay. We know where de gravesite is. Let's head back to that restaurant where we ate earlier and get some grub. I am hungry."

As Bert is looking for a side road to turn around, he asks Duke, "What are we going to do, boss?" Before he even asked the question, he suspected that it was something illegal. Bert has that savvy from the years of being a juvenile hood growing up in Newark.

"After the funeral is over, we need to head back and remove de body from the casket and swap caskets." Duke looks at Bert as if to check for a response, but Bert does not flinch.

Instead, he asks. "How much are you willing to pay? I do not have to be in the mortuary service that long to know that we are robbing a grave." Duke begins to laugh. "That's right. We are robbing a grave and taking back our casket. Are you up for it?"

Bert pulls into an adjacent street and parks the car on the side of the road.

"How much are you willing to pay?" He looks straight into the eyes of Duke. "This is not my first rodeo, and I would expect at least ten grand."

It is this response that confirms to Duke that he is dealing with a hood. He has to steer Bert's attention away from the money that resides inside the casket to another reason for obtaining the casket.

"Hmm. Ten grand is a lot of money," responds Duke as if he is thinking over the cost.

Bert speaks up with, "What the hell do you want to swaps caskets for?" But Bert knows that there has to be something within the casket that is worth a chunk of change, and he is waiting Duke's response. "Come on. I know we aren't just digging up the grave just to get the casket. What kind of stupid idiot do you think I am?" Bert challenges Duke in an attempt to shake an answer.

"Okay, Bert. You've got me. That casket means I will lose my government contract, which is a major chunk of business." A now-you-have-caught-me sort of response to Bert's interrogation as Duke attempts to shift the conversation away from the prize.

"Ha. I thought so. Okay. I will help you get your casket back. But it will still cost you ten grand." Bert reaffirms his service fee.

Duke is relieved from Bert's response and feels that he is back in control of the situation. Bert is quite cerebral at this point and begins spin a tale of his historic scams that he had been involved with. Duke applauds Bert's triumph with a, "No joke ," and a, "Way to go, dude," as Bert continues to spin the tales. It is not long before they arrive at the restaurant and walk in to be seated by the hostess, who supplies them with the menu. They take some time to review the menu.

Bert is reading. "When do you want to do this, boss?" he asks in a low enough tone so that only he and Duke can hear.

"We will have to wait when it gets dark. This reminds me. We will need some rope, shovels, and flashlights. Did you see a discount department store when we were driving in?"

Bert replies, pointing out the direction that he thought he saw the big outlet. Bert cautions that flashlights might not be needed since it is quite clear today and flashlights will only draw attention. It is not long before their food arrives and they start to chow down. There are a lot of grunts and sucking noises as they drink their coffee, along with some crunching and chewing sounds as they eat their toast and chew their bacon. It is not long before their plates have been cleaned and they are sitting back, reviewing the waitresses who walk by as if they are judges reviewing models on a cat walk.

Bert breaks the silence. "We might want to pull into the cemetery right before it gets dark," he remarks as he shares his experience in breaking and entering.

"That's called twilight." Duke attempts to correct Bert.

"Huh?"

"Twilight. That time right before it gets dark is called twi-light," Duke attempts to educate Bert.

"Okay. During twilight then."

The small talk continues. Across the street from the restaurant, in a dark, two-door vehicle, are Bob Garrison and Todd Williams.

"They are in the planning phase and probably reviewing how they are going to lift the casket," Williams speaks up.

"More than likely," responds Garrison.

"And my guess is they will try to lift it tonight."

As they continue to watch the restaurant, Duke pays for the meals. Both he and Bert exit their favorite eatery and jump into their car. Bert is behind the wheel, and he heads toward the general direction where he first saw the discount department outlet when they were coming into town. Not far behind, Garrison and Williams are following. The sun is setting on the horizon, and it won't be long before it dips down and is gone. Meanwhile, Duke and Bert pull into the parking lot of the discount department store and park. They enter the discount department store and begin their shopping spree in search for all the items they will need to transfer the caskets. They pay for the items and depart the discount department store, heading for the cemetery. It is twilight, and Bert makes his way through Lansing, through the quaint, little neighborhood and across the railroad tracks to the cemetery. He pulls up outside the cemetery and shuts his headlights off.

"Wait here," he instructs Duke and steps out of the car to look around. No one is in sight, and so he jumps back into the car. "It's clear."

Bert drives into the cemetery with the lights off. He drives up the driveway, passing the small mounds of snow that cover the smaller gravestones, heading for the site where the body was buried. They pull up to the gravesite with car lights off.

"This is de place," Duke explains; and he exits the car.

Bert jumps out and joins him as they walk over to the gravesite and review the location where the body is buried. Fresh dirt
blankets the ground and, like chocolate crumbs from a cake that
sprawl across a white desert plate, they spread across the snow in
a random pattern from where the body is actually buried.

"I'll get the shovels." Bert heads back to the hearse and opens
the back and retrieves the shovels and returns to the gravesite.
Bert hands Duke a shovel, and they both start digging. "We are
lucky it's a fresh grave. The digging should be easy," Bert explains.
Duke takes it more in stride and continues digging. Bert starts
digging where the head is and Duke where the feet are. After
about twenty minutes, Duke takes a break, but not Bert. Bert is
used to hard labor, and he continues to dig. It is not long before
Bert is almost up to his waist while Duke is about up to his knees.
Bert stops digging for a moment.

"You gotta do better than that. Otherwise, we will be here all
night," Bert complains a little.

"Okay, okay," Duke responds. They continue to dig.

It's not long before Bert realizes that if they are ever going to
make any headway, he needs to change places with Duke.

"Let's change places," announce Bert. A request that Duke
happily agrees to. They move around, exchanging locations, and
continue to dig.

Duke is not used to hard labor and has always tasked his
gravediggers in his cemetery to do any manual labor, to include
his drivers. Although it is around 38 degrees, Duke is sweating up
a storm and Bert has broken one as well. Bert can tell that Duke
is not used to the labor by all the grunts and groans coming from
him. They are both breathing heavy, and the cold air reveals every
breath that they breath out.

Duke places the shovel in the bottom of the pit that he is standing in and hits the top of the blade with his foot. A sound is heard
as if an echo occurred. "Hallelujah! I hit pay dirt! Thank God."

The moonlight reflecting from the snow bounces of Duke's eyes, illuminating the surprise.

"Great. I'm not far behind you."

And they both continue to dig like wild men. As Bert places the shovel on the dirt and gives it a kick, another hollow thud occurs. "Bingo." Bert emanates the same expression as Duke had not moments ago.

They hurry through the remaining work, clearing off the dirt that resides on top of the casket. Moments later, and they both are standing on top of the casket.

"We will need to loop a rope through the top of the metal latches." Duke points to latches on both ends of the casket.

Bert hoists himself out of the grave, works his way over to the hearse, retrieves the rope, and heads back to the gravesite. He throws the ropes into the grave. Duke grabs them, looping them through the D-ring latches, and throws the ropes out of the grave. Duke attempts to hoist himself out of the grave but is unable to. Bert lends a hand that Duke grabs and, working together, Duke is hoisted out.

"Okay. Now what do we do with the ropes?" asks Bert. It is a request begging for the next move in this complicated process.

"Help me get the boards and drill," instructs Duke. They head back to the hearse, pulling out the 2x4's, a battery-operated power drill, along with the drill bits, drywall screws, and a bag full of pulleys. They carry the equipment back to the grave and drop it to the side. Bert inserts a drywall drill bit into the battery-powered drill that he purchased and grabs two of the 2x4's. He lies one on top of the other on the ground so that they resemble the outline of a teepee with about a foot across each other at the top. He fumbles around for the drywall screws and places one screw on the top of the wood where each rests on top of the other and places the top of the drill bit into the top of the screw and starts the drill. The screw turns fast and, before you know it, has traveled through both boards and is buried up to the head of the drill screw. Duke repeats this process again and then grabs one of the shorter boards that he places three feet down from where the screws are holding the 2x4s together and attaches the board to both 2x4's. Like a proud Dr Frankenstein, he raises his creature that, when standing, forms the letter *A*. They move it over to where the ropes are on the ground, and Duke continues to work. The drill whines as Duke throttles its trigger ; and by this time, Bert is getting nervous and is looking around to see if anyone is coming.

"Boss," whispers Bert between all the drilling, "are you almost through?" he asks nervously. Bert is well-aware of his surroundings, whereas Duke is engrossed in his creature feature of construction framework.

"Almost." And Duke continues to work. After a few more whirs, the drill is finally silent and Duke stands up. Before them lie two A-frames with pulleys attached to both.

"Now you grab that A-frame and place it across the grave, and I will grab the other," said Duke as he instructs Bert on the next steps.

Bert follows through, and Duke as well and, standing to the side of the A-frame, they both begin to pull on the single rope that loops through a couple of pulleys. The casket begins its ascent up through the grave, and both Duke and Bert begin to work the pulley system.

"Easy," instructs Duke as they both continue to work the pulleys.

It is a bright, moonlit night. The snow is really helping with the needed light for conducting this kind of work. It is not long before the casket can be seen rising out of the ground.

When the bottom of the casket has exited the ground, Duke commands, "Stop," holding the A-frame in place with one hand and grabbing the handle on the side of the casket with the other. "Okay. You do the same."

Bert follows through, mimicking Duke's position.

"Now pull it toward the edge of the grave and grab the other pulley rope to lower it."

As they both work the casket and the pulley ropes in tandem, they begin to hoist the casket out of the ground until the casket has nudged up to the leg of the A-frame that Duke had constructed.

"Okay. You grab both handles of the casket and hold it in place while I move the A-frames out of the way."

Bert follows the instructions. After Duke has moved the A-frames, he grabs one of the handles that Bert has been holding. Bert removes his hand. Together, with both hands, they slide the casket out of the grave.

By now, Duke is soaking wet with sweat and every muscle is aching; but it is greed that keeps him moving. They both are sitting on the ground, and it is clear to see that this exercise has them winded; and so they take five and rest for a few minutes.

"Let's get de other casket," Duke instructs. They both head to the hearse and remove the casket from the back of the hearse.

The caskets resides on a gurney that springs feet with rollers as if the casket was a large bug backing out of a hole that it dug and is about to stand up. They roll the gurney through the snow and over to the gravesite and remove the casket from the gurney. The casket is light and is easy to lift and is lowered to the ground. The snow crunches under its light weight as if it weighed tons. Duke maneuvers over to the casket that was removed and begins to open it, and he notices that Bert is backing away.

"What's wrong?" asks Duke. "Uh, boss, me and dead people, we just don't get along, if you know what I mean."

It is clear that Bert is nervous, and Duke manages a chuckle and then says, "Bert, dead people aren't going to hurt ya. It's de living you have to watch." Another chuckle follows.

It is not long before Duke pries open the casket, which gives a spooky sort of squeak that one would hear in one of the horror movies as the main character opens the door to cellar staircase. The moonlight slowly reveals the dead soldier's corpse. The mouth is pointed downward in a sullen sort of way and the top part of the head appears to be have a chunk of it missing and is doctored up as best as possible. The soldier is dressed in the typical US Army class A uniform or what is known as the class A uniform. The legs are missing, and so the pants legs are rolled up, with the shoes at the bottom of the casket, side by side, a truly sad sight for a soldier who has fought so bravely.

"Okay. This one isn't going to weigh that much since half his body is missing. Give me a hand to remove it." Bert moves slowly toward the casket and, for a moment, looks away from the body but gradually begins to look downward at the soldier.

"Bert, pull it together," commands Duke as he grabs both of the soldier's shoulders. "Grab him by de hips and lift."

Bert follows the instructions, and they both raise the body; and Duke begins the duck walk, where he gradually turns counterclockwise and begins backing toward the empty casket that will be the new home for the soldier's body.

Duke and Bert begin to position the body over the casket. Duke again commands, "Okay. On three, drop it."

Bert looks at him with a blank stare.

"Three."

Duke lets go of the soldier's shoulder, and the head drops; but the other half of the soldier resides within Bert's grasp, who has not let it go.

"Hey, what are you doing? Drop the body."

Bert then lets go. Duke pauses to stare at Bert. "Ya'll all right?" asks Duke in an almost concerned voice that Duke can muster up.

"Yeah, boss. It's just that I think we are being disrespectful."

That catches Duke by surprise. All along, Duke thought Bert was the typical thug. Lo and behold, there is a bit of decency that Duke had not expected. Duke shakes his head and goes back to the casket to retrieve the shoes. He then returns to the casket where he deposited the body and throws them in and slams the door.

CAUGHT IN THE ACT

"Okay. Let's get the government casket loaded."

Duke walks over and closes it. Bert follows and grabs the other end of the casket. They hoist it, and Bert notices it's heavier than the other casket. They both grunt and groan as they carry it over to the gurney.

"Boss, why is this casket so heavy?" asks Bert more out of wonder than suspicion.

Duke pauses for a moment, thinking of a novel lie. "It is a different model." Duke tries to explain away the question presented. "Ya see, de government has different models, and this model just happens to be the heavier one." Duke is actually proud that he dreamed up a response so quickly.

Bert nods his head and grins in an acceptable sort of way. However, Bert is far more suspicious and if he was not pressed for time would address the suspicion right here and on the spot. *No… Now is not the time… I will get with the boss on this later.* Bert thinks too himself. For now, Bert thinks that Duke is afraid of losing his government contract and thinks he has Duke over the barrel. Bert will have something to talk about after this little scam to his hoodlum friends back in New Jersey.

Ten G's to dig up a body, he thinks to himself. *What a schmuck,* he thinks and is almost chuckling to himself.

They place the casket on the now-empty gurney and begin to move it back to the hearse. They load the casket in the back of the hearse and walk back to the gravesite to clean up their mess when they hear a sound like someone struck a loud match. *Tch!*

They stop and look at each other with a questioned look as if to say, "What da hell was that?" It is not long, and they begin to notice that the ground, although illuminated by the moonlight, is taking on an incandescent brightness as if a candle that had been lit is slowly coming to life. The light begins to increase in intensity; and finally, they realize that it is coming from above, and they both look up.

Directly above them, a bright fire appears to be about the size of a baseball and is growing in intensity. It illuminates a small parachute above it.

Almost immediately, Bert's animal instinct possibly derived from previous juvenile criminal acts back in New Jersey begin to kick in. "Run," he yells; and he begins to run toward the road, slipping and falling as he goes.

Duke continues to stare up at what is a recognizable flare.

"What the hell?" asks Duke in a question more directed at his curiosity than his partner, who is trying to get to his feet from the fall.

Meanwhile, just over the hill ascends four state police cars with lights flashing. As they turn into the cemetery, they turn on the sirens; and now Duke knows why the flare was shot into the sky. It was a signal and, like rats in a trap, they're caught. As the first state police car speeds up the road, the headlights shine directly in Duke's direction. It is the proverbial deer-in-the-headlights look as Duke is staring wide-eyed with his jaw dropped.

"Do not attempt to run," blasts a command voice over a loud speaker. "Duke Pearson, you are under arrest."

The sound alone freezes Duke in his tracks. Meanwhile, Bert is running across the graveyard. In close pursuit are three state police officers, yelling "Halt," at almost every four steps into their strides. The police car comes to a halt. Out of the passenger side steps Bob Garrison, with his weapon drawn and pointed in Duke's direction.

"Duke Pearson, put your hands up," he commands. Without pause, Duke follows the instruction.

Out of the second state police vehicle steps Todd Williams with weapon drawn as well. He moves quickly to the opposite side of Garrison, a police tactic used to catch a prey in a crossfire, should one be needed. They close their distance quickly; and before you know it, they each have grabbed Duke by his arms and are lowering them behind his back.

Williams speaks up with, "Duke Pearson, you have the right to remain silent."

Duke begins to urinate in his pants. The excitement is too much for him to even notice.

Off into the distance, we hear Bert screaming, "I had nothing to do with it." It is a typical criminal response that all the police on the scene recognize as a person who is about to flip on his criminal partner. Bert is not as dumbfounded as Duke, and he puts up a little bit of a struggle as the state police try to get him to his feet. But he is no match for the Michigan state police, who are trained professionals; and it is not long before they have him on his feet, hands behind his back, and the handcuffs are being latched. They begin to read him his rights.

"You have the right to remain silent. Anything you may say will be held against you in a court of law." The officer continues the scripted speech.

But the speech has fallen on deaf ears as Bert's mind is racing toward a quick solution to his problem. "I want a deal," he yells as he is being taken away.

Back at Duke's location, Garrison and Williams open up the casket that is on the ground. As the lid comes open, they stare down at the body. The soldier lies in the casket in a distorted sort of way, with his shoes thrown on top of his body.

"They didn't even attempt to cross the arms on the corpse," Williams says in a disgusted tone.

"Typical criminal. Let's check the other casket," instructs Garrison. They walk over to the hearse and open the back, pulling the casket out of the back along with the assistance of other state police officers.

Once again, the gurney legs spring to life as the casket is pulled from the hearse. Garrison and Williams get to work and open the casket. Once opened, Garrison reaches into his pocket and pulls out a buck pocket knife that has about a four-inch blade. He begins to get to work prying off the silk facade that is attached to the side of the casket. He walks his knife down the entire side of the casket and then pushes on the side and it is pried open. There, in stacks of hundred-dollar bills, about a hundred thousand dollars to a stack, appended to the side of the casket with a piece of white cotton cloth suspending the money, the Franklins are grinning. Garrison turns to the state police officers, who are on each side of Duke, restraining his arms behind his back with hands cuffed. Duke continues to have the deer-in-the-headlights look with the jaw dropped.

"Bring Pearson over here," commands Garrison. The officer walks Duke over to the casket. When he arrives at the casket, Garrison speaks up. "My name is Special Agent Garrison, and this is Special Agent Williams," Garrison goes onto explain. "We are with the FBI, and your partner over in Iraq, Bowe LaDeau, has been apprehended and has given you up."

As Duke is listening to Garrison's speech, he is feeling like he is falling down a deep well, all the while thinking, Crap . *They got Bowe.*

As fear continues its grip on Duke, Garrison continues with the instructions.

"It is in your best interest that you cooperate and tell us where the rest of the money is."

And all of a sudden, that long fall down the well has come to a screeching halt.

They don't know where the rest of the money is. Duke is thinking to himself that this might be a way out. Like a rat being chased across a kitchen floor by a cat, the nearest mouse hole appears to be right in the distance.

"I want a deal!" screams Duke as he tries to hold onto whatever control over the situation that he might have for himself.

"Don't worry, Mr. Pearson. There will be plenty of time to deal once we get you back to the police station." With that, Garrison motions to the state police, who take Duke away.

They open the door to the back of a police cruiser and carefully help Duke into the back. Once seated, the police buckle him in and close the door. The slamming of the door is as loud to Duke as the slamming of the bars that he will soon hear once they have him booked. The officers jump into the front of the cruiser, and they begin to drive off. They pass the vehicle that contains Bert, who is peering out of the back of a cruiser that he was placed in, all the while giving Duke the you-no-good-S.O.B. look as they pass.

Duke is wide-eyed and can't believe he has been caught in the act. *How did they catch on?* he asks himself as the cruiser slowly meanders onto the road that is perpendicular to the cemetery. The drool at the corner of Duke's mouth flows freely now as it makes its way down the corner of his mouth and down the side of his chin, on the way to his double chin turkey gullet below.

The squad car radio interrupts the silence as the police dispatch calls the cruiser.

"Adam Nine, what's your status? Over," comes over the speaker.

The state trooper in the passenger side picks up the radio microphone and responds , "This is Adam Nine. We have captured the suspect and are on our way in."

Back at the gravesite, special agents Garrison and Williams are removing the money from the casket. Williams removes the money from the casket and hands it over to Garrison, who places the stack into the zipper nylon duffle bag.

"I've counted two hundred thousand so far," remarks Williams as he continues to remove the money from the casket.

"Don't bother to count it," responds Garrison. "We will use a legitimate money counter once we get back to headquarters." Garrison continues to stuff the money into the nylon bag.

Williams stops counting the money and immediately hands the freed-up money to Garrison, and the process picks up in pace. Over the hill shines the headlights from another approaching vehicle as it slowly makes its way across the highway. Its signal lights come on, indicating an intended turn into the cemetery. It slows for the turn and slowly makes its way up the hill to where Garrison and Williams are located.

"It's the mortician and his burial crew," announces Williams. "I called them to have the body placed in storage in case we need to collect further forensics," explains Williams. Garrison responds with a nod.

The black limousine makes its way up where the vehicle Garrison and Williams had been parked and stops. Three figures emerge, and one of the three appears to sport a pot belly that is outlined from his overcoat on a short statue of a man. The other two appear to be about in the six-foot range and sport stocky frames. All three make it over to Garrison, and the introductions start with the short man speaking up in a perky, solemn sort of a voice that is evident that he is excited about what has taken place.

"My name is Jeb Brown, and I am an associate mortician." He introduces himself, to which Williams and Garrison both respond, "Glad to meet you, Mr. Brown."

Jeb then introduces the two stocky men next to him. "These are our helpers and gravediggers, Brody and Hank." The two men both outstretch their hand in a handshake to greet the agents who respond accordingly.

"So this is the mess that the criminals left behind," responds Jeb.

"Yes, Mr. Brown. I'm afraid we are going to need the body stored somewhere for further forensic collection, as our forensic team is about to quit for the evening." Garrison points to the three police officers who have "Forensics" spelled out across the back of the nylon jackets. The insignia is so reflective that it almost appears to emanate a bright light of its own as if illuminated by neon. "Well, that's not a problem, Mr. Garrison. We can store the body back in our mortuary services building. We are always glad to help the law, you know," remarks Jeb in a common courtesy response that Jeb thought appropriate.

"Well, we appreciate it, Mr. Brown. Your team has been a big help," responds Garrison; and Jeb smiles in acknowledgement, and then his facial features distort in a look of disgust.

"I can't believe anyone would disgrace our American soldiers in such a manner."

Garrison grimaces in disgust as well and responds, "Yes. I can't agree with you more, Mr. Brown. It bothers us as well."

Williams is quick to jockey for the next response. "About all we can do is catch them and bring them to justice," says Williams with a stern look. "These criminals are not like you and me, Mr. Brown," replies Williams.

Both Jeb, Garrison, Williams, and the two helpers all nod in agreement.

As we leave the group to discuss further requirements for cleaning up the mess, a strong breeze appears as if it came from the wings of the angels guarding the deceased soldier. The breeze rises above the group and above the trees that populate the area where they have gathered. The headlights from the car belonging to Jeb light up the adjacent field absorbed by the snow. The breeze drifts across the snow-white-covered cemetery to the adjacent highway that is darker in color from the day-to-day traffic and the dirty, brown-colored snow packed by tires. It drifts down the highway until it catches up with the state trooper car containing Duke that is just pulling into the parking lot of the jail where he will be housed.

The trooper parks the car and gets out of the vehicle and opens the door to the backseat where Duke is sitting. "God." The trooper grabs his nose as if to protect it from some odor. The odor emanating from the back seat is from Duke, who has soiled himself. "He crapped in his pants," the trooper complains.

"Well, let's get him inside and let the jailers take it from there," responds the other trooper, who has dismounted the front passenger side and is joining in to remove Duke from the car.

They pull Duke out of the vehicle and walk him into the entrance of the building, which is labeled in block letters across the door "Booking," and below it the state trooper insignia for the state of Michigan. Duke has a childlike look of wonderment that is wide-eyed, and it is clear to see that he is scared stiff. They walk him up to a counter that is maintained by three other Lansing officers who are in their bright blue uniforms with large pin stripes down the legs of the pants. The uniforms almost look like they have been pressed to the officer's body, with the seams perfectly perpendicular to the shoulder lapels that bisect both front shirt pockets. The troopers get busy and start the booking process. One of the troopers speaks up. "I wonder where it all went wrong, Mr Pearson."

WHERE IT ALL
WENT WRONG

Special Agent Garrison and Agent Williams are staying at the Marriot hotel in Detroit, Michigan. Both agents work out of FBI headquarters in Washington DC and have booked a room at the Marriot in Detroit during the preparatory work for Duke's arrest in Lansing. Both are early risers and are up bright and early and meet up in the lobby, where they grab a seat in the breakfast cafe. Both are wearing the FBI nylon jackets over their winter coats, which they are quick to shed and hang on the back of their chairs. Almost simultaneously, they grab the menu and begin to review the list of breakfast delights. The odor of English Leather aftershave lotion fills the air, as this is Garrison's weapon of choice for morning aftershave; and it overpowers whatever Williams had been using, who really does not use an aftershave at all. Both agents peer over the menu.

"I think I'm going to have the omelet," pipes up Williams.

He is followed by Garrison. "I'll have ham and eggs with hash browns."

With that, Garrison motions for the waitress, who saunters over to their table and is wearing a light gray dress that almost seems uniform in its presentation, along with a small, white apron tied around her small waist. About five feet four inches in the flat heels that she is wearing, she has a small-framed build and a shapely figure. "Good morning, gentlemen," announces the waitress. "Have you decided on what you will have?" she asks.

Garrison nods to Williams as if to say, "You go first." Williams responds with his order.

"I'll have your Western omelet with hash browns and toast…" Williams continues to add the particulars on what he wants on his toast and what he wants to drink.

"Omelet. Toast. Okay. Got it. And for you, sir?" asks the waitress as she glances over at Garrison.

"I'll have the ham and eggs…" and Garrison continues with his order as the waitress continues to record the order on her receipt book. "That will do it," announces Garrison; and the waitress scratches down the last of the order.

"Okay. We will have that right out, and I will fetch you your drinks." And she turns and walks away.

The waitress disappears through a door entrance to the kitchen area to post her order and returns to obtain the coffee that Garrison and Williams had ordered. Returning to the table, she fills their cups.

"We both noticed you have unusual-colored eyes, with the dark blue mixed in with the brown," responds Williams; and before he can ask about her ancestry, she responds with, "My mother's folks were from Afghanistan, and my father is of Irish descent," she explains. And before either agent can comment, she says, "But both of my parents were born in the US," firming her identity.

"I have an Afghan rug that I obtained from Afghanistan," responds Garrison. This immediately gets her attention as the conversation takes off with Garrison explaining his tenure over in Afghanistan as a special agent and where in Kabul he had shopped for the rug.

The conversation continues; and another couple shows up and takes a seat at the far end of the café, which gets the waitress's attention. She immediately breaks the conversation—"Oh. Another customer. Time to go to work"—and departs the table.

"Interesting place, Afghanistan," remarks Garrison as he picks the coffee up to his lips and takes another sip.

"Well, are you ready to report to the director on this case with Mr. Pearson and company?" asks Williams, who is referring to the FBI director in Washington DC.

Garrison swallows, and returns the cup to its saucer. "Yes. It's pretty much a done deal with all the evidence we compiled." And Garrison continues with, "This was an international crime that spread across many nations. I'm sure that is really going to lengthen the time that they will do in prison."

It's not long before the waitress appears, carrying a tray that is much larger than herself, containing both of the agents' orders. Lowering the tray and supporting it with one arm, she grabs the plates and lowers them to the table in front of each agent. The aroma of the ham and eggs fills the air, adding to the dining experience for this early morning.

After dispersing the saucers to their proper locations, the waitress asks, "Is there anything else I can get you?"

Garrison responds, "No. That's about it, ma'am. Thanks."

Williams responds with a, "No thanks. Everything is fine."

With that, the waitress departs. The agents waste no time in digging in. Before you know it, most of the meal is gone, with only tidbits left on the plate. They both chase the remnants of the meal across their plates with their forks as if they were skilled hockey players and the forks were their hockey sticks. Williams slapsticks his eggs back and forth with his fork as if he is about to make a goalie and—Slap!—the eggs are scooped up and go straight to his mouth. His mouth half opens, giving the appearance of a goalie's net—Score!—and the eggs make it past his teeth and into his mouth. Williams chews his food quickly, for Williams, being a rookie, is always in a hurry and ready to go at a moment's notice. Garrison takes his time, chewing his food as Williams, who has finished his food, waits patiently. As his last forkful is swallowed up, Garrison grabs his cup of coffee to wash it down. By now, Williams is checking out the waitress who has reappeared from the kitchen entrance. She provides Williams with a warm smile that to Williams is as pleasant as the morning sunshine that appears over the horizon during his morning jog.

"Okay. Time to go," announces Garrison. The morning daydream that Williams was having disappears.

The team leaves the hotel cafe and exits to the parking lot in front of the hotel, where they are greeted to a spectacular sunrise that is announced with sunlight bouncing off the clouds to the east with bright hues of orange lighting up the clouds and reflecting off the snow in the distance, giving the appearance of snow on fire. They jump into the two-door sedan with the US government license plate with Williams at the helm.

Williams starts the vehicle and backs out of the parking space. He pilots the vehicle to the nearest exit and onto the main highway. They head toward the main highway, which leads to the FBI's main headquarters in Detroit. The highway has been cleared of snow with the most recent pass of snow plows, and the snow banks on the highway bear the dark scars of the dirt and mud thrown up from the plows that leave spotted streaks of dirt like an artist with black chalk had outlined his masterpiece. It's not long before they arrive at the FBI headquarters and pull into the parking lot and park. Both special agents exit the vehicle and enter the formal federal building with its concrete structure base supporting the ascending floors populated with windows as if they were soldiers standing in formation. They enter the building and are greeted by the security guards, to whom they immediately flash their badges.

Garrison announces, "We are carrying our service weapons."

The guard acknowledges with a nod, and both Garrison and Williams carefully remove their weapons and place them into the gray container, along with the spare clips of ammunition. The containers bypass the x-ray machine and are handed to one of the security guards, and both Garrison and Williams remove their personal items and place them in their assigned gray tray that does pass through the x-ray machine. One at a time, as if they have been drilled in the process, they both step through the doorway of the security machine; and then they both are screened by the security guard, who makes sure they are not carrying anything in addition to the service weapons that they had claimed. They are both cleared, and they retrieve their service weapons and all of their personal belongings.

They then walk to the elevators, and find one that is open.

"Lucky us," pipes up Williams.

They both enter the vacant elevator, and Garrison selects the button for the floor; and the doors begin to slowly close. An approaching young lady that had just cleared security runs quickly to the elevator, and Williams stops the doors from closing. She is in business attire composed of a blue pants suit outfit that is navy blue in color. She is a brunette and is in her mid to late twenties, with dark brown hair and light brown eyes with spots of light blue peering out.

"Thanks," she says with a warm smile, displaying perfectly straight teeth from under her top upper lip, which is well-shaped and curved as if an artist had designed it from a sketch. Along with the warm smile comes the odor of a garden as her perfume fills the elevator floor.

The elevator doors begin to slowly close; and before long, its occupants are greeted with a small lurch upward as the elevator begins its crawl upward. Everyone is staring at the door but Williams, who is slowly eyeing the young lady from his peripheral vision. She is eyeing Williams as well. She is holding a stack of file folders to her chest as if she was nursing them. From her left hand, Williams notices she is not wearing a wedding ring nor an engagement ring. But before Williams can strike up a conversation, the elevator reaches the fifth floor and comes to a halt.

As the door begins to crawl open, Williams departs with, "Have a good day."

And the young lady returns with a, "And you as well," along with that fantastic smile.

The special agents make their way down a hallway of office doors that opens to a breezeway of office workers in an open bay area separated by partition cubicles. They are greeted with conversations from the cubicles as the office workers are carrying on conversations with people on the other end of a phone conversation.

"And then what did you see?" asks one cubicle worker.

"Okay. Right. Got it," says another.

Williams and Garrison leave the chorus and walk down the hallway and pass the open bay area, which enters another hallway with office doors on both sides. On the left is a wall of glass windows with what appears to be a long conference table with four personnel sitting at the table and a large number of vacant seats. The personnel are clad in suits—some of which are dark blue and another which is light gray. Two of the men sitting at the table are about Garrison's age, fifty plus; and the other two appear to be in their late thirties or early forties.

Garrison opens the door to the room. "Good morning, Special Agent Garrison. Glad you could make it," greets one of the elderly, gray-haired men.

Garrison responds, "Good morning, Ted."

The gray-haired man known as Ted also greets Williams, and Williams takes a seat while Garrison whips out his laptop and begins to hook his computer up to an Internet connection that is in the center of the console of the large conference table. At the far end of the table and opposite of where the men are sitting is a large, flat screen suspended from the ceiling. The center of the conference table where Garrison is hooking up his Internet cable is a small console with a number of buttons. Garrison hits the button, and the flat screen comes alive. Meanwhile, there are side bars carrying on between Williams and the four men sitting at the table.

"How did you like Iraq?" asks one man.

"Hot," responds Williams with a look of disgust in his face. "And sandy. Oh yes. I forgot dirty," answers Williams as he elaborates.

"I hear the army was pretty good with what accommodations they had," remarks Ted in a statement that is more of a question.

"Oh yes, sir. They did the best and are a number one team to work with," Williams responds.

"Great," responds Ted.

It's not long before the flat screen TV comes to life, and presented in high definition clarity is the formal FBI insignia.

"Okay. We're ready," announces Garrison.

With that, all men turn in their seats to view the flat screen. Garrison is standing up and presses a key on his laptop, and the flat screen TV clears and is replaced with a PowerPoint representation with large, white letters appearing across the blue background, "Saddam Project," as the title. Below the title is a bulleted list with the first bullet being, "Brief History," and followed by the second bullet: "Notification." Garrison reaches over and turns a knob that dims the incandescent lighting in the room that one would expect to find in a contemporary movie theater, announcing the start of the show.

"Welcome, gentlemen, to project Saddam," greets Garrison. "My name is Special Agent Bob Garrison, and this is my colleague, Todd Williams." Garrison points to Williams, who nods to the adjoining agents in the room. "I would like to start with a brief history of the money confiscated from Saddam Hussein, the well-known dictator in Iraq." A slight pause, and Garrison continues. "In October of two thousand and three, a platoon of Hundred and First Airborne soldiers are on a combat mission in the small town of Al Hila, looking for Saddam Hussein. During the mission, they run across a warehouse which, when searched, they find contains a large cellar. Suspicious and on their guard, they search the cellar only to find it wall to wall with six-drawer filing cabinets, much like the cabinets we have here in this building." Another pause. "Upon opening the drawers of the filing cabinets, they find neatly stacked in rows, hundred-dollar bills."

There is a soft, slight laughter within the room among the agents.

"Must be his shakedown money," responds one agent.

"Or money for another new palace he is about to build," responds another agent.

Garrison continues. "The soldiers found about thirty of the filing cabinets, which were taken back to the US Army base, Camp Trigger. Once received back at the base, the money was counted to find that the filing cabinets only contained three hundred and twenty-five million dollars."

Almost immediately the agents within the room look at each other and then back at Garrison.

"If you are thinking that can't be right, you're correct." Garrison continues to explain. "Looks like the money counters used in the counting process belonged to BCKR, the American contracting company that handles most of the logistics for the troops in Iraq. The BCKR supervisor is known as Bowe LaDeau and, until now, he slipped under our radar.

"Our investigation into Mr. LaDeau revealed that he used to be a prison guard in one of Louisiana's toughest prisons, Angola. The guards we talked to and a few of the prisoners and people within the community where LaDeau had lived, tell a tale of a person that is much of a criminal as the people he guarded. He would shake down family members of the prisoners, claiming that if they did not pay, he would inform prison gangs that would take a contract out on their loved ones."

As Garrison explains, there are grunts of disgust in the room and occasional comments in low tones among the agents.

"But LaDeau did not run this operation alone. He had an accomplice named Bill Smith. It appears that Mr. Smith and Mr. LaDeau had become correctional officers at the same time, and from our investigation, they grew up in the same small town. There was a criminal history of burglaries in adjacent communities, none of which were ever tied back to these two. But from our research of the Angola business, this appears to be a sophisticated operation that would take a schooled criminal within the prison system to put together. From what we could tell, it appears that both LaDeau and Smith both used the Angola job as college training from all the criminals they had communicated with."

Garrison pauses to take a drink of water from the Styrofoam paper cup that he had filled before entering the room.

"LaDeau and Smith got word that BCKR was hiring, and they both landed logistics jobs in areas like Bosnia, Kosovo, Afghanistan, and now Iraq. BCKR hires local nationals in these war-torn countries, and it was LaDeau who had setup the money-counting operation for the money confiscated from Saddam. I might add that while the soldiers were delivering the money back to Camp Trigger, the soldiers were ambushed and one of their own, a Private Bixby, was killed."

A sudden silence, and there is that sudden tension in the room, the kind of tension that you can almost cut with a knife.

"Scum," remarks one agent.

"They're getting rich off our soldiers' deaths," remarks another agent.

Garrison just nods and continues with the presentation.

"The soldiers transferred the money back to Camp Trigger and performed a preliminary count operation before the money was shipped. LaDeau got wind of the operation probably from local shop talk among the soldiers in the dining facility that both soldiers and contractors share. LaDeau had an accomplice, a Joe Manning, who was in on the caper. From BCKR records, we found that Manning had the electronics background and probably had changed the counting logic in the money counters. LaDeau, Smith, and Pearson might have gotten away with this had not the local nationals stumbled across a body in the base mortuary that had a tattoo."

Garrison stops and takes a drink from his cup. "The tattoo was Hot Stuff, the little devil, and was found on his inner thigh, near the right testicle."

Before Garrison can go further, he is interrupted by one of the elderly agents.

"Why were the local nationals messing around with the base mortuary?"

Garrison responds with, "The local base mortuary contains a number of freezers where bodies are stored in preparation for burial. The US Army allows the locals to store the dead bodies of Iraqis who are found murdered along the highways or during the soldier's patrols. The storage of the bodies are a temporary medium until the local nationals either ship them to Baghdad for further identification and from there to their respective town or wherever is convenient. The US Army feels that showing some respect for their dead will further open needed communication channels with the local nationals. When the local nationals are preparing the bodies for shipment, one of their routines is to wash the body prior to shipping it. It was then that they discovered the dead American who was later identified as Joe Manning through an impacted tooth. While he was attempting to disguise the body, LaDeau had attempted to pull out all of Manning's teeth, a good idea if you want to disguise dental records, but it does not hold up to an x-ray that showed an impacted tooth." Garrison pauses for another sip from his cup.

"The local nationals brought the discrepancy to the attention of base security, who got the Army Criminal Investigation Division involved, who then contacted us. Our forensics team arrived at Camp Trigger and, through the analysis of the body and dental x-rays, we discovered the impacted tooth. At Camp Trigger, there was only one American who had an impacted tooth, and he was reported as having quit BCKR and having departed Camp Trigger." Garrison pauses as he raises the cup to his lips for another sip.

"However, in checking the manifest rosters—the US Army keeps meticulous history of who has departed and left the base—we found that Manning's name never showed up. It was this miscalculation that led us to believe that he was murdered on the base. During our investigation, we talked with the commanders and the officer rank in an attempt to find a motive for the murder of Manning. During this investigation, we found that a large cache of money had been found in the small town near Al Hila, belonging to Saddam Hussein."

Garrison is interrupted. "Or from the people he ripped off," said one special agent.

"Or from the people he ripped off," said Garrison. Garrison continues weaving the web of the tale. "We felt that money is always a motive, and so we talked with the officer in charge of the mission, a Lieutenant Armstrong. Lieutenant Armstrong filled us in on the mission and the means of how they had processed the money for shipment to Kuwait. During the interview, Lieutenant

Armstrong had mentioned that his platoon sergeant, a Sergeant First Class Hazard, suspected that the count was incorrect but had no proof and that his soldiers were grieving for loss of one of their own and he thought they needed him and had disbanded further investigation, a wise decision on his part. And I think I would have done the same."

With that comes the nods from the special agents.

Garrison continues. "When asked how the money was counted, Lieutenant Armstrong told us that it is protocol to go to BCKR and ask for any special equipment. It was Bowe LaDeau who took that request. We then talked with the local nationals who work with LaDeau and came across one known as Akhmed. Akhmed was the driver who drove the semi trailer filled with the Saddam cash to Kuwait. Akhmed mentioned that he thought the trailer was odd in that it did not seem to hold the capacity of supplies a trailer should normally carry on a prior supply trip he had taken.

"In communicating this to Lieutenant Armstrong, Armstrong mentioned that a semi trailer truck had been confiscated during one of their combat missions and that it contained a concealed room used by smugglers who were trafficking in stolen linen. Lieutenant Armstrong informed us that BCKR bought the semi trailer from the Iraqis at a steal of a price and that LaDeau was the person who had orchestrated the purchase from the Iraqis. The CID had been monitoring LaDeau from a complaint reported by Akhmed to Lieutenant Armstrong that he thought LaDeau was up to no good but did not have any proof.

"Lieutenant Armstrong had notified CID, and they had begun to monitor LaDeau's suspicious activity during one evening where the semi trailer containing the concealed room had been parked. At that time, the CID had no reason to believe that a crime was being committed but continued to monitor his activity anyway. They noted that LaDeau and Manning had been working around the semi and had been loading something within the trailer through an entrance other than the traditional loading doors of the trailer. Not sure what to think of the activity, they continued monitoring their activity to see if an outcome would manifest.

"Further investigation of the actual semi trailer revealed a trap door in the floor of the trailer opposite of its loading doors. It was there where we found the blood of Joe Manning and that the concealed room had been dismantled. We suspect that LaDeau had dismantled the concealed room and murdered Manning. Obtaining LaDeau's cellular phone records, we found that he communicated with a Bill Smith, another BCKR employee out of Kuwait and the same Mr. Smith mentioned earlier. It turns out that the US Army CID division had suspected Smith in some sort of smuggling operation since they had monitored the weight of the caskets as they departed Kuwait. Apparently, the weight of certain caskets would change, requiring additional fuel. Logistic technicians who monitored the weight of supplies and caskets being shipped picked up on the discrepancy through the additional air flight fuel needed for the shipment and the many logistic records and logs recording the data. Suspicious, they notified CID that they suspected a possible smuggling operation had taken place."

Garrison pauses with, "Are there any questions so far?" and he looks around at his audience in the conference room.

One young special agent pipes up, "Did the CID put it all together?"

"No," responds Garrison. "That is where we came in. It was our forensic team that had searched Manning's sleeping residence and found a plethora of DNA evidence that matched the DNA on the blood that was found in the semi trailer and matched to the DNA of the body found in the base mortuary freezers. We now had a murder, and the most likely motive was the Saddam money found by the US soldiers during their combat patrol.

"Our forensic team also found a printed circuit board in Manning's living quarters, along with a soldering iron and some other electronic tools. When the forensic team searched their database with the part number of the printed circuit board, they found that it matched a circuit board that was used in the BCKR electronic money counters. We asked the BCKR site director if this was common practice for employees to take the electronic board back to their living quarters to be repaired. The site director replied absolutely not and that all work should take place at the BCKR electronics workshop.

"Our forensics team obtained the electronic schematic for the board and began to investigate what changes had been made. They found that one of the chips on the printed circuit board had been re-programmed to count every other bill."

Before Garrison can say another word, he is interrupted by one of the agents.

"And so really they had twice as much cash as they first thought."

Garrison confirms the agent's suspicion. "Exactly. There was more like six hundred and fifty million dollars confiscated during the combat patrol."

one agent speaks up with a, "I thought so when I heard they found twenty-five filing cabinets filled with hundred-dollar bills." And the agent continues with, "I knew that twenty-five filing cabinets filled with hundred-dollar bills did not compute out to three hundred and twenty-five million dollars and fell short from the actual figure."

"Exactly right," Garrison concurs. "Once forensics found that the printed circuit board had been reprogrammed, they swapped the altered printed circuit board with the circuit board of the electronic money counter and conducted a test and found that it did indeed count every other bill." And Garrison continued. "We picked up Mr. Smith at Kuwait and informed him that he was under arrest for smuggling money within dead soldiers' caskets that were being shipped back to the States, and he wanted a deal almost immediately.

"Smith confirmed the caper and that LaDeau spearheaded the entire operation from conception. Smith's job was only to store the money to the sides of the casket and to cover the sides with a silk facade, hiding the cash. Should the casket have to be opened before it arrived at Dover Air Force Base, the money would be concealed. Smith also mentioned that LaDeau had a relative, a brother-in-law in on the caper. When we presented this to LaDeau, he told us that he wanted to see a lawyer and refused to talk from then on."

The elder special agent speaks up. "He probably figured he had more to lose since a murder was involved."

Garrison speaks up. "That is correct, and when we asked Smith about Manning, Smith confirmed that LaDeau had said he planned on killing him."

before Garrison can continue, the elderly special agent speaks up. "No honor among thieves. No honor."

As if in a tag team match, Garrison augments that response with, "No honor is correct. They gave each other up. From what we can tell, we think LaDeau was definitely the leader among the group.

"In talking with Pearson's wife, we are sure she is not involved and was not aware that this caper had taken place. The driver captured with Pearson is a low-level criminal involved with small-time scams, and we suspect he was not involved with the international smuggling ring managed by LaDeau, Smith, and Pearson." And Garrison pauses only to be interrupted by the elderly special agent.

"Have we recovered all of the money?"

"We have recovered three hundred million and, therefore, are continuing to interrogate Pearson on the whereabouts of the remaining twenty-five million dollars. Since the first words out of his mouth was, 'I want a deal,' we feel comfortable in that he will give up the location of where he stashed the cash." Garrison pauses with another sip from his cup. "Well, that concludes our brief, and we are in the process of wrapping up the investigation and all the paperwork that goes along with it." Garrison begins to increase the incandescent lighting within the conference room from the control panel in the center of the long conference table.

There is small chatter among the special agents, and Garrison fields an occasional question as he multitasks between shutting down his laptop computer and positioning his neck tie.

BURIED WITH HONOR

Duke is sitting in a very well-lit room that is bright with fluorescent lighting. It does not contain any pictures on the wall, is dull gray in color, with nothing more than the small wooden table and two chairs opposite from the one that Duke is sitting on. On one side of the room is a large window that appears as a mirror. Obviously, it is a one-way mirror through which the special agents on the opposite side can see Duke but Duke is unable to see them. Duke is wide-eyed in that being arrested was like being hit in the face with a baseball bat. His eyes dart from one side of the room to the other; and he stares at the mirror with his head moving from side to side, as if sitting in an audience at a performing arts hall, awaiting the chorus of entertainers to dart onto the stage and he is checking to see what side of the stage they will enter. However, Duke is not going to like this choir of entertainers.

The door opens, and two agents enter the room and take a seat opposite Duke. The agents are casually dressed in blue jeans and short-sleeved shirts with FBI written on the back of the shirts and plastic necklaces around their necks and FBI badges hanging as if it was a clock pendant just below their sternums. They are both wearing holsters attached to their belts with the standard nine-millimeter pistols mounted inside the holster. This contrasts Duke, who is sitting opposite with a bright orange jumpsuit that contains a belt of chains around his waist attached to the hand-cuffs that are attached to his wrist. This outfit is augmented with the cuffs around his ankles that are attached with a long-enough chain to allow him to walk but not run.

"Good afternoon Mr. Pearson. I am Special Agent Williams, and this Special Agent Garrison. We are here to find out what has happened to the remaining twenty-five million dollars from the three hundred million that you and your crew had stolen from the US Army." And Williams performs a tactical pause and awaits Duke's response.

Duke's eyebrows rise and arch above eyes that immediately radiate surprise as if they were the sun slowly rising at sun-set, radiating the soft beams of light across the sky, making the morning sky aware that a new day has arrived. In this case, an awareness has just arrived across Duke's surprised face.

"What twenty-five million dollars?" asks Duke in a confused reply. "You've got all de money that I received in the eight caskets that were shipped to me, and I told you where the money was," replies Duke almost in a questionable manner as if to say, "What do you want from me?"

At this moment and based upon Duke's mannerisms, Garrison concludes that Duke is unaware of any missing money. However, the questioning continues with Williams at the helm, steering the questions in one direction and then another.

"We know that your accomplice that was arrested with you, a Bert Tanner, was not aware of the money you had stashed back in your office." Williams continues to probe. "You are facing inter-national smuggling charges and RICCO charges that will put you and your crew away for a long time." Williams skillfully baits the hook.

"International smuggling charges? RICCO? I had nothing to do with the smuggling. It was Bowe. He setup the entire thing." Duke begins to drool a lot more profusely and the beads of sweat begin to appear on his forehead.

The interrogation continues for some time, until Garrison reaches over and bumps Williams's arm with his elbow.

"I think we have heard enough, Mr. Pearson. We will be keeping in touch."

both Williams and Garrison rise to leave.

"We had a deal," screams Duke. "I gave up everything I knew about the money."

Garrison affirms, "And we will continue to have a deal as long as you cooperate."

both agents exit the room, leaving Duke sitting alone.

"I don't think he knows where the twenty-five million is, and I am sure that Smith is running his own caper," Garrison explains as both agents make their way through the hallway of the police headquarters.

They meet up with the Lansing police, who are housing Duke in their county jail.

"I think we have gotten everything we can possible get from him," Garrison announces to the two African American police officers lounging around one of the desks in the open bay area of the police station.

"You think one of his crew is holding out?" asks one of the plain-clothes Lansing officers who has a stocky build that could mistake him for a line backer on a professional NFL football team.

"You're correct in that one of the other crew is running one of their own scams, but this guy is definitely not the brains of the operation," replies Garrison.

In a deep voice, the taller of the two Lansing officers speaks up. "We figured that much," replies the Lansing officer who himself could have played on the same NFL football team as his partner.

"He's not the sharpest tool in the shed," responds the other Lansing officer; and all present begin to laugh.

"You've got that right, Officer," responds Garrison. Small talk among the officers begins with Duke's dismal future and eventually terminates with a pause. "While you're in town, you ought to check our local high school hockey team. They're pretty good and have a game tonight at our local high school," remarks one of the Lansing police officers.

Williams looks at Garrison with a nod that says, "Can we?"

"I think we can work that in," answers Garrison. Garrison knows that it is always good to oblige the local law enforcement, and this always seals a good working relationship with any other future FBI endeavors.

The conversation continues with the local Lansing police officers giving the special agents the skinny on the best eateries around Lansing. We leave the police officers to the shop talk.

It's another bright, sunny day in Detroit Both Williams and Garrison are in the process of finishing their morning breakfast. There is a lot of small talk on how they enjoyed the Lansing police officers' suggestion on taking in the high school hockey game and how great the steak dinner was at the local eatery in Lansing.

"Well, we need to beet feet back to Dover to greet LaDeau and Smith. Their plane is due in from Germany this morning, and I will be interested in listening to the lies on who has the twenty-five million," announces Garrison.

"I think you are right from the start in that Smith has conspired to skim the cash from the top of the bounty," responds Williams.

"Yeah. Some skim, twenty-five million dollars," responds Garrison.

The special agents break away from the cafe table and gather their luggage and begin to check out. It's another beautiful day in Detroit as bright, sunny skies greet the agents who exit the hotel and climb into their sedan. They drive on to the adjoining highway and make their way to the airport.

It takes a while to get through security; and the special agents have to explain they are carrying sensitive items, their weapons, and all the particulars are worked out with the local security teams.

Having been processed by the security team, they make their way to the boarding gate and get processed in for the trip. It's a quick trip from Detroit to Dover, and the agents are landing before they know it. They exit the plane along with their carry-on baggage and make their way to Dover Air Force Base. The wait is not long, for the plane from Frankfurt, Germany is already landing. This is not a commercial plane but is an Air Force C17 that is lumbering its way to the landing strip. They pull up to the same location where Duke used to pull up to load the bodies of the US soldiers who had met their fate. They walk over to several other FBI agents who are dressed in blue jeans, wearing the dark nylon windbreaker with the FBI logo on the back of the coat. Garrison and Williams flash their badges, and Garrison introduces them.

"Hello. I am Special Agent Garrison and this is Special Agent Williams, and we are here to accompany the prisoners to FBI headquarters."

All the agents give a nod. The leader of their group, a stout, Latino man of average build with steel gray hair, speaks up.

"I'm Special Agent Perez." special agent Perez begins to introduce the agents to his right and left. "These are Special Agents

Johnson, Trudell, Lambert, and Martinelli." Perez continues. "We're here to escort the prisoners from Dover to FBI headquarters. We have been expecting you, and you're more than welcome to accompany us."

Meanwhile, the lumbering C17 taxis to its assigned position and comes to a complete stop. The tail end of the C17 lowers, revealing the loading ramp that begins to slowly lower; and after some thirty seconds or so, the ramp touches down on the pavement with a thud. The special agents are patient, for it takes another minute and two persons wearing blue jeans and the same FBI windbreaker and leg holsters with pistols exit down the ramp. In between both of the agents is a person in an orange jumpsuit who is shuffling as he walks, for his ankles are cuffed as well and chained together, forcing him to perform the awkward shuffle. From the distance, it is clear to see it is Bill Smith. Following directly behind him is another figure, also clad in the orange jumpsuit. It's Bowe LaDeau, and he also is secured with handcuffs and chains and is accompanied by two special agents by his side. The agents hold each arm of the prisoners, ensuring they do not take flight as they walk down the ramp.

Exiting the ramp, the group heads toward the Garrison and Williams, eventually closing the distance. When the group is about ten feet from Garrison, Williams, and the Perez team, Garrison announces his intentions by flashing his badge.

"Hello. My name is Special Agent Garrison, and I'm here to accompany the suspects to FBI headquarters."

Without pause, one of the agents speaks up.

"I'm Special Agent Burton, and these agents joining me are members of the interdiction team."

Williams intervenes and speaks up, "Welcome to Dover."

Williams and Garrison shake hands with the interdiction team, and Garrison takes in LaDeau and Smith's appearance. Although they are in the orange jumpsuit and handcuffed, there is not the slightest appearance of fear among either one of them. Almost a look of confidence appears that makes them know what their next move would be. Yes, these are going to be hard nuts to crack. They load LaDeau into the backseat of one vehicle while loading Smith into another, keeping the suspects apart so they are not able to discuss any plans. Burton from the interdiction team jumps into the back of Garrison and Williams's vehicle as they pull out of the airport, following the vehicles that LaDeau and Smith are in. They make their way down the highway and into the city of Dover to FBI headquarters, driving into the underground garage.

It's not long before their make their way to the interrogation room that is similar to appearance of the Lansing interrogation room with the one-way mirror. LaDeau is brought in first and seated, and Garrison and Williams are first to interrogate him. They enter the room as they had done with Duke and take their seats opposite of LaDeau.

"Well, Mr. LaDeau. You have been caught red-handed with money and have been given up by your brother-in-law. Do you have anything to say for yourself?"

LaDeau is almost expressionless and looks a bit haggard from the long flight. "Can I have a glass of water?" he asks.

"Sure," responds Williams, who steps outside of the room to obtain the water and returns with bottled water in hand. He unscrews the bottle cap and instructs LaDeau, "We are not going to loosen your constraints. I will put the bottle up to your mouth, and you can take a drink. When you want me to lower the bottle, tap on the table."

LaDeau nods with approval. LaDeau takes a long drink as if trying to delay the inevitable , and then he taps on the table and Williams lowers the bottle. Some of the water drips down the side of his face, and he shakes his head from side to side as in a futile attempt to wipe his chin. After a moment of clearing his throat, he finally speaks up.

"Well, for one, my brother-in-law only knows what we told him."

Garrison's eyes light up and widen slightly. *Could LaDeau be giving up the real leader of this crew?* he thinks to himself, for Garrison thought all along that the leader of the crew was LaDeau.

LaDeau's expression has not changed, for its appearance is that of a hardened felon who is well-schooled in the art of deception. Both LaDeau and Smith had listened in on convict's discussion when they both were working as correctional officers at Angola.

LaDeau clears his throat and speaks up. "It was Joe Manning's idea, and he was de brains of it all. It was Manning who dreamed up of skimming de money, and it was Manning who suggested we ship it back in de soldiers' coffins."

With that response, Garrison begins to pick apart LaDeau's story. "I suppose you are going to tell us that Manning cooperated with your brother-in-law without you knowing it."

LaDeau responds quickly, "No. Manning knew my brother-in-law worked as a mortician from small talk we use to make. What da hell else is there to do in Iraq?"

Williams speaks up with, "Look, LaDeau. You expect us to believe that Manning was the brains of the entire operation when we found Manning brutally murdered with half his face chopped off?"

Again, LaDeau speaks up. "It was Manning's idea, and it was Manning who planned de entire thing. Manning had skimmed some of de money from what was stolen, and he somehow shipped it out of Iraq. We are not sure how he did it. Both Smith and I found out about it. I had found Manning murdered in the motor pool where we were supposed to meet, and I think he was done in by one of de local nationals. He hated them and almost would always treat them like dirt."

Neither the expression nor LaDeau's attitude changed.

"He somehow got a hold of my brother-in-law's telephone number and would always dial the number in front of me, and when Duke would answer, he would pass it to me, giving me instructions on what to say. He would always say, 'You say anything else and I'll have one of these Iraqis kill your butt.'" LaDeau pauses and then says, "He meant it too. He was mixed up with those Iraqis, and over there, you offer them enough money and they will kill ya," LaDeau concludes.

Garrison grimaces in disgust. "Who are you kidding? We already collected the DNA from the semi trailer and know that Manning was killed there, and along with your fingerprints as well."

LaDeau counters with, "That is true I worked with Manning and we both had hid in de trailer's concealed room and stole the money, but I did not kill Manning. Manning had another deal going with de local nationals, and I think that deal had something with him being set up in Dubjai with de money he skimmed, and with that, I want to speak to a lawyer."

Garrison knows that he has to honor LaDeau's request and provide him with the lawyer. "Okay, Mr. LaDeau, but we have you on RICCO charges and international theft charges…" Garrison continues with the list of charges, but this does not faze LaDeau.

Go ahead, law man, LaDeau thinks to himself. *That's it. Take de bait.*

It's not long before LaDeau's interrogation ends and Garrison and Williams meet to take apart LaDeau's story.

"Well, that was unexpected, Manning being the brains of the operation," remarks Williams.

"I don't believe Manning was the brains of the operation, and I still think LaDeau was the mastermind," Garrison says in an assertive manner. "He's is trying to reduce his part in the caper with the hopes of getting a reduced sentence," Garrison annoyingly states.

"But Manning did have the education and the technical knowhow to change the electronics to count every other bill," remarks Williams.

"True, he did have the tech knowhow, but I do not think he had the logistic knowhow of getting the money out of the country, and that is what we tell the US attorney, for this now is an international crime with American citizens at the forefront. We need to interview Smith. My guess is that he will cooperate LaDeau's story."

With that, Garrison calls in Smith for interrogation. Both agents listen to Smith's story; and, like LaDeau, he tells them of his part in the program.

"It was Manning's idea. He knew that the way to get the money out of de continent was to ship it in caskets," replies Smith to the interrogation questions of Garrison. "Manning had buddies all through BCKR, and he knew some of them worked in logistics," Smith goes on. "That little turd was clever, and he skimmed from de entire take. Now I want to see my lawyer." Smith then shuts up. And that ends the interrogation.

Garrison and Williams meet up after the interrogation of Smith.

"I think we have enough to charge them with the theft. Not sure about the murder of Manning," Garrison states.

"Not unless something manifests from the forensic investigations," replies Williams.

"Either way, they are looking at a lot of time in a federal pen for a federal crime," Garrison counters; and with that, we leave both agents to their job.

It's a cold day in Lansing, Michigan as the gravediggers reveal the open grave that was pre-dug during the warmer weather.

"Looks like we have another soldier to bury," announces one of the gravediggers.

"It's a shame that our boys and girls are dying in that war."

The gravediggers prepare the coffin for burial. They grunt and groan as they remove the coffin from the hearse and position it in the automatic lift that will lower the casket into the grave. They clean up the area, placing down a mat of artificial turf around the casket and the grave. This contrasts the snow-covered cemetery, giving the gravesite an appearance that this grass almost grew out of the snow, a ridiculous notion. The long procession of vehicles with their lights on is the signal that the funeral procession is approaching. The first vehicle is a police car with the lights on, which automatically pulls into the oncoming lane, blocking all approaching traffic that might appear and giving access so the funeral procession can make their left turn into the cemetery.

The gravediggers quickly back away from the gravesite and move the hearse out of the area to make room for the funeral procession and its participants. It is not long before all of the cars have driven into the cemetery and parked. Its participants slowly get out of their vehicles, dressed in black suits and dresses appropriate for a funeral. Some of the participants are soldiers who stand to the side of the gravesite in formation with their weapons pointing straight up and down and to their fronts, in a military salute. It's not long before all the members are present to include the young wife of Private Bixby. She is not more than nineteen years of age; and it is clear that she has been crying for some time, with the white of her eyes displaying the red veins of stress of appearing dry from the lack of tears. She is pregnant, which is obvious from the small bulge in her dress, and is wearing a black gown. There are a number of seats facing the coffin; and she is sitting in the center, with her parents and relatives in the adjoining chairs.

The preacher appears and begins with, "We are here to bury Jonathan Bixby, a soldier in the United States Army who was killed in Iraq."

And the sound of that one sentence had the effect of a loud clap of thunder on Private Bixby's young wife, who shuddered as if lightning had hit close by.

The preacher goes on with his sermon, praising Private Bixby's courage and achievements in the army. The preacher concludes with a motion to the army sergeant, who then motions to his small squad of soldiers to come forward. The soldiers and the sergeants are dressed in the US Army dress uniform with the red berets and jump boots that are required for the army airborne uniform that they wear. They sport the airborne badges and infantry combat badges, along with their unit patches and stripes on the right arm from the many tours of duty they have performed overseas.

They position themselves at both ends of the casket, with one soldier in the center of the coffin, as they slowly remove the American flag and begin the slow process of folding it. Starting at the opposite end of the banner of the flag where the stars reside, the soldiers slowly fold the flag into the triangle formation that they are accustomed to doing at retreat from the normal end of the soldier's day. Like the end of the day, this is the end of the soldier's life; and that flag represents that retreat for the young soldier, Private Bixby. The flag is folded into a triangle and presented to his young wife by the sergeant, who slowly salutes and then retreats. With that, the sergeant turns to his squad, who has positioned themselves outside of the circle of people who are attending the funeral. The soldiers are standing in column formation, one behind the other, with their rifles at the ready position.

Upon command from the sergeant, they raise their rifles and fire a round into the air. A shudder filters through the crowd as if they were performing a wave at a football game. Private Bixby's wife shudders as well, as if she had been hit from behind or struck in the back. The sergeant gives another command, and a second round of gunfire erupts and the crowd once again shudders. Finally, the sergeant gives the last command; and the seven soldiers standing in formation fire off the last round of the twenty-one-gun salute. The sergeant yells another command, and the column of soldiers shoulder their rifles and march away from the gravesite. The crowd all files by Private Bixby's wife and gives their best blessings to her and her family. It's not long before they have departed. The funeral concludes with Private Bixby's wife clinging to the top of the coffin, where she had broken down in tears from the pain of her loss. Her parents pry her away from the casket and slowly walk away, trying to console her in her grief. The gravediggers take in the sight from afar; and when they see that everyone has departed, "Okay. It's our time now," announces one of the gravediggers.

They make their way over to the gravesite and remove the artificial turf and flowers and begin to lower the casket into the ground. The casket slowly descends. When it is almost to the bottom, it quickens and lowers with a thud. The gravediggers look at each other.

And one speaks up with, "It must have been an adjustment when the belts were off."

And the others nod and remove the belts from the casket. Once the belts are removed, they motion to a truck driver to back up the truck that contains the dirt that will be used to cover the grave. The gravediggers hop up onto the truck and begin to shovel the dirt into the grave. Meanwhile, inside of the dark casket, if it was illuminated, we can almost make out the figure of Private Bixby. The corner of his mouth is turned downward, as if he is grieving himself. The thud that was heard has shaken loose the silk facade on one side of the casket. There, the padding of the silk facade reveals the smirk of a grin that we had once seen before. Yes, it's the smirk coming from the stack of Benjamin Franklins that line the entire coffin. May they look over this poor soldier for the remainder of their eternity.